Johnny Mac

A novel based on a true story

John Knowles Probst

ISBN 0-7596-5908-7

Library of Congress Control Number: 2002091495

This book is printed on acid free paper.

Printed in the United States of America
Bloomington, IN

Cover Drawing: Jeff Gogué, Gogué Art Studio, Quincy, California

1stBooks – rev. 05/06/02

I dedicate this book to the memory of my beloved wife

Dorothy C. Probst

(1937-1989)

Acknowledgments

To Johnny:

Remember those Thursday evenings after choir rehearsal, when we sat in the Spaghetti Factory drinking beer and swapping episodes of our childhood? My experiences were average and mundane, but yours – yours were a novelist's inspiration to write. I hope I have portrayed you, and those childhood experiences, with a literary justice.

Your old buddy.............. "Knowl"

Also . . . many thanks to Lori and JP Reynolds, who not only encouraged me to publish, but edited the rough copy with an editorial precision, personal care and professional advice.

Table of Contents

Chapter One

Wilcox, Indiana – 1942

Vera McBride lay on her side slowly getting accustomed to the light of the new day. As she awoke, she guessed it to be mid morning. She slowly sat up, leaned on her elbows and saw herself in the dresser mirror opposite the bed. The mirror revealed a woman whose face was gaunt and lined from years of drinking. Even now, the taste of stale whiskey and cigarettes filled her mouth ... a taste she experienced on many mornings upon arising.

'Have got to stop drinking so much,' she thought to herself. She couldn't remember if it was Saturday or Sunday ... "Saturday," she said to herself. "Damn, I guess it's Saturday," she said as she pushed her shoulder-length hair from her face.

Again she caught her reflection in the mirror. For just a fleeting moment, she did not recognize the figure. The face that was reflected back was thin, with indented cheeks; dark circles surrounded her sad eyes, a blue bruise swelled from her lower left jaw, stringy unkempt hair hung shoulder length around her face like a stained picture frame. Her hand went to the bruise; she touched it lightly and winced from the sharp pain.

"Damn him, he's got to stop hitting me," she said and then thought to herself, 'How many times have I said that?'

She realized that it was not the mirrored figure that was so foreign to her, but the changes that had taken place since the last time she had seriously viewed her mirrored reflection.

"When was the last time I needed to fancy up? Why look in a mirror if there's nothing to look forward to?" she asked the empty room.

To the left of the mirror was a picture of herself and Charley, a picture taken by her cousin on their wedding day, twelve years before. The woman in the picture, dressed in white, was the epitome of all the ladies' pictures in the *Look Magazine* soap ads. In the picture, the woman looked adoringly at the man who held her by the waist. Charley McBride, with his cropped hair, bow tie, and dark pinstriped suit was everything Vera had ever wanted a man to be. Tall, thin but muscular. She had always felt secure while in his hold. But throughout their married years, his hold on her had grown from physical strength and restraint while making love to outright brute force.

Vera reached across the bed to the nightstand for a cigarette and remembered that Charley had not returned; she grabbed the last cigarette and crumpled the

1

empty pack. She counted the days since he had left. Monday night. No, Sunday night. Yes, they'd argued; they had both been drunk. What had they argued about?

"Hell, it don't matter; we always argue," she said to no one.

But it did matter. When he had gone off before, the thought of his abandoning her and the boys had crossed her mind, but she had always disregarded it. Charley had gone off before in a fit of anger, but never for this length of time.

"Shit, he hasn't got the balls," she said as she moved to the window seat to warm herself in the morning sun. 'Twelve years with the same man and it's going to end like this?' she said to herself.

"Hell, he ain't got the balls," she repeated to give herself confidence.

Vera lit her cigarette, took a drag, and looked about the room. The flowered wallpaper was faded from years of dirt, and the lace curtains were gray with age. The room's appearance depressed her. She looked out the window. Grass knee high stretched to the highway.

"Damn! Charley said he was going to cut that grass." Across the highway were acres of bright, yellowed wheat stalks ... Then it came to her! What if he did leave her, abandon her and the boys? There was a harvest this month; how would the work get done? They were already in debt. She couldn't afford hired help. She looked at the picture. A tall, strapping man in his mid twenties looked down at a thin, pretty girl in her mid teens dressed in a wedding gown.

"That's the only suit I ever saw him wear," she remarked.

The picture brought to her mind a myriad of memories of her wedding day. Most obvious was the fact that it wasn't really "her" day. Oh, she was married, but it seemed as though for everyone else's benefit, and at her expense. From the beginning, when she'd announced that she was pregnant, her mother had been her only ally, with no real influence in the matter. From the start, her father, Ben, had determined the how, when, and where of the ceremony.

She could hardly remember the actual ceremony, but did recall saying "I do" in an inaudible voice and clinging to Charley until the preacher said, "I now pronounce you ..." After the ceremony, she remembered hugging and kissing her mother, who stood behind her, thin and frail, in her one blue dress, looking like nothing more than a servant to her father during their marriage. Why should she be anything different on her daughter's day of marriage?

"Ma should sit at the head table with Charley and me," demanded Vera.

"I don't give a damn where she sits but someone's got to look after the guests. I ain't payin' for extra help."

After the final pronouncement, to thank her father she extended her hand as though to shake his; she could never remember kissing him or being kissed by him. He stood in front of her, his large, two-hundred-pound frame dressed in his dark blue, double-breasted suit. He grabbed her shoulders and pulled her to him, kissed her on the forehead and said, "You just be a good girl for your Charley," and he was gone in a moment to receive the congratulations of his fellow farmers.

At her father's insistence, the reception was held in the backyard. Charley's "invited" were work hands from nearby farms, the "hangout" crowd from the Buggy Whip Bar, men in their early twenties who made a point of introducing themselves to Vera's young female classmates, to the disgust of the junior high boys who were also invited.

With a beer in one hand and a cigar in another, Ben moved from one table to another, accepting the congratulations from the young guests. Her mother, mute except to ask if everyone had enough punch and ice cream, looked singularly tired and alone among the rollicking group of merrymakers. And when it came time for the newlyweds to open their gifts, her father halted the procedure with a yell that gained everyone's attention.

"Hey, they ain't openin' anything till they get my present first!" And grabbing Vera, while tugging at Charley's coat, he pulled them from their seats. "You young 'uns just keep enjoyin' yourselves. We'll be back in a spell."

And off the trio went, into the house and up the stairs.

"I want you to see something, the both of you, right now," her father kept saying as they climbed the stairs.

Vera looked at the room and remembered the day her father had brought Charley and her to the window. The walls had been newly painted, and the curtains just hung.

The three looked out the window and viewed acres of corn and wheat.

Then her father took each of their hands and cupped them in his. His action surprised Vera; in fact, his complete change of attitude surprised her. Never before had she seen her father so jovial, hopeful, so lighthearted. The fact that he tenderly held their hands in his as though in some ritual was unlike him. Vera only remembered her father giving her, her sister, or their mother, the back of his hand. Ben Roberts, without warning, would slap one of his children for such small infractions as not sitting up straight, or not listening. His wife could expect the same treatment for not being "there" when he called. And now, like a high priest giving absolution, he held their hands and made his pronouncements.

"These fields are my gift, my wedding gift to you and Charley."

The two-hundred-pound man stood in his flowery tie, white shirt, and pressed pants held by suspenders, holding the newlyweds' hands in his and giving away his land. Vera gazed in amazement at her father. 'Do clothes make the man?' she wondered. Before her wedding day, she could only remember her father in boots, baggy pants, and a dirty wool T-shirt, plowing fields or mending fences. All work and no play. As for giving anything away, Ben Roberts was known countywide as that individual who had his price on anything he acquired, and if the buyer didn't accept it, there was no agreement.

"Charley McBride," he said, "you're gonna take over some of the richest land in this county when I die ... all five hundred acres ... and that's my present to you two."

'Well, obviously clothes don't make the man,' she thought. It was apparent from the way he said it that Ben Roberts hadn't changed a bit. He wasn't giving them anything at all. Instead, he was getting something—two free laborers, and Charley would be her taskmaster, as her father had been to her mother. To Vera the present was nothing more than the back of his hand again, only this time it was wrapped in a ribbon of promises, promises only to be fulfilled on his death. 'He'll probably outlive us,' she thought to herself as he finished his proclamation and quickly released their hands.

"Just don't get high and mighty and think that you own the place before I die," he added as if reading Vera's mind.

To Vera, her father's pronouncement seemed not only unusual but unfair. What about her mother, her sister Lillian?

"All of it?" Vera asked. "What about Mom, and ... "All of it!" screamed her father. "You'll be expected to care for your Ma in my place, but your older sister ain't a part of this family no more, not since I threw her out. Now you and Charley have a future here, and I need the help. Just don't forget that, and what I'm doin' for ya. And don't ever speak of that sister of yours to me again," he yelled to them as he singularly descended the stairs, leaving the couple to stare in amazement.

After she and Charley had opened their gifts, danced the first dance, and cut the first piece of cake, the guests, remembering other time commitments, excused themselves. As Vera and her mother cleaned up, Charley too excused himself and ran off with his buddies to the Buggy Whip for just one more drink. When he did return, he was drunk and excused himself for being absent with the story that the boys had handcuffed him to the bar and made him drink bourbon and Seven Ups until "sober" enough to go home.

Vera remembered their first night of lovemaking in the room. Charley recited his canticle of how much he loved her again and again in slurred words. Smelling of bourbon, he sucked at her breasts, and with no thought of foreplay, suddenly entered her with the force of a stud in heat.

Before falling asleep to the tempo of the snoring of her new husband, Vera remembered getting up and sitting at the very window from which she now gazed. Her loins were sore and painful from the rushed lovemaking. Tears fell down her cheeks, and she had looked out to the fields and wondered if her father's gift, her dowry, was nothing more than tying herself to her father's demands and years of farm work. Before falling asleep, Vera feared that the first day of her married life was a sign of what the future held.

"No ... no," she had said to herself. "I'll change him. Things will work for the better, I'll make sure of that."

"Shit ... things don't change," Vera said to the empty room, "not as long as it's a man's world. Things don't change one little bit."

Vera took another drag on her cigarette and glanced across the road. "If Charley's really gone, I'll need to call her; there's no choice in that."

Vera recalled that she had not seen her sister since the day Lillian had hurriedly packed and left the house. She remembered her sister as the most independent female she had known.

"You need to stand up to your Pa like Lillian does," her mother would caution her. "I know I've never been much of an example, but women got to survive the likes of people like your Dad, and some day Lillian will," she would preach to her.

The thought of that day struck fear in her as she remembered seeing her spindly legged sister whose chopped hair and lean face gave her a boyish appearance as she stood up to her father. Her small lean body had been rooted on the spot, her hands firmly on her hips. She remembered hearing Lillian verbally attack her father, and Vera envied her for her spunk.

"No, Pa," Lillian had been saying. "Now I'm takin' responsibility for what I did and not puttin' blame on anyone else. No one is gonna be dragged into marryin' me cause of my condition or 'cause you got to have your pride put right. I know you warned us girls about gettin' pregnant before gettin' married, but it happened, and that's that."

The man swung his clenched fist at his daughter and cut her upper lip as she fell back on the bed.

"You don't tell me what I know and don't know, girl; and, as long as your mind is set, you can just get your gear and get on out of this county, 'cause I won't have no whore for a daughter living on my land."

As Ben Roberts turned to leave, he saw his wife and fourteen-year-old Vera in the hall.

"She's to move out today and never step foot in this house again," he said as he descended the stairs.

'And she never did come back,' Vera remembered as she ground the cigarette out on the windowpane. 'The Bible says the meek shall inherit the world. Well, I was meek and I inherited the damn farm, and look where it got me. She gets thrown out and ends up marryin' a millionaire. Damn! Whoever thought things would turn out the way they did?'

Looking out the window, she realized that she would have to contact Lillian if Charley didn't return. 'That land's a considerable investment out there to be marketed,' she thought.

The thought of his not returning depressed her; she touched the black and blue area where he had hit her. How many times through the years had he been drunk or just angry and forced himself on her? How many mornings had she arisen to look into the mirror and decide how to hide the black eyes and inflamed redness with makeup and scarves? And how many times had she vowed that "things" had to change?

"Shit! As long as it's a man's world, things don't change ... No sir, not one little bit."

Vera rubbed her eyes to erase the scene from her mind. As she listened for noise from the boys' room, she lay down on the bed and looked at the dirty ceiling. Again, thoughts of Charley's abandoning her returned and she sat up. "There's a hell of a lot of work that has to be done around here," she said to herself. It came to her that she missed him for the wrong reason. Did she care about him? Or was she just concerned about his caring for her and the boys? There had been a lot of lovemaking but not much love in their twelve-year marriage.

She had started seeing Charley during her sophomore year, the same year that Lillian had left the house. How proud Vera was when "her" Charley would be waiting for her after school. No other high school girl could boast that she had a twenty-year-old boy friend waiting for her when the last bell of the school day had rung. And there he would be, standing against his buddy's car that he had borrowed, the tallest man any of her high school friends had ever seen. He would be dressed in his clean blue jeans and a tight-fitting T-shirt; the biceps in his arms constricted the material at the end of each rolled-up sleeve. What had really impressed her friends was the fact that he sported a small mustache and a brightly inscribed tattoo of his nickname "Mac." Her friends would stand around and watch as she ran to him. He would pick her up as she grabbed him around the neck. He would press his hands against the cheeks of her buttocks as she kissed him again and again. Then, before getting into the car, she would glance at her classmates to make sure that she had completely impressed them. Some girls were wide eyed with envy, while others had turned away snickering in embarrassment. But as Charley laid rubber, accelerating out of the school grounds, Vera remembered being so much in love that she could care less what the girls and their parents were saying about her romance. And what everyone predicted would happen, did happen. In the beginning of her junior year, Vera remembered having to go to the doctor with her mother when she missed her period.

"I don't care if your breadbasket is full," her father said at hearing the news, "as long as Charley means to buy the whole loaf."

"It ain't necessary that she marry just 'cause she's in a family way," her mother pleaded.

"Oh, is that so, woman? Well, I'm not going to be the laughingstock of the whole countryside; they'll marry, and the sooner the better," her father replied.

It was one of the few times her mother had talked up to her father.

Damn it, she'd talk to Charley when he returned. Things had to change; they had to change. But what if he didn't come home? "Hell, I don't need him." She'd hire men and harvest the crop and sell the damned place. Vera reached for a cigarette and felt the crumpled pack in her hand. "Shit!" she yelled as she threw it across the room. Things would change! "I'll do it with or without him!"

She sat up. "I'll need money." She thought of what money or credit was left to her. Crammer's Corners store was owed about a hundred and seventy-five dollars, and there was that fifty-dollar check Ed Gibbs had given Charley for helping him last month. If worse came to worse, she would hit up Lillian for a loan. With all her money, she couldn't refuse to help her abandoned sister and nephews. "Damn! That woman has done well since she left home," Vera said to herself. She thought again of Crammer's Corners and how much more credit they would allow her. "God damn them!" she roared to the empty room. "I'll just remind them of how they started twenty years ago. My old man gave them this land interest free and never once took it back when they came to the end of a bad month empty handed. You just goddamn well remember who owes who," she rehearsed to herself. Then the memories of past events, of sudden deaths and loneliness, returned to her and she truly felt abandoned.

"Damn it! God damn it! It ain't fair, Charley. It ain't fair!" she cried as she rolled over and pounded the empty side of the bed with her right fist.

Standing in the doorway watching their mother were Johnny and little Tommy. Like uninvited guests, they watched their mother pound her fist at the empty side of the bed. Tommy sucked his thumb and with the other hand held a tattered blanket tightly. Johnny, who stood a half-foot taller than his brother, rubbed his crotch to stop the irritation from his urine-stained underwear.

Vera suddenly looked up. "Why you kids up so early?" Johnny came into the room first. The blond-headed boy was tall and well built for a boy of ten. "I'm hungry, Ma. We didn't have nothin' but apples last night and there's no cereal."

"Oh, there's cereal down there. Leave me alone," she begged and turned toward the wall.

"There ain't nothing down there," said Tommy. The younger boy brushed his sandy-colored hair from his eyes, always holding fast to his dirty blanket. He only removed his thumb from his mouth to speak.

"Thomas, you go down with Johnny. Johnny, you fix Tommy something. Damn it! Just leave me alone!" she screamed.

Johnny pleaded, "But Ma, there's no..."

"God damn it, Johnny," screamed Vera, "you're ten years old and you still wet your pants, and you can't even get some breakfast for your brother! Oh, hell! I might as well do it myself."

With that, she leaped from the bed, put on her robe, and was followed down the dark stairway by her children.

Next to the large stuffed chair by the fireplace was an empty bottle of Jack Daniels. Vera went for the bottle but, on seeing it empty, yelled, "Damn! And no more cigarettes!" as she crumpled up another empty pack. Crossing the room, she went to the china closet and opened the door. Counting eight plates from the bottom, she picked up a set of china saucers and pulled out a fifty-dollar check; he must have forgotten that he got paid. Vera sighed in relief ... 'If Charley did leave, he left with nothing but the clothes on his back,' she said to herself.

She stopped. 'Maybe something happened to him. Hell, I'd have heard by now,' she replied to herself.

"Ma, I want some cereal!" whined Tommy, as he tugged at her slip.

"All right, all right!" she screamed back, and went into the kitchen and took down a box of cereal from the top shelf.

The check would make do for now, but she would need credit at Crammer's Store.

"There's no milk!" yelled Johnny as he slammed the icebox door.

"Just use sugar and that's all. I got to get some stuff," she said as she put bowls on the kitchen table. Vera stopped. What if something had happened to her husband?

"Where's the milk?" asked Johnny.

"Damn it, there's none left. I told ya, just use the sugar. I'm goin' to Crammer's for supplies now. As she headed for the stairs, she began to figure out how to make fifty dollars do for at least a month. By then, she would borrow on the harvest. She could sell the place. And there was always Lillian. Vera went into her room and began dressing. But the real possibility of being abandoned came to her, and goose pimples formed on her arm as she pulled her housecoat about her for warmth against the sudden chill.

Chapter Two

Crammer's Corners — Wilcox, Indiana

Vera brought the 1938 Chevy truck to a sudden stop in the unpaved parking area. Dust blew about her as she opened the truck door. Getting out, she brushed the dust from her print dress.

She stood in front of the store, her image grotesquely mirrored in a four-foot metal Nehi ad that advertised a "Better Day With A Nehi." She dusted off her dress again, straightened her hair, and thought, "Its the best appearance I can make. If they give me trouble, I'll just remind them of who got them started." Vera opened the door and a bell sounded in the back rooms announcing her arrival. The smells of dried wood from twenty-year-old shelving, mixed with vanilla and coffee beans, filled her nostrils as she shut the door. Marvin or Lottie would soon appear. She reminded herself that she must not appear desperate or in need of help, and she must show resolve to gain credit. She reminded herself to buy cigarettes and a half-gallon of Jack Daniels along with other necessities.

Marvin Crammer turned the screw until it was snug in place. Two more screws to tighten, a little soldering, and he could try it out. "Abe," that's what his friends called him. "Abe" because he always dressed his six-foot frame in black britches held up by suspenders that were frayed and old. His lean body and hollow-cheeked face resembled the "Great Emancipator," and everyone, even strangers, reminded him of the resemblance.

"Now what stupid gadget are you working on?" Lottie Crammer said as she sat at her dining room table, checking the week's credits and debits.

"Nothing special, my love. Nothing you'd understand," he replied as he continued to work. "Just an idea I had and thought I'd try out."

"Well, don't break the phone. God knows it costs enough when it's workin'."

"No, no, my love, just something I'm adding to the line. What the telephone company don't know won't hurt them."

Lottie wrote down figures from the various piles of papers before her. Their interests were as different as their figures and form. Marvin was a potential inventor, although his real talent was duplicating and redefining what other people had first invented. He enjoyed his hobby, much to the displeasure of his wife.

Lottie was a realist, a no-credit/cash-and-carry clerk. Each morning she bound her dark hair in a bun and never wore jewelry with her plain black dresses. What she lacked in imagination, her husband made up in invention. What faith

9

"Old Abe" had in his neighboring customers, she countered by demanding that accounts be paid.

"I'd like to see you turn a penny with all the time you put in on some of these gadgets," she growled.

"Oh, don't worry, my love, some day. Some day someone will need one of my ideas," he always replied.

"Well, you'd better hurry, 'cause we're gettin' deeper in debt every month," she answered sarcastically.

"Does it ever get better?" he quietly remarked as he soldered two wires together.

"Well, we'd do one hell of a lot better if you didn't have such a soft heart, Mr. Inventor. I'm tellin' ya, you got to stop lettin' people have so much credit ... it's killin' us," she yelled as she grabbed for a pile of canceled checks.

For the first time, Marvin looked up from his work and spoke in a quiet tone. "They're our friends, our neighbors, Lottie. They're good for it. No one's goin' to skip town ... just have a little faith ..."

"Faith! Huh! That's easy for you to say. You go along electrifying doors and makin' gadgets, but when it comes to the end of the month, I got to figure out how to pay for it all." The bell announcing a customer rang, and Lottie lifted her large frame to glimpse through one of her husband's gadgets, a one-way mirror. As she moved toward the door, she was reminded that her diabetes was worse, and no matter how carefully she watched her diet, she never lost weight.

Vera hoped it would be the more generous of the two—Marvin. She looked at her selections and decided she would use Ed Gibbs's check to Charley to pay something on the bill and charge the rest. If there was any resentment toward what she charged, she vowed to remind them of who had been one of their benefactors.

"Hello, Lottie," Vera said as spiritedly as she could, "I was just driving by and thought I'd pick up a few things."

Lottie told herself determinedly, 'She's going to want to charge it, and I'm going to say something about it.'

"Charley said if I was in the neighborhood to pick up some smokes this morning. My, that man does smoke a lot. How's your diabetes, Lottie?" asked Vera as she darted from shelf to shelf. "And while I'm here, I'll pay something on that silly bill I keep forgettin' about," she quipped.

"I'm fine, Vera. I'll have your bill rung up in just a minute."

Vera carried boxes of cereal and quarts of milk to the counter. "I'll take a carton of cigarettes and that middle-sized bottle of Jack Daniels behind you, if you please."

Before reaching for the articles, Lottie stood her ground and said, "You wanted to pay something on the bill, Vera?"

"Oh, but of course. I nearly forgot. What did you say it was?" she asked offhandedly as she dug through her purse for the check.

"One hundred and fifty-two dollars and seventy-eight cents."

"One hundred and ... what? ... Oh, Lottie, you must be mistaken!" Vera laughed nervously. "I know it wasn't more'n fifty dollars last week, and I haven't been here since then, and ..."

"But Charley was," Lottie interrupted.

"Charley?" questioned Vera. Blood drained from her face as she heard the name.

'She doesn't know ... she doesn't know,' thought Lottie.

"Charley. Of course, Charley ... Why, Lottie, it completely slipped my mind. He did say something about getting something or other yesterday," she replied sheepishly.

'He's gone,' thought Vera. 'That son of a bitch left me all that work ... and all the bills. That bastard left me!' her mind screamed at her, and it took all she had to keep a casual expression on her face.

"Here it is," said Lottie. "He charged over one hundred dollars in one day last week. My husband waited on him. I know it was my husband, 'cause if it was me that waited on him, I would've questioned the wisdom of chargin' so much. I mean chargin' so much all in one day, you understand," Lottie said with a smirk.

"Of course, of course," Vera replied. She was on edge and could not afford to have it show.

"Could I see those charges, Lottie?" she asked, almost gaily. "Just to make sure everything is in order?"

'You bitch,' thought Lottie. 'You just don't know what he bought.'

"Everything's here that he bought. His signature is on the bottom."

Vera tried keeping a look of composure on her face as she read the items that convinced her that he had abandoned her and the boys: one bed roll, a pair of boots, socks, one shovel, a tent, cartons of cigarettes, four bottles of Jack Daniels. It concluded with a check for cash for $50.00, check number 18976.

"Looks like he bought gear for some kind of trip," chided Lottie.

"Oh, of course, of course," laughed Vera to hide the anxiety that grew within her. "He had to go up north ... to Muncie ... eh, to help his brother on his farm. His brother took real sick real suddenly. Well, he wanted to leave the truck for me, so I told him to pick up a few things before he went. It completely slipped my mind."

'Something is wrong,' thought Lottie, 'and I don't like it.'

"I hope your brother-in-law is all right now."

"Yes, why, yes ... Lottie, he's just fine. Everything is just fine ... fine." She had to get out of there ... She was beginning to fall apart.

"Well, how long will Charley be gone?" asked Lottie.

11

"Hard to say, Lottie."

"I thought you said everything was just fine."

"I did ... I did ... but ... that is, his brother's fine ... not so sick ... just not able to handle a day's work ... so Charley will be there a spell."

Vera was rattled; she couldn't think, couldn't remember what she had said. She needed to think, needed time to think.

"Well, how much will you be payin' on your bill, Vera? We don't usually let credit customers charge this much."

"Why, um ... fifty dollars ... yes, fifty dollars," Vera said with a smile. "Charley will be home by the end of the week. Then we'll pay off the rest."

Lottie thought to herself, 'I don't believe it.' She looked at Vera and slowly bit her lip. "You got one week to make this bill straight, Vera. That's all the time we can afford."

Vera thought of reminding Lottie of what her father had done for her and her family when Crammer's Corners was opened, but decided against it. Instead, she smiled and said, "Which reminds me ... I've got to call him today. In fact, right now. Oh, silly me, Lottie. I came in here with only that check, and I don't even have a nickel to make a phone call. Isn't that silly of me?" she said with a nervous laugh. "Could you spare me a nickel?"

"I'll put it on your tab, Vera." And then Lottie thought, 'You don't fool me,' as she slowly reached into her cash register.

"Of course," replied Vera, "I'll just use the pay phone in front," and she was out the door.

Lottie watched Vera as she hurried to the telephone booth between the store and the gas station. In a fit of desperation, Vera dropped the coin the first two times she attempted to put it in the phone. Lottie watched her as she quickly dialed the operator and began giving instructions.

"Marvin!" Lottie screamed. "There's something wrong here. C'mon in here."

"What's the matter, m'love?"

Lottie explained as she eyed Vera through the window. "Vera McBride was just in here, and if my suspicions are correct, she just found out about all that hardware you let her husband charge last week. She's talkin' to him now."

"Excuse me," he said and went back into the living room.

"I don't like it, Marvin. I told you not to let their charges go over fifty dollars. They're into us over one hundred and fifty dollars right now, and it's coming' to no good. There's something wrong, I can tell it; there's something wrong. I don't care. They're not to be chargin' at this store until their present bill is paid in full." Lottie watched Vera bang against the phone booth to drive her point home.

"She's desperate about something, Marvin. I'm witnessin' a woman in a peck of trouble. I could tell from her expression, she didn't know nothin' of him buyin' those goods last week. She ain't chargin' any more here. That I can tell you."

Vera slammed the receiver down and stood in the booth for some time. When she turned toward the store, Lottie backed from the window and walked behind the counter. "I ain't payin' for that family's problems," she repeated to herself.

"Now, let's see," said Vera, as she approached the counter, "where were we, Lottie?"

"You was gonna pay something on this bill, Vera."

"Oh, of course, and I do want these items here and a carton of cigarettes, and a fine bottle of Jack Daniels behind you."

With determination in her voice, Lottie said, "Just how much you payin' on the bill, Vera?"

"Well, I'm sure you can do with fifty dollars. As I said, Charley will pay it all when he returns the end of this week."

Lottie sighed, "All right, Vera, but you're not to charge any more until it's all paid off. I can't afford to hold you any longer than a week."

Vera offhandedly paged through a magazine and smartly replied, "If your husband was waitin' on me, there'd be a difference of opinion, I bet."

"No, there wouldn't, Vera." Marvin Crammer stood at the living room entrance to the store. "I fully agree with my wife."

"Why, Marvin Crammer. I didn't know you were here," Vera said, smiling.

"I'm sorry, Vera, but it's cash and carry for you from now on."

Both women looked at him in surprise.

"I'll take fifty dollars now, and you can charge the groceries. The liquor and cigarettes will have to be bought with cash."

Teeth clenched and making references under her breath to their being ungrateful, Vera signed the check. "The check is to Charley from Ed Gibbs," she shouted.

"We've never had any trouble with Ed's checks," replied Marvin. "Can I put these in a bag?"

"No thanks!" yelled Vera. She picked up her cereal and milk and moved to the door. As she opened it, she turned to them and said, "Some people just forget what others have done for them!" and slammed the door behind her.

"Now, I wonder what she meant by that?" said Marvin with a smirk on his face.

"You know damned well what she meant. What I want to know is, why your sudden change from credit to cash?"

"Well, m'love, that woman's in a bad way, I'm afraid, from what I heard."

"From what you heard?"

"You know that gadget on the phone in the living room? The one I been workin' on? It connects the pay phone to ours, just like it was an extension," he answered proudly.

"Why'd you do a thing like that?"

"Just to prove it could be done, m'love."

"Ain't it against the law or somethin'?"

"I wouldn't be a bit surprised," he answered as he watched Vera slam the truck door and speed out of the parking lot.

"She was bawlin' her husband out for doin' all that buyin' last week, wasn't she?"

"No, m'love. It's far more serious than that. She was callin' a sister of hers in California, a Lillian Breslin in Long Beach, California."

"Her sister? In Long Beach?"

"Well, it seems, m'love, that Charley's gone off and left. She's got nothin' but the change from that check and a harvest with no one to bring it in."

"You mean he ain't coming back?"

"That's right. And, what's more, that sister in Long Beach won't help her; won't help her directly, that is."

"Not directly?"

"Seems she'll support the boys, but only if Vera puts them in that orphanage in Wilcox. What's the name of it?

"St. Helena's?"

"That's it. She'll send money to the orphanage for their care, but not to Vera. It seems Vera owes her money from way back."

"She told Vera to put the boys at St. Helena's?"

"That's right, m'love."

"I'm not partial to Vera, but what a dilemma to put her in."

"Her sister's only safeguardin' her loan, m'love. I don't think the good nuns at St. Helena's will use the money she sends for the boys' care to buy cartons of cigarettes or cases of Jack Daniels."

Lottie walked to the dirty window and looked out. The dust from Vera's truck had just settled. "Would she do it? Would she put them in an orphanage?"

"At this point, I don't see she's got much choice," said Marvin as he moved into the living room. "Unless you want to let her charge here for what she needs."

Lottie turned and followed him into the living room. "I wouldn't mind her charging if it meant the kids, and only the kids, didn't go hungry, but I'm damned if I'd let her charge her cigarettes and Jack Daniels."

Marvin picked up the phone, rechecked the connection and smiled as he said, "That's exactly what her sister in Long Beach had in mind, m'love."

Chapter Three

St. Helena's — Wilcox, Indiana

Sister Jean Theophane laid down the letter she had just read. It was a revelation from the past, and with it came many memories of her days in the novitiate. She picked it up again and reread parts of the letter to make sure she fully understood what she found difficult to believe.

> ... and so, my dear friend, Sister Jean, it is I who instigated a parent company of my husband's corporation to give to St. Helena's the yearly charitable contributions that have been sent since you became Superior eight years ago ... I, as well as you, know so well my limits and that I disassociated myself from the responsibility of becoming a mother. My sister, Vera, should be so wise as to do the same. I still feel completely in your debt for what you did for me so many years ago ... If Vera agrees to place the boys at St. Helena's, I do not know how long they would be in your care, but it is the only solution I could come up with under the circumstances. Again, I must be specific on two points: Although the money for the children's care is of no consequence, at no time is money to be given to Vera for any reason if she decides to give the children to St. Helena's. It is not necessary that the children know who their benefactor is. Again, thank you, dear friend, for what I ask of you now, and for what I asked of you so many years ago. Your friend, Lillian (Roberts) Breslin

The nun put the letter down slowly and knew she was correct in contacting her superior. The situation was such that she did not feel that she could take responsibility for it without further consideration. She again glanced at the letter and waves of memories of her first days in the convent swept over her. Time had moved so quickly; so much had been forgotten and then suddenly revived by a single letter. The nun opened a drawer and pulled out a file as the intercom on her desk rang out.

"Yes?" she asked.

"Sister, I called Monsignor Sabin as you requested, and he will be available to meet with you this morning at his office at eleven a.m."

"Thank you, Sister," said the nun as she snapped off the intercom. Looking at the clock, she figured there would be just enough time to get to the Monsignor's office a block away. But first, she must look at her photo album. Quickly, the nun left her office and spirited herself upstairs to her bedroom. From a closet shelf, she took down an album. Finding the correct page, she became startled and sat back giggling. Yes, there were so many memories. Facing her was a picture of a novice in an all-white habit and, next to her, was another young lady about the same age in a long skirt, sweater, and oxfords.

"Who would have believed that what we dreamed of would all come true?" the nun whispered under her breath.

Then, realizing the shortness of time, she quickly shut the book and replaced it on the shelf. While on her way to the appointment, she hoped she would feel better about the situation after her visit with Monsignor Sabin.

The receptionist escorted Sister Theophane into the Monsignor's office and told her that he would only be a few minutes. As she sat in front of his large mahogany desk, she examined the file she had brought. She checked the figures her accountant had given her. She wished her discussion to go smoothly. From previous meetings, she knew the priest to be somewhat devious. He had a tendency to water down what she considered to be most important. As she mentally prepared to state her feelings about the acceptance of the McBride children, the side door of the office opened. The nun stood and greeted the elderly priest, who shook her hand and said, "Good morning, Sister, and how are you this fine Monday morning?"

"Good morning, Monsignor," she replied, and waited until he was seated before sitting herself. He was a large man physically, and although a gracious and likeable superior, it was difficult to disagree with him. Before talking, the nun reminded herself to make her point and to stand her ground.

"Well, Monsignor, as my secretary stated, I have somewhat of an unusual situation and thought it best that I confer with you about it," she stated as she handed him the letter. "As you will see from this letter, we have found the answer to our mysterious guardian angel that appeared when I first became superior of St. Helena's."

"I see ... I see," said the priest as he continued to peruse the letter. When he had finished, he returned it to the nun and said, "Well, I see you have certainly discovered the source of your angel. I'm curious, Sister. Would you tell me more about her? Your relationship ... if you don't mind?"

"Of course not, Monsignor. I have had every intention of doing just that since receiving Lillian's letter. You see, Lillian and I came from the southern part of the county, near Dale and Coix. We lived about twenty miles outside Wilcox. Our fathers owned adjoining farms. That was until we were thirteen."

"I see," he said, sitting back in his chair.

"My parents wished me to continue in a parochial school; so, when I began high school, I attended St. Cecilia's Academy."

"I remember you as a freshman," interrupted the priest. "I would come to say mass there on holy days, and you would put the vestments out. Did I ever tell you that?" he said laughingly.

"No," the nun said and blushed. "I do remember you coming to say mass and wanted to be of some service to the church even then."

He was very likeable, and the nun felt she must stay to the point. "As I was saying, I attended St. Cecilia's and Lillian went to Wilson High, but we kept in contact. Our families were acquainted. In fact, when my father retired, he sold part of his farm, the adjoining part, to Lillian's father. Well, anyway, I graduated and went directly to the novitiate. In those days, the novitiate was part of St. Helena's, and ..."

"Did you ever believe, Sister, that one day you would be asked to supervise that wonderful institution?" he interrupted with a boyish grin.

"No, Monsignor. I just wanted to join the Holy Claire's order because of their missionary work and teaching work. I never really saw myself as an administrator."

"Well, Sister, we seldom meet, except at administrative functions, and I never get the chance to thank you for the wonderful job you are doing at St. Helena's," he continued.

"Thank you, Monsignor," she replied. His compliments were appreciated, but she wished he would not interrupt her train of thought. 'Is he really listening to me?' she thought. Maybe she was drawing out the explanation too much.

"Well, to make a long story short, Monsignor, I graduated from the Academy and went on to the novitiate. Lillian lived at home and worked at different jobs in town. Once in a while, when time permitted, she would visit me during the year. Then, one day in late May, she came to me, very late at night, right to my room at the novitiate. She was very distressed. She had found out she was pregnant, and refused to name the father. It went deeper than that. Lillian's younger sister, Vera, was preferred by her father. The pregnancy only heightened his prejudice against Lillian. In any event, to further punish her, her father told her to leave the house until she would tell him the name of her lov ... the father of the child. Lillian was adamant. Under no circumstances would she reveal his name. Having no place to go, she came to me for help."

"Didn't the mother have something to say about all this?"

"No, Monsignor. Mrs. Roberts had nothing to say about anything in that household, and was treated most unjustly by her husband in front of the neighbors and children. It was a very unhappy household."

"A most perplexing problem, I would say." the priest replied.

17

"Yes, Monsignor. In any event, she came to me with nothing but the clothes on her back and a small suitcase of personals. And, so, there in the middle of a May night, there at the novitiate, sat two young girls, crying, one out of rage and frustration, the other out of compassion. Well, I immediately called my superior, who at that time was Sister Catherine."

"Sister Catherine? Of course," he interrupted. "How is she? Where is she now?"

"Sister Catherine is administrator of our hospital in Arizona. She's doing very well." The nun wished he would not interrupt and began to shorten her story.

"Anyway, I told Sister Catherine, and she made arrangements for Lillian to stay at the novitiate until her situation could be worked out. Mr. Roberts never relented; only Mrs. Roberts knew where she was. As it worked out, Lillian stayed with us until the child was born. It was her wish to give the child up for adoption to St. Helena's and to get as far away from Indiana as possible.

"Where did she go?"

"To California, Monsignor."

"California?"

"Yes, we have several schools there. She stayed at one of our novitiates in Long Beach until she found a working position."

"And the child, Sister?" he asked.

"The child was adopted out of St. Helena's several weeks later to a couple that moved to the northern part of the state."

The priest sat back in his chair and said, "That's most interesting, Sister. And, so, because of your friendship and the benevolence of your order, St. Helena's Orphanage has been debt free since you became Superior."

"Yes, Monsignor. Lillian married into quite a bit of wealth, and we have been accepting this guardian angel contribution for the amount of ..." The nun paged through the papers until she found the report. "Over the past eight years, Breslin Corporation, under the name of Breslin, Inc., a company owned by Lillian's late husband, Lou Breslin, has contributed the amount of $22,798.00," the nun said as she handed the priest the financial report.

"Her husband is dead?" he asked.

"Yes, Monsignor. Lillian was the sole heir of a great fortune. Actually, if you notice, the contributions started anonymously under another name. Probably when she first married."

"I see," he said, pausing to look at the report. "Tell me, Sister, is she insisting that we take in her nephews?"

"No, Monsignor. Only asking."

With a caution that precluded his discussing a sensitive issue, he asked, "Is there any indication that ... we owe her a favor ... that we ..." He fished for the right phrase, "that is, that we are expected to take the children or that further contributions ... would stop?"

That he would consider the possibility after all that Lillian had done irritated the nun, but she bit her lip and said, "You have read the same letter I have, Monsignor. I believe Lillian is just saying that it is the only way she will be of help to Vera without giving her sister any personal help."

"Yes, of course," the priest said as though excusing his indiscretion, "Well, in light of what she has already contributed, I would say that we certainly owe someone something, wouldn't you, Sister?"

The nun recognized his statement as an attempt to convince her to accept the children without really studying the problems and circumstances that would accompany them.

"Monsignor," she said emphatically, "I am most reticent of this situation. Most of the children that are in our care are abandoned. Parents have either given up their rights or are not directly involved with the children any longer. Children at St. Helena's are placed there under court orders. These court orders allow us to decide what is best for the children. In effect, the parents of our wards have no control over their children while at St. Helena's. Now, allowing the mother to just drop those children off until she is financially prepared to pick them up again, leaves a great many questions unanswered. But, worst of all, it sets an administrative precedent that I consider most unwise."

"Well, we would, of course, have the children follow your usual entrance procedures; physical examinations, paper work, et cetera."

"Monsignor," the nun replied, "the children will follow those procedures, but what I want to know is, how do we handle the legal aspects; the rights of the mother, while the children are with us, visiting rights? How long are they to stay?"

"Of course, you are right, Sister, and let me assure you, these considerations will be taken seriously. But, in good time, Sister, in good time."

The nun felt she was fighting a losing battle. He was being evasive, playing the difficulties down, and extending any final decisions to future meetings. She had to make her point, and now. "Monsignor, I do not believe we should accept the McBride children, no matter how much their aunt has contributed in the past."

"Why, Sister, as I am not inferring that we have an obligation to accept the children, but accepting the children without court orders has been done in the past."

"If you're referring to the Crawford case, you will remember, Monsignor, that the situation turned out to be an embarrassment for the institution."

"Yes, I do remember, Sister, but, unlike the Crawford case, we do have the continuation of financial support to consider."

The nun sighed and stated, with a steadied patience, "But I also do not want St. Helena's to go on record as a high-priced babysitting institution."

The priest was taken aback by the directness of the nun and responded politely, "Well, now, I tell you what, Sister. Mrs. Breslin has done us a great service over the years. I believe, in all Christian charity, that we do owe her something. I'll tell you what: We will accept the children, temporarily, that is, and you have Mrs. McBride see me personally if she brings the children. No matter what time of day or night, you have her see me. I will personally take control of this situation," he said emphatically.

The nun knew she had lost, and, with hesitation, asked, "Do you wish to contact Lillian Breslin regarding your decision, Monsignor?"

"No," he said slowly, "I think you should handle that."

As the nun got up, she said, "I will, of course, follow your directions, Monsignor, and await your decisions on visiting rights and length of stay."

"Of course, Sister," he replied. "Really, it's not as complicated as all of that. I'm sure we can work everything out."

"Yes," she said with reluctance, "I'm sure we can."

"Well, now, you keep me posted on this."

"Yes, of course," she replied, "and I will have to confer with Sister Maureen at St. Helena's if the children become our wards. They will be schooled there."

"Of course, Sister. Make whatever plans are necessary."

The nun began to leave, and the priest stood and extended his hand. "You know, Sister, the children might not even be brought here for our care."

"That's exactly what I'm praying for," she replied while shaking his hand. "It would make things much simpler."

"True," replied the priest. "True, but God works his will in wondrous ways. We are not to reason why, but be a servant to Him without question," he said smiling.

"Yes, of course," she replied as she opened the door.

"Thank you, again, Sister, for coming. Tell the other sisters I send my regards, and don't hesitate to drop in again."

"Oh, thank you, Monsignor," she said, respectfully. "If the children are brought to our care, you will be hearing from me with God's speed."

Chapter Four

St. Helena's

The little girl balanced the tray of food in her left hand as she quietly knocked on the office door.

"Come in," said Sister Maureen, looking up from her desk. "Oh, Jeannie, you are a dear. Just bring it in and set it up there on the table. I see we're having tuna sandwiches and soup today. Tell me, dear, how is the sixth grade these days?"

"Oh, it's fine and you know it, Sister," she said as she put the tray down. "You always ask me that when you see me."

The nun laughed as she placed some papers in a file.

"Sister," asked the little girl, "why are you eating in the office today?"

"Because Sister Theophane called. You remember Sister Theophane."

"She taught us when you got ill last year."

"That is correct. Well, she called and wants to talk to me privately."

"She wants to talk to you how?"

"In private, dear. With no one around. And, since I have so much work to do today, Sister Theophane and I are going to eat lunch right here and have a nice private talk."

"When I have to talk private with you, can I eat lunch in your office with you, too?"

The nun leaned back in her chair laughing and said, "Of course, you may, dear. When you have something private to talk about, we'll have lunch, dinner or breakfast right here in the office."

"You'd better watch out, Sister Maureen. Word of these private lunches might get around and then you would have the entire student body asking to share lunches with their favorite principal," Sister Theophane said as she walked into the office.

"Oh, Sister, so good to see you. You remember Jeannie Willits?"

"Of course," answered the nun. "How are you, Jeannie? And how is the ... ah ... sixth grade?"

"I just asked her myself," said Sister Maureen. "I'm afraid we are a bit redundant."

"A bit what, Sister?" asked the child.

"Never mind, Jeannie. It's time for you to go. One new word in your vocabulary a day is enough," she answered as she escorted the child out of the office door and closed it behind her.

21

"These children today ... so grown up!" she exclaimed as she returned to her desk.

"Oh, Theo, your call has put me wondering. Here, I had your lunch brought in. We won't be disturbed. Now, tell me all. What's going on? And who is your guardian angel?"

Sister Theophane sat down at a small table and put the napkin in her lap. "Mo, you'll never believe this. Here, read this while I start on the soup."

The nun took the letter and quickly read as Sister Theophane began her lunch. When she finished reading, she returned the letter, saying, "Theo, I can't believe it. You were just talking about it the other day. Remember? And you were right."

"I know, Mo, I know."

"You said to me, 'What if my guardian angel was Lillian?' Those were your exact words, right here in this room. I remember."

"I know, Mo. This whole situation is quite unreal."

"... and now her nephews might be coming to St. Helena's?"

"... and attending St. Helena's elementary school," the nun replied as she sipped from a cup.

"Of course."

"That's why I'm here, Mo. But first, I need to talk to someone about all this. In private," Theo said, teasingly.

"Oh, of course, dear friend. But tell me, Theo, what did Swinging Sammie Sabin say?"

"Oh, Mo. That's absolutely profane!" Theo said as she laughed.

"If he cares as much about the institutions under his management as he does his golf scores, we'll all be better off," Sister Maureen said sarcastically.

"True, true. I got his usual 'I will be handling this case personally,' and, of course, you know who gets left calling the police on irate irresponsible parents."

"Oh, you poor dear. Here we go again, eh?"

"I tried to explain to him, Mo, that you can't let children into St. Helena's without some kind of legal custody for our sake; but, of course, he sees the possibility of Lillian's checks not coming at the end of the year, so ... 'I will handle this case personally'," Theo replied, mimicking the priest.

"Oh, Theo, I don't envy you your position."

"I tried to explain to him. I reminded him as gently as possible about the Crawford case."

"That's the one where the mother was ..."

"Where the mother was given carte blanche access to her children which were here in our care, thanks to Monsignor Sabin. Her family was old stock in the parish. The mother called or visited all hours of the day and night, and, more drunk than sober. Oh, it was terrible, Mo. Those unexpected visits would always end up with the police dragging her out the front door while she screamed profanities at us."

"I remember, Theo. She came to the school several times, too."

"I tried to impress on him that we have to have certain rights when those children are in our care, and when the parents are still involved. And, it could happen in this case, Mo. I even told him I didn't want the case."

"How long will they be staying, Theo?"

"Ask Swinging Sammie Sabin."

"Oh, Theo," said the nun, laughing, "You really are upset, aren't you?"

"Do you blame me?"

"The letter said the children were ... how old?"

"Eight and ten, Mo. They are two young boys brought up with an alcoholic mother and a father that just abandoned them."

"You knew Vera, didn't you, Theo?"

"I was in the Roberts' house several times as a child. That was years ago. I don't expect Vera would know me, but I shall never forget her or her poor mother. Mrs. Roberts led a persecuted life in that house. They weren't even sure that her death was accidental."

"Oh, my God in Heaven," yelped Mo, as she made the sign of the cross. "How did she die, Theo?"

"She fell down a flight of stairs ... stairs that she had used for twenty years. Before the accident, she had confided to a neighbor that she was pregnant and that she had not told her husband. The neighbor had described how distraught she was about the pregnancy. Anyway, after she died, several friends of hers were of the opinion that she threw herself down the stairs to avoid having another child. It was just hearsay. Nothing was proved one way or another."

"Oh, Theo. You've got me on pins and needles. What was wrong with that household?"

The nun wiped the crumbs from her mouth and continued, "Well, Mo, Mr. Roberts' word was law in that house on all subjects. His wife was given no say or opportunity to ever express herself in any regard. The last time I was in that house was for Lillian's fourteenth birthday. There was a party. About six or seven freshman classmates were there. Vera, who was ten, was also there. She had some friends there, too. I remember Lillian had just blown out the candles. We had just sung 'Happy Birthday.' Lillian was going to open her presents when Vera glanced at her father, saying, 'Could I blow out the candles, too?' Her mother replied something about it not being her birthday, but Mr. Roberts became very demanding. So, to ward off any embarrassment, she took time to light the fourteen candles. Well, some of the kids blew out the candles, and Vera became very bratty and looked at her father for them to be relit. Mr. Roberts again insisted. Mrs. Roberts said something to the effect that there were presents to be opened, that it was not her birthday. Well, no one was really paying attention to all this until Mr. Roberts yelled a profanity at his wife and screamed, 'You light those G.D. candles right now! If my little girl wants to blow out birthday candles on someone else's cake, then that's what she's gonna do!'

"Oh, I can tell you, Mo, the conversation and enjoyment in that room came to an immediate halt. Some children snickered, but Lillian, myself and others were so embarrassed, and, of course, Lillian's mother was so humiliated! Lillian started to cry and ran to her room. I made some excuse and left the party. So did the others. I remember after I got my coat and was heading for the door, I took one more glance at the party table. The smaller children were sitting quietly, content in eating their ice cream and cake. Mrs. Roberts left the room. Presents sat on the table unopened, and Vera stood at the head of the table; a smile of satisfaction was on her face, and slowly, so very slowly, she blew out those birthday candles one ... by ... one."

"Oh, Theo, that's not only sad, that's sick, very sick."

"Oh, yes, Mo. There was a sickness in that house. I had glimpses of it. I had heard my mother talk about it."

"You were friends in high school?"

"We became friends during high school, and after graduation I went into the novitiate. She worked in various jobs in town. Then she got pregnant and Mr. Roberts threw her out of the house. That's when she came to me. She didn't know where else to get help. Sister Catherine gave her a position at the orphanage and kept the whole matter confidential. Mrs. Roberts would come to see her when she could. Her husband never knew where she went, before or after the child was born. To my knowledge, Lillian never saw her father again after she was thrown out."

There was a big silence between the women as they both thought of what had been said. Then Mo turned to Theo and said, "Theo, who did it?"

"What?"

"Who got Lillian pregnant?"

The nun put down the sandwich slowly and looked at her friend.

"Mo, you're a very dear and trusted friend, but I did give my word that I would never divulge his name."

"Oh, of course, Theo. I have no right. Lillian's child must be about ten now?"

"Eleven, Mo. The child is eleven," she answered quietly.

"Well, I'll never forget when you mentioned during one of our 'Chapter of Faults,' Theo, that your real intention for visiting Sister Angelus in the hospital was really to view Lillian's newborn baby."

"Oh, Mo, do you remember those sessions of 'telling it all,' sitting in a circle, the whole community, and explaining each one's wrong doings for the previous week to everyone?"

"Thank God that barbaric practice has been eliminated," Sister Maureen replied.

"I did see that baby when the three of us novices visited Sister Angelus at my suggestion. 'To cheer her up,' I said. The poor dear died of cancer. I remember, soon after we arrived and were visiting her, I made some feeble excuse to leave the room. I went to the nursery and asked the nurse to show me the Roberts baby. It was beautiful, right down to the little birthmark on its left cheek. After I confessed my real intention for the hospital trip, I was punished. 'You are not to avail yourself of any information regarding that child,' Sister Catherine warned me. But, as fate would have it, I accidentally found out more."

"How?" asked Sister Maureen anxiously.

"After Lillian gave birth, the State handled all the paperwork for the adoption, but St. Helena's was the foster home until placement could be made. One day, this couple came to the novitiate to see the Roberts child. They mistakenly thought the novitiate was the orphanage. I was on duty alone; everyone else had gone on convocation. I did not want them to walk all the way around the block, so I took them through the novitiate, which backs the orphanage. During our walk, I asked their names so that I could tell the sister at the orphanage they were coming in the back way. 'Phillips,' they said, and introduced themselves as Jack and Theresa. The woman had lived in Wilcox years ago before she married, and then moved away. She was unable to bear children."

"You found this all out in one walk through the novitiate?"

"I took them the long way, through the library and around through the kitchen."

"No wonder you were recognized so early as administrative material, dear friend."

"I was told later that the child had been adopted—not by whom, just adopted."

"But you're still curious, aren't you, Theo?"

The nun laughed, "Yes, I am. I must admit I was emotionally involved then. Even now, I would like to know what happened."

Again the nuns sat quietly; then Sister Maureen asked, "When could you expect Vera's children?"

"Well, Lillian didn't say, only that they might be on their way. It's Vera's decision."

"Well, maybe there's nothing to worry about."

"Thanks, Mo. You're sounding like Sammie Sabin."

"You haven't finished your sandwich. Now, how are we going to keep the administrator of Wilcox's finest orphanage well and in good spirits?"

Sister Theophane laughed, "By having a private lunch and a good talk with the administrator of St. Helena's school."

They both laughed as the phone rang.

"I told the good Monsignor I was coming here to inform you on the latest happening, or what might happen. Really, Mo, I pray that Vera doesn't bring her children to us."

As the phone rang, Sister Maureen reached for it and said, "I'm with you, Theo. Kids from normal home settings are difficult enough to handle without asking for offspring from parents like the McBrides. Excuse me, Theo ... Yes, Mrs. Campbell?" Sister Maureen handed the phone to her friend. "It's the orphanage. They want you, Theo. They found out you were back from the Monsignor's office."

Sister Theophane took the phone. After listening for a minute, her face became crestfallen. "Yes, of course," she said, as she shoved the rest of her lunch aside. "I'll be right there." She handed the receiver back to her friend. "I think I'm going to be sick, Mo."

"What's the matter?" replied Sister Maureen.

"They just told me that a woman and two boys are waiting to see me. Their name is McBride."

Chapter Five

St. Helena's

As Sister Theophane crossed the play yard that backed the grade school and orphanage, she was greeted by the children playing at their afternoon recess. As she passed each child, she greeted him or her by name and yearned for the days of having just the responsibility of teaching the third grade. How she would gladly change places with any grade school teacher for the post and responsibilities she found herself involved in now. Her head began to ache and she lacked any enthusiasm for the meeting that was about to take place. She looked about, realizing that forty of the two hundred children in the yard would return to the orphanage at the end of the day. The rest would board busses and return to their homes in Wilcox and throughout the countryside. She was about to agree to take two more children and the whole affair strained against her better judgment. The door to the orphanage was opened by Sister Ann, and, from her facial expression, it was obvious that she was upset.

"I'm sorry to have interrupted your meeting, Sister, but I had to call you."

"No problem, Ann," Sister Theophane said abruptly.

The two nuns walked briskly through the long narrow kitchen. Sister Ann was hardly able to keep up with her superior.

"They have only been here for fifteen minutes, but all that time, the boys have been running up and down the hall. They nearly knocked over the St. Anthony statue."

"Yes, Sister," Sister Theophane said impatiently.

"Their mother just sits in your office, smoking and using your inlaid glass paperweight for an ashtray."

"Yes, Ann," the nun said emphatically.

"... And the language I've heard! Well, I'm glad they're not our children!"

Sister Theophane came to a sudden halt and faced the nun. It was clear from her tone, that she was tired and impatient, "Sister Ann, that woman out there is Mrs. McBride. She has come here to make arrangements for her children to be placed in our care. Before you start asking questions: Yes, Monsignor Sabin has accepted the case, against my better judgment. No, I don't know how long they are going to stay, but while they are with us, we are going to have to put up with much more than scuffed hallways, inlaid paperweights used as ashtrays, and the Lord's name taken in vain."

"I'm sorry, Sister. I was not aware of the situation." Sister Ann said apologetically.

"Well, now you are, Ann." Sister Theophane leaned against the wall and rubbed her forehead.

"You have one of your headaches again, don't you, Sister?"

"Yes. I'm sorry, Ann. It's been a long day, and it's not over yet. I could use your help right now."

"Of course, Sister."

"Interrupt me in a few minutes after I begin talking to Mrs. McBride, then suggest the children go on a small tour of the main building. Return them to the chapel and keep them busy until I am done talking with Mrs. McBride. I will have them say their goodbyes there."

"Of course, Sister," the nun said and promptly left.

Sister Theophane stood before the kitchen door leading to the hallway. She wondered if Vera would recognize her; if Lillian had told her who she was, should she acknowledge knowing her. There were too many questions that came to mind and her head ached. She would play it by ear. The nun entered the hallway and walked across to her office as she heard, "Quit runnin' around, God damn it!"

The nun stopped at her office door, and her presence startled two boys who were running toward her.

"Oh, shit! You scared me!" said the older boy who was bumped from behind by his younger brother. The nun looked at the boys. They looked like they hadn't bathed in days. Their clothes were filthy, shoes were untied or without laces. 'They will certainly need to be isolated. They probably have lice,' she thought.

"Damn you! Stop running, I said." Vera looked up and saw the nun framed in the doorway. "Oh, Sister, I am sorry. These boys are the death of me." She continued to discipline them and attempted to introduce them to her as they scampered around the room playing tag. Sister Theophane moved behind her desk and introduced herself. The boys roughhoused as Vera explained why she was at St. Helena's.

"I have been contacted by your sister, Mrs. Breslin, regarding arrangements for having the boys stay here temporarily," Sister Theophane explained.

Lillian had obviously not told Vera who she was.

"Now, you know they ain't goin' to stay here forever," Vera said while trying to put some humor into a very nerve-wracking conversation. "It's just that I'm down and out right now. Charley, my husband, is North, workin'. I need to work the farm. There's no one to take care of the boys, so my sister Lillian made this suggestion. She said she'd help by payin' for the boys to stay here until this … until I'm on my feet again, and it's just a perfect plan." The woman rambled on and on. The smell of whiskey was all about her. She talked as though to convince herself of what she was doing. The more she rambled, the more tension was heard in her voice. Sister Theophane looked at the woman as she continued to talk. It was obvious Vera did not recognize her. The woman who sat in front of her had aged beyond her years. Sister Theophane could see no resemblance to the little girl she had known so long ago.

"This arrangement is strictly temporary, you understand, Sister. We're goin' to sell the place right off. You know, it's worth a fortune, some of the best land in Vincennes County." The woman licked her lips and puffed on her cigarette.

Sister Ann came into the room and was introduced. The boys sat on the couch poking each other, oblivious to the nun's entrance. The adults made small talk, and then Sister Ann made the suggestion that she take the boys on a small tour of the building. The boys jumped at the chance to leave the room, and the nun and the children left. When they were alone, Sister Theophane partially shut the office door and returned to her desk.

"I need to know exactly how long you expect to leave the children in our care, Mrs. McBride."

"Well, as I've said, things ain't goin' our way." The woman swept her hand through her uncombed hair, as though to trim up her appearance. "But, it shouldn't be more than a couple of months. My husband is up north right now, and, well, he's sick of farmin'. As I said, we're goin' to sell the place. It's an awful burden, you understand. Why, I wouldn't be surprised if everything was right-side-up again by the end of the month."

"Of course," the nun replied, giving no indication that she knew the woman was lying about the whereabouts of her husband.

"Mrs. McBride," inquired the nun, "I have talked to my superior, Monsignor Sabin, and he wished to discuss this matter with you at your earliest convenience. I would suggest that, after you leave here, you go directly to his office regarding the placement of the children."

She handed the woman two legal forms.

"The first one is in regard to our right of legal guardianship while the children are in our care. That one you take to Monsignor's office. The second ..."

Vera quickly took the papers from the nun and stuffed them in her purse. It was obvious that she was not able to face up to the realities of leaving her children.

"Mrs. McBride," demanded the nun, "I need that paper signed before you leave here, giving us the right to administer any medication or to call a doctor in your name." The woman slowly took the papers from her purse.

"I'm sorry ... I'm in such a hurry."

Sister showed the woman the paper, and without a word, Vera affixed her signature. It was obvious to the nun that any discussion of rights and other institutional procedures was out of the question. Vera wet her lips and kept trying to put her hair in place. All the while, she shyly smiled to keep some pretense of dignity about her. She handed the nun the paper, saying, "I know you'll do the right things by my boys. They're really lookin' forward to stayin' here. I told them all about this place and all the friends they're gonna make."

The nun could see through the partially opened door that Sister Ann was taking the boys into the chapel.

"I do wish to remind you, Mrs. McBride, that Monsignor Sabin is most anxious to see you. He will explain that other paper to you regarding our right of guardianship while the boys are in our care."

On seeing that Vera was anxious to leave and in no condition to continue any conversation, the nun suggested that she go to the chapel to say goodbye to her sons. The nun stood as the woman reached out to shake her hand. She again reassured the nun that the situation was only temporary; things would work out, and the boys would be home within the month. The nun sat down as Vera made sure of her directions to the chapel and left, leaving the door open.

"Don't forget to go to the Monsignor's office," Sister Theophane said as Vera waved goodbye.

The nun rubbed her forehead and sat back in her chair. She felt a migraine coming on. It was no surprise; they often accompanied her on a full day of work. She clicked the intercom on her desk and instructed her secretary to contact the Monsignor's office. "Please notify the Monsignor that Mrs. McBride was here and is now on her way over to see him," she said as she rubbed her forehead.

The first visit had not gone well. The nun knew it. The boys were not prepared to stay at St. Helena's. It was obvious that they understood very little of what was going on. She could hear the faint voices of the children as they argued with their mother. Children saying goodbye to their parents was always emotionally upsetting to her. Being Superior had given her the advantage of leaving the emotional separation to someone else. Their voices rose and intermingled with the noises of laughter from the playground. Soon the nun could not distinguish the different sounds, and, then, as in a dream, she saw herself driving a school bus. It was a dream she could not wake from ...

... All the other buses were going in the opposite direction. They were full of children laughing and waving out the window. In her bus, there were just the McBride boys, sitting across the aisle, solemn and hateful. She was taking them to town, to St. Helena's, and they didn't want to go. It was a holiday, and all the other children were going home. She continued to drive them past the many buses loaded with children that waved and shouted. Suddenly, everyone began to honk their horns at her to tell her to turn around. She drove faster to avoid the noise. The boys pleaded with her to stop the bus. The faster she drove, the louder the honking and the more persistent the boys.

The nun suddenly awoke with a start; the intercom on her desk was bleeping. "Yes?" she answered, pressing the button.

"I have contacted the Monsignor's office, Sister, but he is not there. It seems he is playing golf," her secretary replied. "He left word that he would not be in for the rest of the afternoon."

"Thank you," Sister Theophane said as she flipped off the intercom.

Sister Theophane sat back. "The nerve of that man!" she thought as Sister Ann opened the door.

"I see what you mean, Sister Theophane," she said. "Those children are going to be a real headache."

"The children are in isolation?" inquired Sister Theophane.

"Yes, Sister Emory is with them. Oh, Sister, it is not going to be easy."

"Were the children upset when their mother left?"

"They argued somewhat, but became resigned to stay the week."

"The week?" Sister Theophane shouted, taken aback.

"Why, yes," replied Sister Ann, "Mrs. McBride was quite emphatic about that. She said she would be back no later than Saturday night; that she would pick them up right there in the chapel. She kept saying to me, 'Be sure to have all their things packed,' that she didn't want her boys staying a minute longer than they had to."

Sister Theophane put her hand to her forehead. Pain throbbed in her temples. Quickly, she picked up the phone and asked for Monsignor Sabin's office.

"Is anything the matter, Sister?" Sister Ann asked.

While waiting for the connection, she said, "Sister, Vera McBride sat right here and told me that it would be at least a month. I know it's going to be longer than that. She lied to me about her husband's whereabouts. Only God knows how long we will have them with us; and our Superior, who told me explicitly that he was going to handle this case personally, is out playing golf ... and now she has lied to the children with regard to when she will return for them."

A receptionist answered on the other end of the line, and Sister Theophane requested to speak with the Monsignor.

"He is still out playing golf, Sister. I really don't expect him back this afternoon. Could I take a message?"

"Yes. Sister Theophane requests his presence at dinner at St. Helena's Convent Sunday evening, around seven?"

"I'll give him the message, Sister," replied the secretary.

Sister Theophane hung up and sat back in her chair, tapping her pencil angrily.

"Excuse me, Sister Theophane," asked the nun, "but isn't our Mother Superior dining with us that evening, too?"

"Yes," asserted Sister Theophane. "And when Mrs. McBride comes to pick up her boys, we'll invite her, too."

31

"What if she doesn't come?"

"Don't worry, Sister," explained Sister Theophane. "Either way, we'll have plenty to discuss over dinner."

Chapter Six

St. Helena's Chapel

Tears fell down the cheeks of the boy as he sat looking out the frosted glass windows of the chapel. He twirled in the seat and looked down the long aisle which ended at the altar. Three candles flickered on the altar and, because there was no light, the shadows of statues and the painted pictures were gruesome figures on the walls.

Johnny McBride could hear the chant of the other children as they prayed over their evening meal. He knew that one of the sisters would soon arrive with a tray of food to tempt him from his vigil. How long had he been here? He reckoned since yesterday noon, and he wondered how long he could last. His stomach ached as he smelled the prepared food, and it brought a revulsion of tears and hysteria which he held in place. He would not relent; there was nothing to relent for. He was right; they were the liars. She would come. She would arrive. She had promised.

If only his brother, Tommy, had not left. His own brother, and he had given up! Johnny was confused and tired. They had both decided to wait yesterday at noon, and they had been granted the right to wait. Johnny insisted that Tommy stay with him until their mother came, even during the night. But sometime during their sleep, Tommy had gone; maybe they took him away. The boy tried to convince himself that it didn't matter. He would wait it out alone. Even when they had brought his brother to him after Mass, and Tommy had said, "Really, Johnny, it's all right here. C'mon to breakfast. I don't want to see you sittin' here all day," Johnny recalled screaming about the importance of waiting. It was important that they wait in the chapel where she said she would pick them up. They were lying; she would come. He remembered the sisters pulling him off his brother, and for the first time, they were angered by his insistence.

"All right, Johnny," said the Irish nun, "If you're goin' to be so insistent, you can stay; but your brother has more sense. We'll leave your luggage here, just as you insist. But, I'll be tellin' ya this, young man, for a ten year old, you certainly have your own mind, and I'll have no pity for ya, boy. You can sit in this chapel until you know better, for all I care!"

Johnny remembered watching the nun march his brother up the aisle and to the door. Before leaving, she stopped and said to him, "And, we'll not be leavin' any electric lights on, Mr. McBride. You'll do with the candles, since you insist on waitin'. But it's no use. It's no use, young man. She'll not be comin', no matter how long you wait."

Johnny turned again to the windowpane and opened it to view the outside. His eyes followed the path that led to the main entrance. He remembered being brought up that path by his mother. He remembered being assured and reassured. He remembered how she kept wiping her nose and eyes with a handkerchief. Her actions irritated him and made him nervous. "Johnny, it's going to be fine ... just fine... There's lots of children here... Tommy will be with you... Actually, I won't be gone long ... just for a few days."

Once again, the boy turned in the pew and sat facing the chapel. Above the altar hung the big wooden cross with the figure of Jesus stretched across it. In the flickering candlelight, it seemed as though the eyes would open and close. The facial expressions changed, and all sorts of contortions could be imagined.

Then he heard noises. Someone was approaching the chapel entrance. They would be coming to entice him with a tray of food. The boy quickly went to the Holy fount and took the sponge from its center and squeezed the water into his mouth. With his mouth not so dry, it was easier to refuse the contents of the tray. Then he hurriedly sat down at his place as the janitor, with his broom and mops, walked across the chapel. When he saw the boy sitting at the end of the room, he stopped and shook his head.

"You're a stubborn one, that's for sure," he said. Then he took his equipment and put it in a small room behind the altar and was gone.

Again the boy's lips were dry and, as he had done before, he rose from his place and walked across the room and up to the fount. He took the sponge from its place, wet his lips and sucked at the liquid.

"Johnny McBride, put that down!"

The boy turned in fright. He had not heard her enter, yet there she stood. It was the nun from the kitchen. She was silhouetted in the light of the hallway. A tray was in her hand; her long black gown surrounded her like a shroud.

"That holy water is sacred, mister. It is not for drinkin'."

The boy returned to his seat and sat stiffly, as though pretending not to hear. The nun approached him, put the tray down, and said, "John, you are ten years old. You know the difference between right and wrong. Now, you cannot stay here in this chapel any longer, just waitin'. I know what your mother told you, but the instructions to us were different."

The boy sat motionless, as though there was nothing to hear. The nun moved closer to him. "I've brought you something to eat ... you must be very hungry. You've not eaten since yesterday."

When he did not reply, she knelt down, took his chin in her hand, and slowly turned his eyes toward her. "Now listen to me. When your mother brought you to this place, three days ago, it was with the understandin' that you would stay with us longer than just a week. She should have made that clear to you." The boy wrenched from her hold and scurried to the other end of the pew, where again he sat stiff and erect in protest. Then while giving a sigh, the nun slowly rose to her feet. "Young man, you've won your way again, but not for long. Time is running out. I'm afraid that something will be done."

Johnny sat very still, saying nothing. "I will leave this tray of food. You really should eat, John. You'll only make yourself sick." And, as quietly as she had come, she was gone.

Tears fell again down his cheeks and he cried as silently as possible. He could not let them hear him. He felt panicky inside; his stomach ached. He felt dizzy. The boy thought about the situation. He would go somewhere else. He didn't know where, but he would have to go. But first, he would sleep. His mouth tasted bitter from the water he had taken from the fount, and, although the food was tempting, he was determined not to eat. Again the dizziness came, and he laid his head down slowly. He would sleep for a moment, and then he would get up and go somewhere, but not so far. He had to be here when she came. He must be there when she came ... when she came ... when she ... came ... when ... she ... came...

The boy was not aware exactly what it was that awakened him, but on awakening, he knew he was not alone. He sat up in the pew. He wondered how long he had been sleeping. It had grown very dark outside. As his eyes became accustomed to the dim light, he saw four figures standing at the end of the aisle. They were talking about him. They were whispering something about him awaking. There were two nuns and two men. One of the men was the janitor; the other was the doctor that had examined him after arriving at the orphanage. Their mumbling was hardly understandable, but he knew they were talking about him. As they began to approach him, he sat up very erect, as though he had never fallen asleep, as though he had been waiting. The four approached him and stopped abruptly in front of him. He recognized the nun who had brought him the tray from the kitchen. The other nun he had met the first day he had come to St. Helena's.

"John, my name is Sister Ann. Do you remember me? I showed you the orphanage the first day you arrived here." The boy sat silently, ignoring them. "John, your mother will not be coming for you. She did not come yesterday. She will not be coming today." The boy sat very still, trying to blot out the words. "Nor will she be coming in the near future. Your sitting here will not make her return. She should have told you that she would return for you at a much later date." The boy sat perfectly still, as though the others did not exist.

"John, you cannot sit here waiting for her. I know what she told you, but she will not be returning. You must understand this."

He turned toward her. He was tired, angry, and suddenly, he did not want to hear any explanations about his mother's absence.

"She will come! ... She will come! ... You're lying to me! ... You're lying ... I hate you!"

As the doctor began to undo the black bag, the nun began rolling up her sleeves.

"Johnny, I don't care what you think, you cannot stay here waiting for something that is not going to happen. Doctor Neven has something to help you sleep, something to help you get over this idea that you must stay here and wait for your mother."

Instinctively, the boy knew it was time to move. They had not come to reason; they had come to end the situation. He scampered to the end of the pew, then down the middle aisle, and he crossed in front of them to get to the other side, to get to the exit door. He reached for the handle, but it would not open. It had been locked. When he turned around, they stood in front of him. He dove at them, but he was caught by the doctor.

"I got him! I got him! Get a good hold of him, Sister!"

As he tried to pull away, an arm circled his head and an arm caught him at the throat.

"I've got him," said the janitor. One of the nuns turned the light on.

The boy pulled and screamed, "You liars ... liars! ... Bastards! Let me go! ... She will come! ... She will come!"

With the doctor and janitor holding him, the kitchen nun held his legs so that he could not kick. "Hold him still. I don't want to hit a vein," the doctor said as he pressed his fingers against his arm. From his black case, he withdrew a syringe which had a large needle at one end. The doctor began rubbing something pungent on John's arm as all three tried to hold him in a still position.

"Should we be doing it this way, Doctor Neven?" asked the kitchen nun.

"There's no time to argue about that, now, Sister," he replied.

The boy began to break free.

"I'll take care of the rascal," said the janitor, and he lowered the boy to the floor. While pressing his knees to the boy's chest, he grabbed his wrists and stretched out his arms.

"Now you can stick him, Doctor," the janitor said triumphantly.

"I want my Mom! Let me go, you bastards," the boy cried as he tried in vain to move under the man's weight. Then he felt a sharp pain in his left arm, and when he looked to see its cause, he saw the needle of the metal container being pressed into his arm. He could feel his arm filling with something. He kicked his legs and lurched his head back and forth in hysteria, but for all his efforts, he could not begin to free himself.

"She's coming! ... She's coming! . . Don't, you bastards! . . Don't ... You lyin' bastards! ...She's comin'!"

The kitchen nun knelt close to him and pleaded that he be silent, and to the boy, she seemed more afraid than he was. Then the dizziness set in, and he resisted less and less. Then, the pressure was released from his chest and he tried to resist, but did not have the strength. He looked at the altar and could see the form of Jesus on the cross. Everything became hazy, and the form on the cross seemed to smile at him. The nun at his side prayed that the boy would forgive them. And, in a last effort at resistance, he uttered, "She's coming ...You're liars ... I hate you ... She's coming ... She lied . . I ... hate ... you ... I hate ... you ... you're coming ... she lied ... she ... lied ... I...I'm coming ... I hate ... I hate her!"

Chapter Seven

Kansas City — 1945

He stood at the corner of Ellis and Stuart streets in a gray security uniform given to him by Earl Bates. Earl was one hundred pounds heavier and about six inches shorter than Charley McBride, so Charley felt ridiculous standing on a street corner in an outfit that hardly fit him. The name "Universal Security Company, Inc." was embroidered on the right-hand side of his jacket. The nameplate on the left side had a plain piece of paper in it. Charley put his suitcase down and, after wiping the sweat from his forehead, shoved his hands in the unfamiliar pockets. He felt unsure and nervous about what he was about to do. He looked at a clock in the window of a jewelry shop. At one-forty, Earl was ten minutes late. 'Damn,' thought Charley. 'Where the hell is he?' he thought to himself.

Charley sat on the bus stop bench and thought of the plan. When Earl explained it, the plan sounded so easy. But, when left alone, Charley felt unsure. The waiting heightened the question of whether he had made the right decision. He had never done anything illegal. Well, not this illegal. "What if it doesn't work?" he said quietly to himself. But, if it did work, he'd have more money than he could possibly use.

He looked at the jewelry window clock again and swore to himself. "Damn! Where the hell is he?" he said. He reached into his shirt pocket and pulled out a pack of cigarettes and quickly lit one. Perspiration poured from his forehead and he wiped it away impatiently. He sat down on the bench and held the suitcase on his lap. A patrol car moved up and stopped for the red light. Charley's heart raced as he tightened his grip on the suitcase. The patrol car slowly moved on as the light changed. Charley wiped his forehead and cursed his friend for being late.

A dark blue 1938 Chevy drove up to the corner and the driver, dressed like Charley, bent over and opened up the door.

"Damn it, you're late!" yelled Charley as he threw down his cigarette and got in the car.

"It's O.K. Relax. We still got plenty of time," shouted Earl, "Did you get a piece?"

Charley opened the suitcase and showed Earl the weapon.

"Oh, for Christ's sake, Charley. I said a piece, not a damned machine gun."

"What the hell am I supposed to do? I got twenty bucks to my name. How the hell am I supposed to buy a piece? I cut the end off my shotgun last night. It'll work fine."

"Slide it up your sleeve when you get ready to use it."

The men sat silently as Earl drove the car through the traffic and turned off Ellis onto Archer Drive.

"How far we got to go?" asked Charley.

"Just a few blocks," replied Earl, "Let's go over it once more while we got the time."

"Suits me," said Charley as he wiped his sweaty forehead.

"I'm going to park in back where the security truck is going to park."

"Earl, what if there are more than two guys makin' the transfer?"

"Damn it, Charley, I've told ya. I worked for that company for three years. I know them. This is a regular run. All the time I worked for them, they only used two men on the regular runs. One rides shotgun and doubles in the security compartment and as a driver."

"All right, all right," sighed Charley, trying not to show his nervousness.

"Now, I'm going to park in back of where that security truck will park. We wait until the man riding shotgun gets out and goes into the bank."

"If he opens the back of the truck first ... " interrupted Charley.

"If he opens the back up first, we know there are three men and one of them is in the back, and we just drive off, but, I'm tellin' ya, Charley, there ain't goin' t' be three men. That's why I know this is goin' t' work," insisted Earl.

"All right. I just want to get it straight!" yelled Charley.

Earl made another left turn onto South Street and continued his explanation. "After we're parked, we'll have a ten-minute wait. When the man riding shotgun gets out, he'll go right into the bank. We wait until he comes out with the first load. It will be small coins and checks, worthless paper. Large bills always come last. He'll open the back of the security compartment and put the stuff in. He'll shut the door, but it won't be locked."

"You're sure it won't be locked?" interrupted Charley.

"If he locks the damned thing, we can't go through with it. Does that satisfy you, Charley?" yelled Earl as he slowed down for a red light.

"O.K., O.K., retorted Charley, who was getting mad at Earl for his impatience with him.

"Charley, I know what I'm doin' on this take. Now, relax. We aren't goin' to take any chances. Locked! Hell! I worked for this company for three years, and I've seen them hold those back doors together with rubber bands, then go in for the next transfer because the locks won't work."

"All right," said Charley as he sat back and tried to relax.

"When the guy comes out and puts the coins and paper in the security compartment, it looks to anyone who don't know like he locks it, but nobody ever does. He'll just slam the door. Nobody, I mean nobody, ever bothers to take out his key and lock that door. O.K.?"

"O.K." answered Charley.

"Now, when he goes back in the bank for the second load, I get out and go into that security department. At the same time, you are sticking that shotgun into the driver's face. Maybe it's best that you brought that thing. It's a hell of a lot scarier than a hand piece. You got buckshot in it?"

Charley nodded yes.

"Good. I'd rather go to prison for armed robbery than for murder 'cause you got nervous and shot someone's face off."

"Yeah, O.K.," answered Charley, who was getting impatient with Earl's sarcastic remarks.

"You have to take his two-way radio and gun off him. Put them on the floor. Tell him to get in the security compartment. I'll open the door to the cab from the inside and have my piece lookin' right at him. When the guy comes out from the second transfer and opens that door, I'll grab him and the money, slam the door, and get in this car. Then you just follow me."

"This place we drive to is your brother-in-law's ranch?" asked Charley.

"Yeah. The son of a bitch is loaded. He's got a beautiful spread right out of town. Talk about someone with money! Anyway, they're on a trip. There shouldn't be any life in the place. If there is, we'll just have to go somewhere else to split the money."

"Yeah, I guess so," said Charley nervously, as he lit another cigarette.

"After we split the money, I'll drive the guards out to an abandoned cement factory and put them in one of the buildings."

"What if someone sees us moving in and out of the truck?" asked Charley.

"It's a chance we take to split what I think will be a fifty thousand dollar transfer. Now, I'm ready to take a chance for that kind of dough. Are you?"

"Yeah, I guess so," answered Charley.

Earl turned right on Scott Street and said, "The bank is at the end of this street, about a block down."

"I thought you said you tried this once before, Earl."

"No, I didn't say I tried it. I said I planned it right up to the day before it was to come off, then they fired me. I thought maybe they suspected something, but the boss wanted to hire his brother. I was the last hired, so they gave me the boot. Anyway, it spooked my partner, so we didn't do it. Since then, I've been lookin' around for someone like you, someone who would be interested in gettin' rich on a sure deal."

"Yeah," said Charley hesitantly, as he nervously took a puff on his cigarette.

"This is the place," said Earl as he stopped in front of the Kansas Security Bank. "We're in luck. I'll back up two spaces so we're not obvious.

Charley began to perspire. He wiped his forehead and the sides of his face. "Shouldn't we have bags over our faces or something?" he asked.

"Hey, you're really thinkin' there, Charley. You'd look real cute sneakin' up to the driver with a damned paper bag on your head. Relax. It's going' t' be hard enough carryin' that piece of yours. Be sure to keep it hid in your sleeve until you got to show it."

The men smoked and kept silent until a gray security truck with the name "Universal" came to a stop ahead of them.

"It's here, Charley. They're gonna make the transfer," said Earl.

Charley could feel his armpits oozing with perspiration. The truck pulled a car length ahead of them and a man in a gray uniform got out on the right-hand side. He adjusted his belt, looked up and down the street and walked into the bank.

"They have to look like they know what they're doin'," Earl said jokingly.

"He didn't open the back door," replied Charley.

"I told ya, Charley, there's two, just two, guys. I'd bet my life on it."

They waited in silence, and then the bank door opened. The guard appeared carrying a metal box and dragging a mail pouch.

"There's coin in the pouch, checks, securities in the box," Earl said quietly.

He unlocked the back door to the truck and disappeared inside, shutting the door after himself. When he did not immediately reappear, Charley asked, "What happened? Do you think something's wrong?"

"Hell, no. He's just talking to the driver or something. Relax," replied Earl.

The door opened, and the guard jumped out and shut the door.

"He didn't lock it," said Charley, feeling more confident.

"I told ya. Nobody, but nobody ever takes the time to lock up between transfers," said Earl, almost in a whisper.

When the man had reentered the bank, Earl said, "O.K. It's our turn. Let's go. Let me get in the back, first, then you go for the cab."

Charley watched as Earl walked to the back of the truck. He looked up and down the street. Except for a mother and child walking by, it was almost deserted. Charley got out of the car as Earl slowly opened the truck door. The light had turned green at the intersection; cars were moving in the traffic lanes. Charley quickly moved to the front of the truck. Standing just in back of the driver's door, he realized he could be seen by the driver in the rear-view mirror. They looked at each other. The driver was puzzled. He was a middle-aged man with receding hair. He began to roll down the window to ask something. Words began to form on the man's lips, as Charley stuck the shotgun through the open window.

"Open the door. Put the radio and gun on the floor, God damn it!" Charley grunted.

The man moved quickly and did as he was told.

41

"Now get in the back," said Charley as he moved into the front seat.

Without saying a word, the man opened the small door to the security compartment. Charley heard Earl command him to lay his ass down on the floor. It was working, just as Earl had said it would. Charley felt good. He felt almost calm. He picked up the driver's gun and radio and put them in the glove compartment, and sat at the wheel, waiting. He could hear Earl tying up the driver. Then he saw the bank door open and the guard walked into the street, carrying two large mail pouches. Charley froze with fear.

"He's coming, Earl," yelped Charley.

"O.K. I got him," replied Earl, "Start the motor."

The back door to the compartment opened and Charley could hear Earl yelling at the guard angrily. Then he heard bags being pulled in and the door slam. Earl continued to make threats as he bound and gagged the two men. When he had finished, he came through the small door to the cab.

"O.K., they're secure. I'm going to get in the Chevy. You must follow me." He left by the passenger door, and Charley waited until he saw the blue car pull into the traffic. He felt more excited than fearful. It was almost over. The worst part was done.

Charley watched as the blue Chevy turned off the main highway, then, after a few miles, onto a dirt road. He could see a white house to his right as he drove into a dirt driveway. The Chevy stopped and Earl got out and waved him on to the back of the house and into a barn. It was just large enough to accommodate the truck. Earl stood facing the back of the truck as Charley got out.

"Get your gun on those guys when I open the doors, just in case they're loose."

Charley leveled his gun at the truck as Earl cautiously unlocked the back doors. The men were still securely tied up and gagged. After transferring all the money to the dining room of the house, Earl shut and locked all the truck doors. "When we've counted the money, I'll drop those guys off."

"Hey, they won't suffocate in there, Earl?"

"Hell, no. There are vents all over these rigs," replied Earl as he locked the last door.

The two men entered the house as Earl said, "My sister and husband are on a vacation. There ain't no reason we should be disturbed. We can split the money and stay for a couple of days. You're welcome to stay if you want."

"No, let's divvy it up. I'm going West as soon as possible," replied Charley as he sat at the table looking at the bundles. "How much you figure we got, Earl?"

"Probably close to twenty thousand dollars, but some of it we won't be able to spend right away," said Earl as he started pulling packets of bills from the pouch.

"What do you mean, we won't be able to spend it?" yelled Charley.

"Well, not right away, Charley. Look at it." He threw Charley a packet of money wrapped in a brown paper wrapper.

Charley looked at him. "Why? 'Cause they're so clean?"

"No, Stupid! It's the serial numbers on the bills. They follow in a row. They're new bills the bank hasn't used, and they know the serial numbers. You spend one of those bills within a hundred miles of here, and they'll have a fix on you in two days."

"Earl, you didn't say nothin' about bills we couldn't use."

"How the hell am I supposed to know what's in the transfer and what's not, Stupid?"

Charley threw the bills on the table and yelled, "I ain't stupid, Earl, and I ain't never done nothin' like this. Now, you're the one that come up with this idea. You're the one that asked me to come along on it. You're the one..."

"All right. All right," said Earl, realizing Charley was to be feared when upset. "You're not stupid. It's the chance you take, gettin' marked bills when you hit on a transfer. You just don't spend them right away, that's all."

"All right, then, what do we do with the money we can't spend?" Charley said, slowly sitting down.

"I know a guy that can launder money."

"Launder?" asked Charley. "What's launder?"

"You give him, say, ten thousand dollars in marked bills, and he gives you seven thousand in unmarked bills."

"Why only seven thousand?"

"You don't expect him to do it for nothin', do you?"

"The hell with that!"

"You can always put it in a safety deposit box and sit on it for a couple of years."

"A safety what?"

"Deposit box, Charley. They're in every bank. Don't you know what a safety deposit box is?" Charley glared at Earl. If he called him stupid again, he was going to hit him.

"I never had enough of value to own one," replied Charley sarcastically, "but I suppose you own those boxes all over town."

Not wanting any trouble, Earl explained the benefits of putting marked bills in a deposit box, and told him of a situation where a man had robbed a bank and then put all he had taken in one of their own deposit boxes and left it there until the bills could not be traced.

"How long does it take, Earl?"

"It all depends, Charley. Usually around seven years."

"Seven! Jesus! That's the craps. I don't want to wait no seven years!"

"I'll tell you what, Charley. Instead of splitting the money, let's go, say, a third of the bills are untraceable. You take those bills and all the coin, and I'll take the rest. That way, you can spend yours night away."

Charley looked at Earl. He had never really trusted him; he could not be sure he was being told the truth right now. He stood up as though challenging Earl to differ with him. "We split the money fifty-fifty, just like we agreed, Earl. I guess we'll just have to take our chances with them marked bills," he said in a determined voice.

"Suit yourself," Earl said casually. "Help me move some of these bags of coin onto the floor and we'll have room to count the bills together."

Both men worked in silence as they placed the bags of coin onto the floor.

"How much money is in one of these sacks?"

"Depends on the type of coin and how many rolls," replied Earl.

Then, suddenly, Earl stopped moving the bags and looked at Charley.

"Yeah?" Charley said as he continued moving the bags.

"I don't know," said Earl as he rubbed perspiration from his forehead, "I feel funny."

Charley dropped the bag and looked at Earl. "No, honest, Charley. I feel funny." Then he grabbed at his chest and began falling to his knees. He reached out to the table to stop his fall, then fell among the bags on the floor.

Charley grabbed for his gun and pointed it right at Earl. "What the hell you tryin' to pull now, Earl?"

"No, honest ... Charley ... I can't breathe ..." He continued to grab at his chest and gasp for breath. With every breath, his face turned whiter, and his eyes strained in wonder at what has happening to him.

"Charley ... help me ..." he gasped.

Charley put his gun on the table and knelt down beside him, unsure of what to do. Then Earl spewed vomit on the floor and continued to gag and gasp for breath. The smell made Charley sick, and he backed away. Earl gasped for breath, and his left arm went out to Charley, as though pleading for him to do something. Then he stiffened, made gurgling sounds, and fell back and lay very still. Charley covered his nose and looked closer at the man. He was dead. His eyes were still open, but Charley was sure he was dead.

He became aware that he was alone, alone with a dead man staring at him. He felt scared and he wanted to vomit himself but held it down. The longer he looked at Earl, the worse the feeling got. It was the same feeling he had as a boy when locked in the hall closet or bedroom. His mother would lock him away when his father drank. "It's for your own good," she would say, as she closed the door and locked it for the night. Then he would hear glass breaking; his mother would be slapped and cry, and images and fears would grow in the boy's mind from hearing without seeing. He would hold his hands to his ears and rock back and forth, eventually falling asleep, exhausted, lying in his own urine.

It was the wetness in his crotch and the smell of vomit and urine that broke his stare at Earl's open eyes. His only thought was to put as much distance between the room and himself as possible. He jumped up and grabbed his suitcase. He threw as much paper money into the case as it would hold. Then he hurriedly stuffed his pockets with as many rolls of coins as they would take. He ran out of the back door, and while getting into the Chevy, heard the guards banging against the truck door. As he slammed the car door, he decided to drive for several hours and then notify someone of their whereabouts. "Ain't gonna have them guys suffocate and have a murder rap to boot," he said to himself as he drove into the dirt road. When he reached the main highway, he turned toward Denver, Colorado. When he reached Calpine, Colorado, he was too exhausted to go any further. He entered a liquor store and bought a quart of Jim Beam, being careful to pay the clerk with a well-used twenty-dollar bill. Once outside, he went to a pay phone and called the Highway Patrol.

"Highway Patrol. Officer Belmonet talking. May I help you?"

Perspiration beaded over his body as Charley said, "There are two men tied up in a truck five miles east of Kansas City," and hung up. Glimpses of Earl's face staring up at him and the smell of vomit returned to him. He drove around town until he found a motel that suited him. The parking lot was in back of the main building and the car would not be seen from the highway. Once inside his room, he sat on a chair opposite the bed and guzzled the whiskey. He opened the suitcase and looked at the money. As he drank and counted the different packets of bills, he relaxed, and the fear of being caught was replaced with the possibilities of being rich.

"Tomorrow, I'll get rid of the car and put some of this in one of those deposit boxes," he thought. Then grogginess began to fog his thinking. He took one more swig and lay back on the chair. His sleep was so sound that he was not aware that the cigarette he held burned to the second and third fingers of his right hand before smoldering out. On the bed, in the opened suitcase, lay an assortment of bills and rolled coins totaling over twenty thousand dollars. Each packet was neatly secured in bank wrappers labeled "Kansas Security Bank."

Chapter Eight

Wilcox, Indiana —August, 1945

Sister Theophane rubbed her forehead. It was obvious to the boy who sat in front of her that she was in pain.

"You got another headache, Sister?" he asked.

"Yes, Johnny." She hesitated a minute and then continued. "Now, to continue. I can't excuse this type of conduct."

"Yeah, I know, Sister," he said while playing with a loose thread on his jacket.

"Johnny, I want your full attention."

He sat very still and looked at her.

"You will give Sister Wilma a sincere apology. Do you hear me, young man?"

The boy looked down at the floor; his face muscles tightened. He clenched his teeth. "She doesn't like me, y'know. I mean, she really doesn't like me," he said, shaking his head back and forth slowly. "Well, that is still no excuse for what you said to her."

"She never liked me," he continued, "not since I've been here. I mean, I'm never good enough for her, y'know? I mean, she waits for me to screw up, and that doesn't take long for me."

The nun appreciated his honesty and was finding it more difficult to continue the conversation.

"Johnny, it's obvious that you and Sister Wilma have a communication problem."

"Communication problem!" he answered as he sat up, "Sister, she's got it in for me! All the time she was tutoring me this summer, I couldn't do nothin' right. And now I'll have her for all this coming year in the seventh grade."

"Johnny," the nun said as she stood and went to the window. She moved slowly and used the time to phrase her answer, to put it in the right perspective. "Sister Wilma is a bit over zealous in her duties, but a good teacher. And, as far as your talking back to her, there is nothing to discuss. You were wrong. What you said was insulting, disrespectful and an apology is in order."

The nun returned to her desk; the headache seemed to worsen. She looked at him. He was small for his age, but she knew that his curiosity for learning and quickness to comprehend would quickly advance him among his peers. She had every intention of making him aware of his talent.

"As for Sister Wilma and the tutoring this summer, that was my idea." The boy looked up, surprised at what she said. "With a little additional help, I see no reason why you can't skip the seventh grade and proceed to the eighth this September."

"You mean I won't have Wilma the Witch? I'd be in your class?"

"Johnny!" the nun scolded.

"I'm sorry, Sister, but that would be neat. Hey, man, I'd work for you, ya know." In his excitement, the boy stood up to make his point.

"Sit down!" yelled the nun. "First of all, her name is Wilma, *Sister* Wilma. Secondly, I have not completely decided to allow you to advance, and thirdly, if such advancement takes place, certain promises are to be kept regarding your attitude and conduct toward your superiors."

The boy sat down sheepishly and said, "Yes, Sister."

The nun regained her composure. "First of all," she continued, "I will consider this promotion only in exchange for the following conditions." She looked at him. The nun had always challenged him, and he respected her for it. If he wanted to be promoted, he would have to earn it.

"Since you have been at St. Helena's these past three years, you have had this organization of friends in the dorm which has a tendency to control other boys, their actions, and possessions."

"Organization, Sister? I don't understand."

The nun leaned across her desk. "Let's not play games, John McBride. Many of the boys trade off kitchen and hall duties with you and some of your friends, to your betterment. Other boys' possessions and clothes find their way into your locker, and your friends' lockers. And, when asked how they got there, these boys seem very reluctant to explain. You and your friends hold some power over them. I want this stopped. Is that understood?"

"Yes, Sister." he answered reluctantly.

"I want it stopped immediately. Is that understood?"

"Yes, Sister."

"And, furthermore..."

A knock on the door halted the nun and she asked, "Who is it?" Sister Maureen popped her head inside.

"Sister Theophane, may I see you?"

"Sister Maureen. Why, of course."

The nun looked at the boy. "Johnny, we'll continue this after lunch. Until then, do not repeat what I've said until we have completed our agreement. Is that understood?"

"Hey, Sister, you got no problem. Things are going to work out. You just wait." He wished them both a good morning and quietly shut the door behind him.

"Was that the McBride boy, Theo?" asked Sister Maureen.

"Yes, Mo. That was Johnny McBride," she said as she sat down at her desk.

"Well, you have done wonders with him, Theo. I remember when he came here. He was some problem."

"There's been a lot of improvement, Mo. He's a bright kid, a real leader, full of imagination. It just has to be pointed in the right direction. I've had him tutored this summer to get him ahead and out of Wilma's class."

"They don't get along?"

"Don't get along! Mo, it's one continuous feud, and the boy is not completely at fault."

"Knowing Wilma, it doesn't take much to cross her."

"Well, Mo, since his mother left him, anyone that crosses him is in trouble. But, befriend him, and he is your friend for life."

"Does his mother ever visit, Theo?"

"No. Except for a package on holidays or birthdays, she has not contacted either of the boys since the day she left them."

"How long has it been?"

"Over three years, and although his younger brother has settled in, it's left a mark on Johnny."

"A mark?"

"Yes. He only sees things in black or white. You're his friend, or you aren't. If you're not his friend, you're never off his hit list."

"Hit list?" You sound like a gangster, Theo."

"Just shop talk, Mo. Thank goodness he hasn't discovered girls yet."

"Girls!" Sister Maureen yelled. "That's why I've come to see you, Theo. What I've got to show you isn't going to make your day any easier. Theo, unless it's some kind of unusual coincidence, I'd bet that Lillian Roberts' child is returning to Wilcox," the nun said as she handed a student file across the desk. "Theo, I just received this from a Sister Katherine in South Bend, Indiana. She informed me that a Mrs. Phillips would be putting her child in St. Helena's. She mentioned that the woman is returning to her mother's home here in Wilcox after going through a messy divorce. The girl's name is Frances."

Sister Theophane looked wide-eyed as she perused the information in the file.

"From what you told me, Theo, I can't see that it would be anyone else but the Mrs. Phillips that adopted Lillian's child some ... was it twelve years ago?"

"Thirteen years ago, Mo," the nun said quietly as she studied the file. "Well, Mo, the birth date and hospital are certainly correct." The nun rubbed her forehead. The pain drummed again in her head. "Mo, what grade will she be going into?"

"The eighth, Theo."

48

Sister Theophane slowly put the file down and walked to the window. She wished she could just get up and leave her office; she wished she could just walk away from it all. Her headache seemed to heighten.

"So will Johnny McBride. I just promised him, if he behaves, I would let him skip to the eighth grade."

There was a long silence as both nuns thought of what had been said.

"Theo," said Sister Maureen, "they're going to be in the same grade, the same class this year, your classroom?"

"Yes, Mo."

"They're first cousins and they're going to be in the same classroom, and they won't even know they're related."

"Yes."

Again the silence permeated the room. Sister Theophane looked out the window, but was so engrossed in thought that she did not see one of the children wave as he passed by. Then, while rubbing her forehead to ease the pain, she said, "Mo."

"Yes?"

"You're wrong."

"I am? About what?"

"You're wrong about them being cousins.

"They're not?"

"But I thought you said..."

"I did, Mo, but there's more to it."

"More to it?"

The nun turned from the window and stood looking at her friend across the desk.

"Mo."

"Yes, Theo?"

"Promise you won't repeat this?"

"Of course, I..."

"They aren't cousins, Mo."

"No?"

"Lillian's child was fathered by Charley McBride, the same man who married Vera two years later. Lillian swore me to secrecy."

"By Vera's husband!"

"They're half brother and sister, Mo, and there's no way in God's world it can be told, much less proven."

Chapter Nine

Long Beach, California — January, 1946

Lillian Breslin watered the carnations that grew next to magnolias and poppy seedlings at the south end of her greenhouse. Through the windows, though covered with mist, she could make out the figure of a man turning the corner by the tennis courts and approaching the greenhouse entrance. As he looked about, it was obvious that he was determined to find someone on the estate.

"Damn it, he must've rung the doorbell a minute ago. I guess I'm not going to be able to avoid him," she said, turning off the water tap. From his shabby appearance, she concluded he was looking for a job, or just a handout. As the man approached, it made her nervous and she tightened her grip on the metal hoe in her pocket. Then, something in his walk seemed familiar to her. When he reached the greenhouse, she was positive she had met him before. He rapped on the door and waited for an answer. She studied his glossy shape as she approached the door. When she opened it, she recognized him immediately.

"Hello there ... ah ... excuse me, I'm looking for Lillian Breslin," he said.

Behind the wrinkles and puffiness, she recognized a face she had not seen for more than thirteen years.

'What the hell is he doing here?' she thought to herself.

"Hello, Charley," she said.

Charley McBride squinted his eyes, then realized who he was talking to.

"By God, Lillian, I didn't know you."

"If I'd've seen you on the street, Charley, I wouldn't've recognized you, either."

"You're probably surprised to see me," he said, smirking.

They stood motionless in an awkward moment, both not knowing what to say next.

"Nothing you ever did really surprised me, Charley. What do you want?"

"Can I come in a minute?"

"For a minute, I guess."

He came in and she shut the door. He looked much older than his years. He smelled. His clothes were filthy, and his hair was matted from the wind and road dust.

"You wouldn't have a beer ... for old time's sake?" he asked with a boyish grin.

"I was just about to take a break. C'mon in the kitchen."

"Nice place you got here, Lillian."

"It beats makin' a living," she replied as they entered the kitchen. He sat down on the barstool as she handed him a beer. The silence between them became awkward.

"Hey, you got a nice place here."

"You said that."

"You're probably surprised to see me, ain't ya, Lillian?"

"Yeah, I'm surprised, Charley. Now what do you want?"

"Well, I wanted to see you."

"Well, I don't want to see you, Charley."

It was obvious to her that he had something to say and was having trouble putting it into words.

"You're probably still mad as hell at me for not ... I mean ... for not helping out ... for when your old man threw you out and..."

Lillian could see herself crossing the wheat field, her bag in her hand, toward the McBride place, cursing her father's name and vowing, with Charley McBride's help, that she would get revenge.

"Look, Charley," she interrupted him, we were just kids then. It's water over the dam. I don't want to talk about it, and I have no feelings for or against it. Now, what did you come for?"

"I always wished it could've turned out different, Lillian."

"Charley, we both made a mistake; but, with a little perseverance, I landed on both feet. Let's leave it at that. Now, how about saying what you got on your mind to say and getting the hell out of here."

"Sorry, I know how you must feel."

"I told you. I have no feelings about you or anyone else in the past, thank you. I do get damned tired of picking up after your mess-ups, though."

"What?"

"I survived our relationship, thanks to a good friend at St. Helena's Orphanage; and, then when you decided to run out on Vera, I had to contact this organization again so that your children, that is, my nephews, would get fed properly and have a roof over their heads," she said angrily. Charley took a sip of beer and, without looking at her, said, "How's she doin?"

"My, I thought you'd never ask, Charley." Lillian puffed nervously on a cigarette and then quickly put it out. "Vera called me the minute she realized you were gone. Since I don't trust her any more than I trust you, I suggested that the children be put in the orphanage and told her I would pay for their keep."

"I heard that's where you had our kid."

"You heard right, Charley ... Jesus Christ! And they say that history doesn't repeat itself," Lillian yelled as she banged her fist on the bar and turned away from him.

There was a long silence as Charley sipped at his beer. And then he said quietly, "We had something once, didn't we, Lillian?"

She turned toward him, her face contorted in anger. She picked up his beer and threw it in the sink.

"God damn it, Charley, get the hell out of here. You disgust me! You need money, I'll give you just enough to get out of my sight and stay out! Just get your ass out of my house and I don't ever want to see you around here again."

Charley got up. "1 don't blame you, Lillian, for feeling that way. I don't mean nothin' ill toward you. I just need a favor from you, that's all."

"Sure. For old time's sake, Charley." she said as she grabbed her purse and pulled out a checkbook," How much you want? The sky's the limit up to a thousand dollars, but you got to promise me you'll never see me face to face again."

"I don't need money, Lillian," he said as he gave her a printed card, "I need for you to sign this card."

"Are you crazy? If this is one of your schemes... If you think I'm signing a loan for you..."

"No, no, Lillian. It ain't no loan. Y'see, I put your and my name on a safety deposit box in a bank in Denver, Colorado. You got to sign this card so's they have your signature. Then they'll send you a key. That's all."

"Why me?" she asked sharply.

"'Cause I don't trust no one else, Lillian. If something happens to me, it's all yours. It's sort of my way of paying you back for what I didn't do."

"What's all mine?" she asked suspiciously.

Charley surveyed the room, and with a smirk on his face, said, "It ain't nothin' you can use now, but if something happens to me, it's yours to do with for what you want, that's all."

Looking at the card, she said, "I'll think about it, Charley. Now, will you please leave?"

Lillian opened the door.

"I'm goin' up North, Lillian, to a place called Sonora. I can make a lot of money choppin' wood."

"Don't expect a postcard from me, Charley."

Charley put his hand on the door and looked at Lillian.

"Our kid, Lillian ... what was it, a boy or a girl?"

Lillian looked at his eyes, between the wrinkles and redness from too much drinking, she caught a glimpse of a young boy whose innocent smile raised feelings within her that she had long buried.

"Wait a minute, Charley." She went to the bar and picked up the card he had given her. She quickly read the instructions and then scribbled her name next to his. Then, handing it back to him, she said, "I didn't wait around long enough to find out, Charley."

"They'll be sending you a key for the box." Then, looking at her, he smiled and said, "I won't bother you no more, Lillian. That's a promise."

She shut the door behind him.

Lillian stood at the door watching him walk through the greenhouse. He stopped once to smell a gardenia, and then, after letting himself out the door, was gone. She returned to the bar and made herself a strong martini. Gulping it down, she winced from the sting in her throat.

"Why did I ever bother to open the door to that bastard?" she said to the empty room.

Suddenly, she felt a need to be with other people. "I'll call Roberta ... No, I'll call Barry and let him take me dancing tonight."

Halfway up the stairs, Lillian decided to buy herself the most expensive dress she could find.

Chapter Ten

Wilcox, Indiana — June, 1946

Vera awoke suddenly. The bedroom was bright with the mid-morning sun. She could smell coffee brewing, then recognized the sound of wood being chopped. 'Hank has been up,' she thought to herself. She looked about the room. The new window curtains and freshly hung wallpaper raised her spirits, as they did every morning, for she always awoke expecting to see the drab water-stained walls and twenty-year-old draperies she had so long ago gotten accustomed to. The smell of the coffee made her gag and confirmed what she had long ago suspected. Vera sat up in bed. "This is a hell of a time to get pregnant," she thought. She knew Hank would want her to get "fixed," as he put it, but there was no time to worry about that. She had more pressing problems to deal with.

Vera reached over and opened the drawer to the nightstand by her bed. Her hand trembled as she took out the letter. She knew its contents, but reread the words to emphasize their importance.

The Faculty and Class of 1946
Cordially Invite You to Attend
The Twenty-Third School Graduation
of St. Helena's Orphanage
June 8, 1946

"My God!" she said to herself. "To think my oldest is graduating from grade school!" As she looked at the invitation again, feelings of guilt closed in on her and she wished she had paid more attention to the boys in the last four years. Their stay was meant to be no longer than a few weeks, but the weeks passed into months and the months into years, and by then it was easier to forget them than to harbor guilt for not having visited them.

Now she knew they could no longer be forgotten. From the envelope, she pulled out a second paper. On its heading was written <u>Michael S. Simmons and Sons, Attorneys at Law</u>. She glanced down the page and reread the final paragraph. "... and since you have not shown an interest in the boys, or returned my letters of inquiry regarding their future, their care will be referred to the Juvenile Courts of the County of Wilcox for the purpose of a hearing with regard to abandonment. We request that you contact us at the earliest possible date with regard to this matter." She put the letter down and looked at the ceiling as she tried to think of a solution.

She knew Hank would never agree to their being brought home. He would never agree to her pregnancy. Vera bit at her fingernail as she recalled the last time she had mentioned the boys in conversation.

They had been at Obie's Bar and Grill. They had been drinking for most of the evening. Vera remembered being very drunk and feeling sorry for herself. She kept talking about the boys and how she missed them. Then she would cry and take a drink of Jack Daniels. Several times he had told her to shut up, that he wasn't interested. And, when at last she continued to harp on the subject, he reached across the table, slapped her across the face, then grabbed her by the neck and screamed, "I ain't interested in your damned kids. Is that clear, Vera?" Then he pushed her back in the seat and her head banged against the wooden back. He downed the last of the whiskey and the conversation at the surrounding tables stopped until he slammed the front door and pulled her through the front parking lot.

Vera picked up a cigarette on the nightstand and lit it. 'Maybe he really didn't feel that hateful about children,' she thought. She had brought up the subject in bad surroundings. They had both been drinking. Maybe, if the time was right, he would be more interested in talking about the boys. His personality was far more amiable when they made love. The act was always precluded by the use of some type of birth prevention. It always disgusted Vera, but it was a preliminary she had gotten used to. "Is it your time of the month?" he would always ask. Other times, he would just withdraw and hold himself to her until he spilled himself on her belly. But, after the lovemaking, he was very agreeable to her comments and suggestions.

Vera got up and went to the window seat and sat down. From the side of the house, she could see Hank Kidder chopping wood and neatly piling it into a cord. She took the new curtains in her hand and pressed them to her face. They smelled so new and clean. To herself, she thanked Hank Kidder for his arrival. Times were better. The place was beginning to look like it did when her father was alive. She watched from the window as he chopped at the wood and was reminded of the first day she had seen him. She was sitting in the living room when he appeared at the screen door. "I hear you need a handy man about the place, ma'am. All I need is a place to sleep and something to eat."

Vera watched him strike at the wood with the ax and place it on the pile with precise evenness. She realized she didn't know anything about him. He never volunteered information about himself, and when she asked questions, he would always change the conversation. If she persisted, he would grow angry, and now she had learned it was better not to probe. Two weeks after he arrived, they began to sleep together. One night, he just walked into her room and crawled into bed. She was not quite awake when they made love, but it was not much different than if Charley had come in late from a weekend of drinking.

Watching him, he would size up the logs, and if one was too long, he would attack it with the ax and make it fit with the rest. The actions were typical of the man. He was neat and precise. It came to Vera that when he first arrived, he asked her what he was to do. After they began sleeping together, he took it upon himself to do what was needed, and it was now Vera that needed his permission to do what was nothing more than routine. Vera pressed the new curtain material between her fingers. Hank had made the place profitable. They had a future. Because of it, she didn't want to lose him. But, the boys must come home after graduation. Hank would have to be convinced; even if it meant the possibility of losing him, the boys had to return. She would not abandon them any longer.

Vera watched from the window as he struck at the wood logs. He was dressed in only his pants, and his long, lean body gleamed as he perspired. Beads of sweat would roll down his back and front and soak into the waistband of his briefs that showed above his belt. The sight gave rise to sexual feelings in Vera. 'I'll seduce him, and when the time is right, he'll listen to me and agree,' she thought. 'Yeah, I'll get him in bed. He's never denied me anything when he's on his back.' She snickered to herself. Vera opened the window and yelled, "Hank, what you doin' down there?"

"What the hell's it look like I'm doin'?" he yelled back.

"Do you have to do it right now?"

"If you want a hot stove to cook on, I do."

Vera leaned out the window and let her dress fall open. "Why don't you forget that and come on up here?"

He looked at her while shading his eyes from the sun. Vera brushed her hair back and said, "C'mon ... C'mon up here."

He stood for a moment, and then said, "Yeah, I'll be right up."

Vera closed the window and returned to the bed. She undressed and slid naked under the covers. Seeing the envelope, she quickly returned the letters to the drawer and pulled the covers up to her neck. 'If I handle this right,' she thought, 'I'll have the boys home, and Hank, too.' Suddenly, she sat up in bed. "What if they don't want to come home?" she said to herself. "Oh, God, if only I had paid them more attention," she cried. "But why wouldn't they want to come home? How could anyone want to stay in an awful place like that?" She lay flat and pulled the covers up as she heard footsteps on the stairs. Her stomach twitched. 'My boys come first,' she thought. "As for you," she whispered while patting her stomach, "I'll deal with you when you start showing yourself."

* * * * *

"C'mon," he said, as he led the young girl by the bushes that ran against the brick wall.

"We shouldn't be here, Johnny. I just feel it," she said as she hesitated to follow.

"It's all right, Frankie. I come here all the time, and nobody in the orphanage knows it," the boy said as he stopped at the dusty window. He pulled at the sill and it opened. "Honest, Frankie, I come here all the time. It used to be the furnace room that heated all the buildings, but now it's used to store tools and stuff." The boy opened the window and jumped in. "C'mon," he pleaded and then helped the girl through the opening.

"Why do you come here?" she asked as she jumped to the floor.

"'Cause it's just quiet and peaceful; and it's mine, all mine. Nobody knows about it."

The girl looked at the large brick room. In the middle stood a big furnace from which pipes of various sizes emerged. An old picnic table stood in the corner. An assortment of tools and school lockers lined the dirty walls. The air was stale and dust covered everything.

"It stinks in here, Johnny."

"You get used to it," he said as he walked around the room. "C'm'ere," he said to Frankie. "Look through this window. I come here when I can. I come here and smoke. I just stand in front of this window, smoking and looking out. But the other kids can't see me. Nobody can see me. I guess it's the dust on the glass or something. Anyway, I just stand there smoking, and nobody knows it. Once, I was standing right here, and the old witch walked right up to the window. I was sure she saw me. She just looked in. I was standing right here, blowing smoke, and she didn't even see me through the dust."

"You mean Sister Wilma?"

"Yeah. She just stood there lookin' at me and here I was smokin', and she didn't even see me. Hey, Frankie, you want a cigarette?"

"No."

Johnny went to an old desk in the corner and, from the bottom drawer, he pulled out a pack of cigarettes.

"Why do they call you Frankie?" he asked as he lit up.

"Just a nickname. My real name Is Frances. My father called me Frankie when I was small, so everybody else did. Your friends call you Mac, don't they?"

"Yeah, sometimes." Johnny sat on the broken picnic table, smoking.

"Why'd you bring me here?"

"I don't know. I guess 'cause I'm leaving St. Helena's after graduation, and I've had this place to myself for about a year now ... anyway, I just wanted to show it to you before we graduate."

"Do you mind the kidding the kids give us?"

"You mean about our names. Frankie and Johnny?" Johnny took a puff from his cigarette. "About the song?"

"Yeah," Frankie giggled, "Frankie and Johnny were lovers," she repeated.

"It's just a song," he said, smiling at her.

"You're going to Damien House, aren't you? I mean, after you leave here?"

"Yeah, Sister Theophane set it up. There's this guy that's going to teach me drafting when I get there. He works in the courthouse. That's why I wanted to see you alone, Frankie. You're going to St. Cecilia's girl's school, aren't you?"

"Yeah. It's just a couple of blocks from here; and, during the summer, I'm working for Sister Maureen here to help pay for tuition. Johnny, what happened yesterday when you were in Sister Theophane's office? Why'd they take her to the hospital?"

"I don't know. She was going over my speech with me, that I got to make for graduation, and she put her head down and didn't say anything. I got scared when she didn't say anything or answer my question, so I called Miss Wayne from the library. They sent me out of the room and then took Sister to the hospital."

"I wonder how she is?"

"I don't know, but I do know they got the witch doing the graduation. That's where I got to go in a few minutes, to see her."

Frankie brushed some dust from her arms. "Let's get out of here, Johnny. It gives me the creeps."

"Sure."

"We won't be going to school together ... can I come to see you when I'm at Damien House? I could come and see you, and ... I could write you, too, at your house?"

Frankie looked up and smiled. "Sure. Damien House isn't very far from my grandmother's house."

"Hey, that's great, Frankie. You're livin' at your grandmother's house?"

"Yes, with my mother."

"Where's your old man?"

"My mother divorced him." The girl looked hurt as she said it.

"My old man's gone, too." he replied.

"Gone?"

"Gone. One day, he just left ... We woke up and he was gone. That's why my old lady put me and my brother in St. Helena's."

"How long you been here, Johnny?"

"Almost four years. That bitch of a mother of mine told me and my brother Tommy she was only droppin' us off for a couple of days! ... 'Sunday, I'll be back Sunday, Johnny,' she told me. Shit!" The boy took a deep drag of his cigarette. "Well, Sunday came ... Monday … and Tuesday..."

"She never came?"

"Never came? ... Hell! She sends us packages on our birthdays and Christmas. That's all! Tommy and I have never seen her in four years. And, as for me, that's all I care to see of her! She's a ... a bitch and I hate her!"

"Johnny!"

"Oh, shit, Frankie, it don't matter. She never cared much for us. She just sat around and drank. That's all I remember of her. Even if she wanted us, I wouldn't go home. And, after next week, it won't matter."

"Next week?"

"Yeah. Next week I go to court because my old lady abandoned me and Tommy."

"Abandoned?"

"Yeah. It means she left us and Tommy at the orphanage; and since she doesn't care about us, Tommy and me become part of the courts or somethin' like that. Anyway, Sister Theophane explained it to me. My old lady can't have us back after the judge says so next week, and that's all right with me. The bitch!"

"That's sounds awful, Johnny."

"No, it ain't. It's been good here at St. Helena's, and Damien House will be even better. Hell, I wouldn't go back to live with my old lady for nothin', anyway."

The girl looked alarmed at what he said.

"It's all right, Frankie. Hell, my old lady will never turn up after all this time. Hell, the lawyer representing the school says it's just a matter of procedure. Anyway, he says it's something they got to go through so we're wards of the court or something. Then she can't have us."

The girl was obviously distressed at what he said. "I don't know how anyone could feel that way about his mother ... no matter what. I love my mom very much, and my father, even though they divorced."

"Yeah, well, I guess I shouldn't have brought it up."

"Let's get out of here, Johnny. It stinks in here."

"You'll write to me at Damien House, and I can visit you sometime?"

"I'll have to ask my mom, but ... I would like to see you again."

"Hey, that's neat," Johnny said as he took a final drag on his cigarette and threw it on the floor. "Maybe we ought to get out of here." He opened the window and looked both ways. "O.K. All clear." They jumped out of the window and he shut it behind them. They walked around the building and onto the playground. "I'll be seeing you tomorrow, Johnny," Frankie said.

"Yeah ... tomorrow. I got to see the witch about graduation ... Hey, Frankie!"

The girl stopped and turned toward him.

"I'm glad you're gonna write me when I move to Damien House."

"I'm glad you asked me to, Johnny," she said, smiling, and then waved as she headed for the front gate.

Johnny entered the school and headed for Sister Theophane's office. He began reciting the graduation speech he had memorized for her.

> 'On behalf of the class of 1946, I have been asked to speak. Whether we live at St. Helena's or are day students, we have a lot ...'

"No, that's not right," he said to himself.

> '... we have much to be thankful for. I would like to thank Sister Theophane for all she did for me.'

He smiled to himself ... yes, he would add that line to the speech, just at that point, but he would tell no one. It would just be his surprise. He stopped at the door and was reminded that she was not inside.

"Damn!" he said to himself, and wondered how Sister Theophane was doing as he knocked at her office door.

"Enter."

He opened the door and thought how unusual it was to see someone else at Sister Theophane's desk.

"You're late, young man," complained the nun.

"Sorry, Sister Wilma, I forgot."

"Sit down, young man. I have some surprising news for you."

"About going to Damien House?" he asked excitedly.

"It involves that, yes," she said as she picked up a letter. "As you know, I am taking Sister Theophane's place until she recovers, and ..."

"How is she, Sister?" he interjected. "Is she real sick?"

The nun glared at the boy. "First of all, I do not appreciate being interrupted in mid sentence. Secondly, your question is totally inappropriate. Her medical condition is a matter between her and her physician."

Johnny sat up and decided to speak only when spoken to. He was angry, but only had to deal with her for a few more days. A glass sphere paperweight sat on the table next to him. Johnny picked it up and shook it. Snowflakes fluttered about a house and a snowman inside.

"Just put that down and listen to me, young man," demanded the nun.

He did as he was told and sat attentively.

"When I speak, I expect your full attention, young man."

He sat very still and said nothing.

"As you know, John McBride, your mother was informed by our legal staff that if she did not respond regarding you and your brother's status by graduation, that you would be transferred to Damien House and become a ward of that institution until you were eighteen. This was explained to you?"

Johnny smiled. "Yes. Sister Theophane explained it to me before she sent the letter to my mom. I go to court next week."

"Sister Theophane has done a great deal for you during your stay with us."

"Yes, Sister."

"Much of it I personally disagree with, but it doesn't matter."

The boy smiled at the nun's displeasure.

"As I said, I have exceptional news for you. Yesterday, we received a letter from your mother. It seems she has every intention of attending your graduation and taking you and your brother home afterwards."

His eyes widened; the boy could not believe what he heard. The words, 'home afterwards' kept repeating in his mind as the nun continued.

"She asked us to tell you this before seeing you. I'm sure this will make you and your brother very happy. Your mother also called and said that she will be accompanied by a Mr. Kidder."

"Wait a minute!" he yelled. "You mean I'm not going to Damien House?"

"That is what I said, John. You are going home where you belong."

"But Sister Theophane said..."

"It is not a matter of what Sister Theophane said, young man. Your mother was given an option, and she wisely decided to take you home."

"But I don't want to go home," he pleaded.

"You don't want to go home?" the nun replied. "Young man, you should be grateful you have a parent that has found the means and the wisdom to have you return."

"But I don't want to go home. I like it here," he pleaded again.

"You wouldn't be staying here in any event, even if your mother did not respond ..."

"No ... No ... I mean Sister Theophane fixed it so I could go to Damien House early and this guy, this draftsman, was going..."

"I know exactly what Sister Theophane had arranged, but that has all been changed. Your mother has decided to take you home."

"But I don't want to go home." Tears welled in his eyes.

"Listen, young man, whether you like it or not, that is the way it is going to be. First of all, if Sister Theophane was here, she'd be telling you the same thing. Secondly, because I'm here makes no difference; your mother is coming to return you to your home," she repeated.

He couldn't believe what she said. Somehow, if Sister Theophane was well, nothing would change. It wasn't fair! No one asked him what he wanted, and that angered him. He stood up and shouted to the nun, "I don't want to live with her! I hate her! I hate my old lady! I want to..."

The nun stood up, in shock from what he'd said. "First of all, your mother is not to be referred to, in my presence, as your 'old lady.' Secondly, you are going home. That is final, and you should be grateful there is a place to go to. We have an orphanage full of children with nowhere to go, no one to live with or love them, and you ... you ingrate, stand there speaking this way. And in my presence! How dare you!"

For a moment they stood looking at each other. Then Johnny turned from her gaze and picked up the glass paperweight and smashed it against his clenched fist again and again.

"What are you doing! Seat yourself, young man! I am not through talking to you."

"I want to know how Sister Theophane is ... I want to talk to her ... now ... Now!" he screamed as he smashed the glass sphere against his fist.

His knuckles reddened and bruised as he continued to smash the glass ball against his bloody fist.

"You will sit down and leave that paperweight alone before I have anymore to say to you!" bellowed the nun in desperation.

Johnny turned and headed for the door as he trembled and shook the winter scene into a frenzy.

"Our meeting is not over, Mr. McBride! You will sit down immediately!" yelled the nun.

"Sister!" he yelled, framed in the doorway.

"Now, I am tired of your insubordination. Give me that paperweight."

"Sister!" he again screamed as tears welled in his eyes.

The nun moved around the desk as she yelled, "It's acts of insubordination like this that demonstrate just how much of a problem you really are! I have told Sister time and time again! Now, give me that paperweight!"

"You witch! ... witch ... witch!" he screamed as he threw the glass sphere. It banged against the front of the desk and broke. Tiny flakes of white splattered on the newly polished linoleum.

"What do you think you're doing?" screamed the nun, gasping. She backed up in fear of the boy.

"Bitch! Bitch!" he screamed.

The nun gasped.

Then, with all the dignity he could muster, he said quietly, "Sister, go fuck yourself on a ten-foot broomstick," and he ran down the hall, crying uncontrollably.

Chapter Eleven

St. Helena's

At the last strains of the ceremonial march, the line of graduates broke. Parents and other well wishers congratulated the robed children for their accomplishment. Nuns moved about the crowd gathering the ceremonial robes and received congratulations on the afternoon's presentation. In the midst of the well wishers, Vera stood opposite her oldest son. She watched him as he took off his robe. She was nervous and felt uncomfortable. She berated herself for leaving the boys so many years ago. She watched as her son handed his robe to the nun. She hardly recognized him. He was growing up, and she knew there was no one to blame but herself.

"You sure are grown a mite, Johnny," she said, just to say something.

It was obvious to Vera that the meeting was painful for both of them.

Tommy ran up to them, munching on the cookies. "Hey, they got lots of cookies and stuff to drink on the porch."

"Yeah, I know," Johnny said sullenly.

"You want some, Johnny?" Vera asked.

"No, I don't want nothin'," he replied.

Another graduate ran by, yelling, "Hey, Mac, we're free!"

Johnny nodded and waved to the boy.

"They call you Mac? Your friends gave you a nickname, eh?" chided Vera.

Johnny looked at her sullenly. "Sometimes."

"The baggage is in the trunk, Vera," Hank Kidder yelled as he approached them. "You ready to go, Vera?"

"I thought Johnny might want something to eat or drink before we go?" she replied.

"I said no."

"Well, let's go, then. I want to be home before dark," insisted Hank.

"I got to tell Sister thank you. What was her name, Johnny?"

"Wilma. Sister Wilma."

"Yes, Sister Wilma. I got to thank her. You boys go on to the car with Hank. I won't be a minute."

Hank and the boys moved toward the car, and Vera approached Sister Wilma. "I want to thank you for everything you done for Johnny and Tommy."

"You're welcome, Mrs. McBride. I'm sure you will be happy to be reunited with your sons."

"Oh, Sister, I am happy ... but ... there's one thing I wanted to ask you."

The nun shifted robes to the opposite arm. "Yes?"

"Well, the valedic ... valedic ..."

"The valedictorian speech?"

"Yes. Well, it said on the program that my Johnny was to give that speech, but when it came time, a pretty girl got up and spoke instead. I was just wondering why ... 'cause Johnny's name was on the program and all..." Vera ended sheepishly.

"I'm afraid it's a matter you'll have to take up with your son, Mrs. McBride. Now, if you'll excuse me, there is so much to be attended to."

Vera sensed the tone of finality in the nun's voice, and so, made her final goodbye. On the way to the car, she wondered if it was wiser not to ask her son about the program change.

"This car—it's almost brand new, boys. How do you like it?" asked Vera as Hank pulled on to the road. "Hank bought it from a feller who needed money awful bad, didn't ya, Honey?"

Johnny frowned at his mother at the use of the term, 'Honey.'

"As I mentioned over the phone, boys, your daddy left us, over three years ago. That's why I left you at the orphanage. I didn't have much choice. Hank, here, he come along, and things have been really fine since then. Wait'll you see. You won't recognize the place. It's been repainted, and there's new wallpaper everywhere. Hank's a wallpaper hanger, aren't you, Honey?"

Johnny frowned again. Hank did not answer.

Vera continued to enumerate everything that was new or that she could think of. Hank turned on the radio and dialed in the Chicago White Sox game.

"We got a new tractor. Hank has done all sorts of things with it, plantin' and fixin' things up. New barn doors and fences; it's a brand-new place. You won't hardly recognize it, boys."

As the "Star Spangled Banner" announced the beginning of the game, Johnny looked out the window at the passing countryside. He hated his mother for taking him away from school. He hated her for taking up with Hank. He didn't like the man. He was upset with Tommy for being so receptive to him. He sat opposite him, playing with a rubber ball Vera had bought for him earlier.

After a while, Vera asked, over the announcer's description of the list of baseball players, "Say, Johnny, I was wondering ... I noticed in the program that you was supposed to make a speech, but when it came time, a girl did it instead. I was just wondering why."

Johnny ignored the question and looked out the window. Hank was not sure that Vera had been heard over the announcer's monologue.

"Your ma asked you a question, boy," yelled Hank over the announcer.

"I heard her," he said.

"Then answer her, boy," Hank insisted.

"Oh, it's not important," Vera said, laughing. "It was just that I saw your name in the program and was awful surprised when it was your turn to speak and you didn't get up, that's all."

Johnny said nothing and Tommy kept throwing the rubber ball into the air and catching it.

"Why didn't you make that speech, boy?" Hank asked, then turned down the radio.

"'Cause she didn't want me to," Johnny replied abruptly. 'I don't have to answer none of his questions,' Johnny thought to himself.

"You mean Sister didn't want you to, Johnny?" Vera asked over the hum of the engine.

"Yeah, something like that," he replied shortly.

"Well, why not, if she went to all the trouble of putting your name in the program?"

"She didn't, that's all," he yelled out.

"O.K., O.K.," said Vera. From the sound of his voice, it was obvious to her that she should not press the point any further.

Hank turned the radio down again. "Your ma asked you a question, boy, and she expects an answer," demanded Hank.

"Oh, it's all right, Hank," insisted Vera. "It really don't matter if..."

"No! It ain't all right," he insisted. "You asked him a question; you should get an answer! Now, why didn't the sister want you to make that speech, boy?"

"'Cause she didn't, that's all."

Hank turned off the radio with a snap. "That ain't no answer, boy. Now, why didn't she let you make that speech?"

"Hank, it's really not important. Say, why don't we stop somewhere and get something cold to drink? I could stand..."

"Shut up, Vera! When you ask a question, you get an answer. Now, why didn't you make that speech?"

From the tone of his voice, Johnny knew he meant business. 'I don't owe him any explanation of anything,' he thought to himself.

"None of your business," Johnny mumbled to himself.

Hank yelled, "I can't hear you, boy."

"It's none of your god damned business," he screamed.

Vera thought the car had blown a tire as it swerved to the roadside and came to a sudden halt. Before anyone knew what was happening, Hank was halfway over the front seat. One hand held Johnny by the throat and the other slapped at his face back and forth.

"God damn it! You better damned well remember, and quick!" screamed Hank as he battered the boy. Little Tommy sat frozen in his place, his new ball pressed against his mouth, thinking he was next to be hit.

Hank grabbed Johnny by the ears and pulled him to his face. "Now, in one goddamned complete sentence, you just tell me why you didn't make that fuckin' speech, boy!"

"Because ..." Johnny gasped for air, "'cause I sassed ... her ... I talked back ... to her."

"Well, you little son of a bitch, I can see that's a real bad habit of yours; one which I aim to cure real quick." Then he backhanded the boy in the face, sending him into the back seat. "And, if you are ever asked a question or given a command by me, boy, you jump. You got that? You jump ... you just jump, boy, and we won't have no trouble between us. Got that?"

"Yes," Johnny whispered, as he gasped for breath. "I didn't hear you, boy, and it's 'yes, sir' to me, boy!"

"Yes, Sir," Johnny yelled with difficulty.

"... And don't you ever forget it, boy," Hank continued. Then he turned on the radio and started the engine. Vera sat frozen in the front seat, looking straight ahead. Tears streamed down her face.

"It shouldn't start this way ... it shouldn't start this way," was all she could think of as Hank pulled onto the road.

Hank lit a cigarette and turned up the baseball game. Everyone sat very still and listened to the announcer as he described the play of the game. After the score of one-to-nothing was announced, Hank looked at Vera. Her cheeks were wet with tears. "What the hell you crying for, Vera?" he asked as he laughed. "You got your answer."

Chapter Twelve

Sonora, California

> "Oh, it's not that she's pretty,
> Or enchantingly witty,
> The girl of my dreams
> Who is the same girl it seems ..."

Kelly Keenan leaned against his maple wood bar and sighed. "That's Charley McBride again. He's tying one on tonight," he said to the last two customers.

"Say, Kelly, you should be happy to have an entertainer who would bother to perform in a dump like this," chided Michael Marr as he and his wife laughed at Kelly's predicament.

"Go on, laugh," said the bartender, 'but it gets a bit old when it's the same drunk singing the same tune every night."

"Why don't you throw him out, Kelly?"

"Yeah, who owns this joint, anyway?" continued Mike's wife.

"It's because he needs as many customers as he can get," replied her husband as they both snickered.

"Seriously," asked Mike, "who is this Charley McBride?"

"Well, Mike," he must've come into town, two, maybe three months ago. He got himself a job at the mill. He'd come in here and tell me about his farm in Indiana, that his family is gone or dead or something. Anyway, I felt sorry for the fella, so ... I rented him a room upstairs."

"Kelly, your Irish heart is too soft, or ... you saw a chance to sell a hell of a lot of Scotch."

"It's Jack Daniels that he drinks, thank you, Mr. Marr. Go on with ya! He's all alone, and got his problems, and he's no problem, so I rented him a room."

> "The woman is so stupid and a bore
> But the stupidity you can ignore
> Because what whore
> Isn't one hell of a bore?"

The couple giggled as they listened from the end of the bar. Then Michael stood up and, in a commanding voice, announced, "Oh, Mr. Kelly, my wife and I do apologize, but we're unable to stay for the rest of the concert."

"Yes," imitated Milly, "we must be on our way, even though your bar is recognized as the cultural center of Sonora."

"Oh, go on with ya, you got to stay for the whole act," retorted Kelly.

"There's more than just the singing?" asked Milly.

"He's got a curtain closer that will curl your hair, young lady," laughed Kelly.

"No matter what she's like in bed,
It can always be said,
That she's great at gettin' a head."

"That's it for me," insisted Milly. A bit too crude for me. Let's go, Honey."

"Hey, you there," screamed Charley. "Happy days ... Happy days!" he yelled as he became aware that he was being noticed. "Hey, what's your name?" he asked as he strolled toward them.

"Let's go, Honey," Milly said as she pulled at her husband.

"Hi, I'm Charley. Kelly, here, is my old buddy. Ain't ya, old buddy?" Charley spilled part of his drink as he leaned against the bar.

"Charley, we all know who you are, and I think it's time you were gettin' upstairs."

"All I want to do is meet your friends, Kelly."

"Customers, they're just customers, Charley," said Kelly as he came around the bar to help him. "Now, look, Charley, I'll sell you the rest of the bottle so you can be takin' it upstairs to your room, but no more at the bar."

"No ... No, damn it, Kelly! I just want to have a drink with my friends. What did you say your name was, buddy?"

"I didn't say, but it's Michael. This is my wife, Milly."

"Charley. Charley McBride. Here, have a drink. Kelly, give my friends a drink," Charley insisted.

"No, we really can't," said Milly. "We have to go. It's late."

"No ... No ... No, there's plenty of time," slurred Charley. Then he half sat on the barstool. "Hey! You want to see something? I mean something you've never seem before in your life?"

"Please, now, Charley," pleaded Kelly, "why don't you go on upstairs?"

"Hey, get this," Charley said as he stood up and nearly fell backwards. "Now, just give me a minute. One minute." He turned his back to them and bent down while holding his glass of Jack Daniels to his face.

"It's the finale I warned you about," said Kelly.

"What's he doin?" asked Mike.

"You shouldn't have encouraged him," replied Kelly.

Suddenly Charley whirled around, and, while extending the glass in his hand, he said to the trio, "Here's lookin' at you! ... get it? ... Here's lookin' at you." Then, while tottering in place, he let out a drunken laugh.

"Oh, for Christ's sake," gasped Mike "That's sick!"

"The glass, Milly. Look at the glass," implored Mike.

Charley laughed and then gulped the liquid contents of the tumbler and shoved it in Milly's face.

"Here's lookin' at you, Baby," he screamed again.

"Oh, God!" she gasped as she pushed the glass away, "Let's get out of here, Michael."

At the bottom of the glass was a blue and white glass eye.

"It's mine, all right," yelled Charley. "Got stabbed in the eye in a bar fight," he said as he pointed to the empty socket in his face.

"Let's get out of here," pleaded Milly.

"Oh, you don't have the stomach for a real drunk, eh, Mr. and Mrs. Marr?" chided Kelly.

"You're one up on us, Kelly. I'll remember this, you old leprechaun!"

"Let's go, Michael."

"No, you and Michael wait here. It's his Eminence that is going to part our company," pleaded Kelly.

"Drinks all around, Kelly," yelled Charley as he danced about.

"C'mon, my friend," said Kelly as he put his arm around Charley and led him down the bar. He picked up the half-empty Jack Daniel's bottle. "The party's over, Charley. Time to go to bed. Put the glass eye in the socket like a good boy."

"So long, Charley," yelled the Marrs as Kelly moved him into the back room and up the stairs.

"Oh, God, I don't think I will ever look at the bottom of a bar glass without remembering, 'Here's lookin' at you.' God, how disgusting!"

"Well, maybe it'll cure you of chomping on your ice like a Cocker Spaniel when you finish a drink."

Milly's jaw dropped in mid motion and she spit the half-chewed ice cube into her glass. "That's sick, Michael! That's just plain sick."

Charley thanked Kelly for walking him to his room and insisted it was not necessary. He slammed the door and put the half-empty bottle of Jack Daniels on the bare table. Pouring himself a drink into the glass that he had the glass eye in, he held it out and yelled, "Here's lookin' at you!" and drank it in one swallow. It amused him when he thought of the woman's reaction.

"To Milly and her husband," he said, and poured himself another drink. As he drank it down, he felt dizzy and sat down to keep his balance. He laughed to himself and relished the feeling of lightness as the alcohol took effect. Then the bare ceiling light seemed to flicker, then dim, then go out as he felt himself fall to the floor. When he regained consciousness, his nose was pushed against the leg

69

of the chair. The first thing he noticed was the light was burning, yet he remembered it going out. He got up and felt his forehead. There was a lump and blood where he had fallen. The Jack Daniels bottle was still gripped firmly in his hand, but it had spilled. He got up and went to the mirror. He touched the bruised spot above the empty eye socket. He winced with pain when he touched it. His left elbow was also bruised, but there was no feeling in his arm. He stripped off his clothes, which were damp from the spilled liquor. The pungent odor of alcohol and urine permeated the room.

"I pissed my pants," he said to himself. He threw his wet clothes in the corner and lay down. Sunlight came through the window. It came to him that he had been unconscious for some time. He wondered how long he had been out. His head ached.

Turning on his side, he looked across at the glass on the table, which held the blue and white eye. "Got to stop drinking so damned much," he whispered to himself. Dizziness engulfed him when he closed his eyelids. Sourness gripped his stomach as he resisted the urge to vomit. 'Damn! I didn't just pass out,' he thought to himself. He turned to the wall and tried to relax. "Got to stop drinking," he repeated to himself, "Got to stop drinking..."

Chapter Thirteen

Wilcox, Indiana — 1947

Johnny scratched at the weeds around the rows of pea vines. It was starting this morning, and nothing was being done to stop it. Hank had been drinking, and now he was starting on Tommy. "Honest Hank, I did what you told me!" Johnny knew the scenario. Hank would find something wrong with what he had told him to do. He would accuse him of being lazy, or just disrespectful. It didn't matter. Eventually, when he had his reason, he would take off his belt and the exercise on the boy would begin. Johnny scratched at the dirt, and his anger mounted as his brother pleaded not to be hit. "I'm sorry, Hank, please ... don't hit me!"

Johnny looked to the house. He could see his mother peering through the curtains and crying. They had been home almost a year, and not once had she intervened. Johnny could hear his brother's pleadings coming from the barn. He knew she could hear them, too. "Please, Hank. I did what you said ... Don't Hank! Please!" He watched as Vera shut the window curtain and walked away.

'It ain't right,' he thought to himself. "Why don't she do something?" Johnny grumbled as he dug into the earth. "He ought to stop it. It ain't fair!"

"Don't, Hank! ... Please!"

Johnny looked to the barn. As soon as his brother was reduced to bruises, it would be his turn. He looked to the window. "Shit! She's as scared as we are! It ain't right!" Johnny gouged at the same hole over and over as he listened to the screams from the barn. Suddenly he stopped. "Why should I wait for it? Why should I let him do this to us if she ain't goin' to do nothin'?"

He threw down the hoe and ran toward the barn. With each step, he feared for his brother more than for what Hank would do to him. "It ain't fair," he repeated again and again to give himself courage.

When he reached the barn door, the screaming had stopped. Hank stood several feet away. He was panting hard, and he clutched the familiar black belt in his right hand. Sweat poured from him profusely. In front of him lay Tommy. His face and shoulders were red with newly drawn blood. Tommy did not move. The scene so upset him that any fear he had of Hank was overwhelmed by hatred. And, to arouse the same hatred in Hank, Johnny screamed, "You bastard! ... you bastard! ... I hate you! ... I hate ... your bastard guts!"

Hank turned toward him and re-gripped the belt as he prepared to put it to use. In self-defense, Johnny picked up the closest object at hand. As Hank came toward him, he raised the stick, and, with eyes closed, ran at Hank waving the

71

stick in front of him. He felt it scrape him here, then there, and, as he opened his eyes, he gave his last effort with a single plunge. Hank fell back, and Johnny realized that he had struck him with a four-pronged, heavy-duty pitchfork. The prongs were lodged in his throat and shoulder. Hank staggered back and forth. First he was down, and then he was up on his knees, always unsuccessfully trying to remove the object from his throat.

Johnny watched in horror as the grotesque figure screamed and reeled in pain. He could not take his eyes from the streaks of blood, which ran down the length of his torso and formed a ring around his belt line. While watching his attempt to gain release from the fork, Johnny felt a release of frustration and rallied with excitement at what he saw. Then, as though he had found the source of his misery, Hank turned and came at him, always reaching out, but never able to grasp him. Johnny lurched from him as the freakish thing reached out for him. Then, while attempting to run from it, he tripped over the body of his brother.

The hideous form of Hank fell on him. Johnny screamed. He could not bear it, but felt it coming for his throat as he wrestled in the hay with the bloody form of Hank and his brother. Back and forth they rolled until Johnny got a footing and stepped out of Hank's reach. He looked down and saw that he was standing on his brother's face. He ran around Hank, who was just getting to his knees, and into the fields of corn which flanked the barn. As he ran, he could feel the cool breeze dry the matted blood and mud on his face. Tall cornstalks beat at his face and cut into him as he ran in and out of the rows of corn. The terror of what he had just been a part of was foremost in his mind. Then the ground angled downward; the cornstalks became fewer and smaller; the earth became soft and slushy, and he knew the river and swamp were close by.

When he reached the river's edge, he stood for a long time feeling his body shake and quiver. The longer he stood, the more apparent it became to him that he was losing control of himself. He bolted his arm straight out in front of him and watched as his bloody hands and fingers trembled uncontrollably before him. He wrapped them around his body to stop the shaking. Then he began to laugh and cry, cry and laugh, and then he fell into the water to cleanse the dirt and filth he felt inside.

It was the choking from the water in his lungs that brought him to his senses. He swam from the shallow water and let himself float around the bend in the river, then crawled up on a sandy beach. He lay under some bushes. The heat of the sun relaxed him, and he fell asleep. It was dark when he woke, and he had no idea how long he had been there. Quickly he cleansed himself in the river and ran to the highway. He would to go St. Helena's, to his furnace room. There he would be safe... he could rest. He could think, and plan and rest.

He was not on the highway ten minutes when a black four-door coupe slowed as it passed him, and then cautiously turned off the road and stopped.

"Where you goin', son?" asked the elderly man.

"Up the road," Johnny replied.

"O.K., I'm goin' that way ... get in."

He was a man in his sixties from the looks of his hands and face. Johnny surmised he was a farmer or worked with tools. Once inside the car, he felt better.

"Been on the road long, boy?" inquired the old man as he drove off.

"No, just gettin' started. Hitchhiking."

"You goin' to Wilcox, or you want off sooner?"

"To Wilcox. That would be fine. I'll get off there."

Johnny realized he was stammering for answers and needed to show some assuredness in his replies.

"You ain't in no trouble, are you, boy?"

"Trouble?"

"Yeah," demanded the old man. "You ain't got no luggage; you're dirty from head to foot."

"Oh ... no ... no ..." Johnny answered with half a smile, "My sister ... my sister ... I just came from my sister's place."

"Sister's place?"

"Yeah, she ... uh ... she just had a baby.... Her husband's away, so I came to keep her company until he got back."

"Well, ain't that something?" the man said. "Now that's real nice."

"Her husband came home today, so I just left to go home."

"What'd she have?"

"Have?"

"Yeah. The baby. What'd she have?"

"Oh ... the baby... She had ... a ... a ...boy ... yeah, a boy."

"Well, I'm not from these parts. I come up here from Kentucky to bury my sister."

"Oh"

As the man continued to talk, Johnny thought of the afternoon's events. He hadn't meant to hit Hank with the fork ... He wasn't even aware of what he had in his hand until it struck him. He grimaced as he thought of stepping on his brother's face. He wondered how Tommy was. He hadn't meant to do that, either. Suddenly, he felt guilty. It was his fault. As much as he hated Hank, he was partially to blame. If anything happened to his brother, it was his fault.

"It's his fault, you know," the old man said.

"What? ... Whose ... whose fault?" stuttered Johnny as he came out of his reminiscing.

"My brother-in-law. It was his fault ... not looking after his own. He should have provided for it before she died; that's what he should have done."

"Oh ... yeah ... sure," Johnny replied, as though interested.

73

As the old man talked on, Johnny began making plans. Then it came to him: What if he had killed Hank? ... What if he was dead? The thought made him sick to his stomach. In any event, he would have to hide. He couldn't go back home. Tonight, he would stay in the furnace room. No one would find him there; he would be safe. But, after tonight, he would have to make plans.

"I've made plans."

"What?" asked Johnny

"I said, I've made plans. When it's my turn to go, nobody's goin' to have to bury me. It just ain't right to have your relations have to bury you."

"No it ain't right to have your relatives bury you," Johnny answered as though interested.

"Yeah, it ain't right," the old man continued, "Hell, you can't depend on nobody these days, anyway. You know what I mean, boy?"

"Yeah," Johnny replied to keep the man talking so that he might continue his train of thought. The drone of the man's voice and the hum of the car's engine relaxed him and he began to doze and wake, doze and wake.

"Hell, you might as well do what you got to do yourself, anyways. You can't count on nobody these days," the old man continued. "And the reason you can't count on nobody is 'cause no one ever tells the truth no more. I mean, if a guy gets in a jam, he'll just lie his way out, and most everyone's so gullible they believe him. Mark my word, boy, ain't no one tellin' the truth these days, I can tell you that. Why, just a couple of hours ago, I come from that doctor's hospital in Wilcox where they took my sister's body. I had to make plans to move the body to Kentucky. I'm gonna bury her at home. Her husband didn't like it, but, hell, if I'm payin' for the funeral, I ought to be able to say where she's goin' to be buried.

"Anyway, I was makin' arrangements, and this guy comes in lookin' for first aid. His wife brought him in. He says he fell on a pitchfork! Fell on a pitchfork! Why, hell! I've been workin' on a farm long enough to know someone forced that fork on him, the way them wounds was. But the Doc believed him. I knew different, but I didn't say nothin'. None of my business. I tell ya, someone gets in a jam, these days, they just lie their way out. That's not my generation. Ya know what I mean? It's puttin' money out to bury your sister. Ya know what I mean?" The man looked at his passenger and saw that he was sound asleep.

"Well, boy, I guess you're as tired as you are dirty," the man said to him and then cursed at the car that passed him going twice his speed, "Go on, ya damned fool. Hell's not half full!"

Chapter Fourteen

St. Helena's

Johnny knelt by the running water. The crystal clearness and gentle flow gave him a feeling of well being. But, then, it always began with that feeling of well being. As the water flow moved faster, he knew what to expect. Slowly, at first, it began to churn and move in many directions. The mud would be next. As the movement of the water accelerated, the color turned from gray to black. His heart began to gallop with the rapid flow of the water. From behind him, Johnny could see it coming at him. He couldn't make out the thing through the underbrush, but he knew what it was and what to expect. There was nowhere to turn. There was no choice but to wait for the pain. His pulse accelerated as he waited for the thing to approach. As the water whirled and splashed, the thing was upon him and beating him. The water foamed and bubbled. Beads of sweat poured from Johnny's skin. Then the water turned red, blood red. It was his blood, as the whip lacerated his back and arm, Johnny looked into the water. It eased his pain to look at the water. But this time it was different. A figure could be seen emerging from the pool of blood. It was a face, a distorted face, as though someone had trampled, mutilated and gouged it. It came out of the blood-red pool, arms extended, pleading to him for help. Johnny recognized his brother, Tommy. His mutilated mouth contorted into a scream. But it was not Tommy screaming. Johnny sat up. His whole body was soaked with perspiration and he gulped air as though each breath was his last.

"That damned dream," he said to himself. It had acquired new extremes since he last experienced it. He lay back on his elbows; woke up to his surroundings. He was not in his bedroom, but in the furnace room at St. Helena's. A chill ran through him as he recalled the fight in the barn, the pitchfork, running through the cornfield and being picked up on the highway by the old man. What was it the old man had said to him when he dropped him off in town?

"I'll wait right here 'till that porch light goes out, then I'll know you're safe."

He had picked a house with a front porch light because the old man was so adamant about returning him to a waiting house.

"You can't take chances these days," the old man repeated again and again. "I'll be waiting here 'till that light goes out, then I'll know you're safe," he yelled as Johnny crossed the street and disappeared behind the porch-lit house.

Then he ran through the back yard and down the alley. At the end of the alley was St. Helena's playground and the safety of the furnace shed.

Johnny tucked the old carpet around him for warmth. Tomorrow he would find one of the boys on the playground to help him. With luck, he would be where Hank could never get to him – that is, if Hank were still alive. Oh, why did he hit him with that pitchfork. As he thought of the experience, he realized that he had been unaware of what he was holding. Johnny fell asleep repeating, "I hope he isn't dead... " and his last thought, as the darkness came, was of the shining of the porch light. He wondered if the old man who gave him the ride was still waiting for it to go out.

It was the turn of the key and the pull of the door chain that awoke him. Johnny scampered behind a broken blackboard and watched as the folding door at the end of the room opened. Herman Mueller, the gardener, stood in the open door wiping the sweat from his brow. Johnny watched as the old man entered the room and began pulling the cord on one of the three lawn mowers. When the motor did not respond, he moved to the next while swearing under his breath. "Damned nuns; they can't buy new equipment. I got to work with these antiques ... they always expect me to keep 'em runnin'." After working with one machine until it started, he grabbed a rake and pulled the mower outside pushing the door half-shut behind him.

Johnny went to the window and watched as the gardener dragged the machine across the playground. He looked at the bare playground and the buildings surrounding the yard. He recalled the contents of each building and, with each remembrance, appreciated his stay at St. Helena's all the more.

Mitchell, a seventh-grader, came out of the kitchen door and ran into the schoolyard.

"Mitch! Mitch!" yelled Johnny from the opened door. From the expression on his face, he recognized the voice, but could not find its source.

"Mitch, here at the shed," yelled Johnny.

The boy threw a box into the disposal and ran toward the shed door.

"Hey, Mac, what you doin' in there?" the boy said as he entered. He smelled of pancakes and syrup.

"Hey, Mitch. Anyone see you come in here?"

"I don't know. Hey, Mac, what you doin' in here? You comin' back?"

"It's a long story, Mitch, but I don't want anyone to know I'm here, O.K.?"

"Yeah, sure. Hey, you in trouble?"

"Yeah, sort of. Hey, Mitch, I haven't eaten since yesterday. Can you get me something to eat?"

"Sure, Mac." Mitchell looked at him as if he had found his own personal treasure. "What kind of trouble you in?"

"It was an accident. I sort of got mad at my old man. We got in a fight. Can you get me something to eat? I'm really hungry."

"Sure, Mac. Just stay right here. I'll be right back."

"Mitch, don't tell anyone I'm here. That's important. O.K.?"

"Hey, that's our secret. I got to make one more run to the disposal. I'll come back with some breakfast for you."

Johnny watched as he ran across the yard and into the kitchen. He thought of telling Sister Theophane about his predicament. He could trust her. Maybe she could fix it so he could stay at St. Helena's. If he could just talk to her in private, he might be able to work something out. He watched Mitchell as he returned from the kitchen. He threw a bunch of boxes in the disposal and returned to the shed.

"We had pancakes this morning, Mac. I got you a whole bunch."

Johnny took the box and immediately began eating.

"Hey don't eat so fast, Mac. I can get you more."

Johnny gulped down the pancakes and used his finger to smear the syrup.

"What you doin' here, Mac? Why did you leave home?"

"'Cause."

"'Cause, why?"

"'Cause. I told ya. My old man, he was always on us for no reason. Anyway, we had a fight."

"What happened?"

"We just had a fight, that's all," Johnny said between bites.

"You hit him?"

Johnny stopped and looked at the boy. "Never mind, Mitch. We got in a fight, and I left. That's all."

"What you gonna do now, Mac?"

He licked the syrup off his fingers and said, "I ain't sure, but you can help me."

"Sure, Mac."

"But you can't tell no one, Mitch. You got to keep my bein' here a secret."

"Sure, Mac. A secret between you and me."

"O.K. Now listen, Mitch. I got to see Sister Theophane. You go tell her I got to see her. Tell her you got to show her something. Don't tell her I'm here. You got it?"

"I can't, Mac."

"Why not?"

"'Cause she ain't here."

"What'ya mean, she ain't here?"

"She ain't been here since she went to the hospital."

"She ain't here?"

"No, and I heard the witch tell one of the sisters that she won't be back for a long time. She's got something wrong with her head."

"Her head?"

"Yeah, she keeps fallin' asleep or somethin' like that. Hell, I don't know. But she won't be back for a long time, I know that."

Johnny walked over to his makeshift bed and sat down. He slowly wiped off his mouth with the end of this sleeve.

"Mac, you want me to get you some more to eat?"

"No ... no, Mitch ... I ... got to think for a minute."

"I can get you all the food you want. Hell, they never know it's gone. I always take rolls and stuff and put it in my locker so I can eat it at night. I'd've gotten away with a whole plate of leftovers at lunch yesterday, but Frankie caught me takin' 'em and..."

"Frankie!" yelled Johnny.

"Yeah, Frankie. She made me put them back."

"She's here?"

"Yeah. She works for Sister Maureen. Cleaning rooms and stuff like that."

Johnny got up and went to the window and looked out. A smile crossed his face.

"Mitch, I got something for you to do."

"Sure, Mac. You want something more to eat?"

"No, Mitch. I want you to get Frankie. Tell her I'm here. Just don't tell anyone else."

"Hey, you can count on me. I'll be right back."

"Just tell Frankie to come here."

Johnny watched as the boy darted across the playground and into the kitchen door. He walked around the room, reassuring himself that Frankie could be trusted. He thought of the plans they had made after graduation. So much had changed. He looked out the window and saw Frankie walk into the yard. Mitch was next to her, explaining something. An expression of surprise came over her. Then Mitch pointed to the shed. She stopped for a moment, then ran to the shed door. Johnny threw open the door.

"Johnny," she said while catching her breath, "What are you doing here?"

"C'mon in, Frankie." Mitch followed her in.

"Hey, Mitch, do me a favor," asked Johnny.

"Sure, Mac. Just name it."

"Get me something to eat again."

"You got it. I'll be right back and I won't tell anyone."

"Are you in some kind of trouble, Johnny?" Frankie asked.

They sat down on two broken desk chairs, and he explained how he and Tommy returned to the farm after graduation. He told her how he hated his mother's boyfriend.

"I hit him with a pitchfork. I didn't mean for it to happen. I was trying to save Tommy from gettin' hit again. That's why you can't tell anyone I'm here. They could be lookin' for me."

"Oh, Johnny! What are you goin' to do now?" she said as she reached out for his hand. Johnny clasped her hand. It was the first sign of concern someone had shown for him in a long time, and he felt a surge of love for her.

"I don't know where I'm goin', but I've got to get out of here. Hank might be dead. I might have killed him."

"No," she said. "You can't just run away. Let me tell Sister Maureen; she'll help you."

"No. I got to find somewhere to go and some money to live on."

"Money. I know where some money of yours is."

"You do?"

"Yes. I work for Sister Maureen, and there is an envelope with money in it. It's got your name on it. She had me put it in a file."

"What file?"

"The Graduation file. There is this letter addressed to you, with some money in it. I think it ... your mom was to get it and give it to you. It's in the Graduation file."

"Go get it, O.K. But don't tell anyone."

"Johnny, Sister trusts me. I can't just get it out of the files."

"Please, Frankie. I don't know what else to do. Just go see if you can find it."

Oh, all right, but I'll have to tell Sister when she finds it missing."

"O.K. But not now. Please, just get the envelope. Let me see what's in it."

As Frankie ran toward the back entrance, Johnny looked out at the playground and memories of better days came to him, playing ball with his classmates; and while waiting for the recess bell to ring, he would talk to Sister Theophane of his future plans. And now ... now he was hiding in the tool shed. How many times had he been in here to gain a bit of privacy, never realizing it would become his refuge from breaking the law.

"I got it," Frankie said as she entered the shed. "And no one saw me."

"Great. Let me look," Johnny said as he grabbed the envelope. On the front was

> To: John McBride
>   c/o Vera McBride
>   St. Helena's Orphanage
>   Wilcox, Indiana

Johnny opened the envelope to find two $10 bills. And two notes. One was addressed to his mother and said,

> Vera, please give the enclosed money and note to John as a graduation present from me.

On the second note was written

> Hello, John McBride. I am your Aunt Lillian. We haven't met because I live in California, but I wanted to buy you something for graduation. I wasn't sure what would be appropriate, so please accept two new $10 bills as my gift. Some day, if you ever get to California, you must come visit me. Congratulations on your graduation from grade school."
> Lillian Breslin

"Wow! Johnny yelled. "This is from my Aunty Lillian. I've heard my mom talk about her – and she wants me to come to California!"

I think maybe Sister Maureen forgot to give it to your mom after graduation and kept it until she saw her another time."

"Yeah, well, I got it now, and boy do I need it. Look on the back of the envelope – it's her address in Long Beach. Hey Frankie, I'm goin' to California. To my aunt's place in Long Beach. She can help me, I know she can."

"California" breathed Frankie. "It's so far away."

"I don't have no choice, Frankie. I can't stay here." He felt an urge to hold her, but was too unsure.

"Oh, Johnny, I'm scared for you," said Frankie, and she rushed to him and put her arms around him.

He held her. "I'm scared, too, Frankie, but I got no choice."

"No," she said, "Let me tell Sister Maureen. She'll help us. I'll bring her to you. She'll understand."

Johnny pulled back from her. "No, Frankie. I can't take any chances."

"Please, Johnny. Let's talk to Sister. She'll know what's best. Please, Johnny. For me?"

He walked to the window. As scared as he was, he might try it. 'For her sake,' he thought to himself. "I don't know," he said.

"Johnny, I'll bring Sister here. I won't tell her why. If you don't like what she says, you can always leave. Please, Johnny, try this ... for me please?"

He looked up and saw the tears in her eyes.

"Please, Johnny. I'm so scared to see you run off."

"I don't know, Frankie. Maybe, if you don't tell her why she's comin' out here."

"I won't, Johnny. I'll be right back. Just don't you move. You wait. Sister will help us. I'll be right back ... Don't leave ... Please!"

He watched her run over the yard and disappear into the kitchen entrance.

Sister Maureen was dusting off books in the library when Frankie entered. "Sister," she said urgently, "I've got something to show you."

"To show me? What are you talking about?"

Frankie realized how ridiculous that sounded and said, "Sister, Johnny McBride has run away. He's in trouble. He's hiding in the maintenance shed."

"What!"

"He ran away from the farm, Sister. Now he wants to go to California."

"Ran away ... California? Please, Frankie, calm yourself."

"Sister, just come with me before he changes his mind."

The nun began to follow the girl. She continued to talk.

"...and he's really scared, Sister. He said he'd talk to you. You've got to stop him from running away to California."

They crossed the schoolyard, and the nun began to realize the seriousness of the situation. When they reached the shed door, it was partly open.

"Johnny!" she yelled as she looked first behind the metal lockers and then the door. "He left. Sister ... He left," she said as she began to cry. "He didn't wait like he said he would. Oh, Sister, I'm so scared for him!" She fell into the nun's arms, crying.

"All right, all right," Sister Maureen said. "Quiet down. We'll think of something." She led the girl from the shed as Mitch came running up with bottles of Coke and candy bars bulging from his pockets. He looked at the nun in surprise. "Where's Mac?"

"Put those bottles back where you got them," insisted the nun quietly.

"What's the matter with Frankie?"

"Never mind, Mitchell," said the nun, "Just put those things back in the kitchen."

Sister Maureen helped Frankie across the yard, explaining to her the need to notify his parents.

"... but he doesn't want anyone to know where he is, Sister. He's afraid of them ... very afraid ... because of what he did."

Herman Mueller approached the shed door. He saw the nun and the two children leaving and wondered what they were doing in his shed. He dragged the lawn mower inside and looked around.

"She must have found those damned kids fooling around in here," he muttered to himself. He put the lawn mower against the wall and noticed the cement bags and carpet out of place. "I should've locked that door before I left," he said to himself. He moved the bags into the corner and uprighted a broken blackboard. He squinted his eyes to read what was written on it.

> "Frankie, I can't wait. They'll take me back to the farm
> ... I'll write you. I love you."

"Damned kids," he muttered as he placed the board against the wall. The man picked up the door lock he had left on the shelf and walked out of the shed, pushing the door shut behind him. As he placed the lock on the latch, he muttered to himself, "Got to remember to lock this when I go out. Can't trust them damned kids. Got no better sense than them fool nuns that teach them."

Lillian waited at the open door for the mailman to bring her the packages and letters. "Morning, Mrs. Breslin," he said as he handed her the letters first. "Ya got lots of mail today."

"Yes, thank you," she said while taking the mail.

"End of the month really keeps me hopping."

"Thank you, Gary," she replied as she picked through the letters and packages.

"Everyone gets a free can of soup today from a new manufacturer. I sure wish they'd quit inventin' new products."

"See you tomorrow," she said as she shut the door. She sat down on the sofa and continued to look through the letters. From the pile she picked up the envelope with the return address Colorado Key and Lock Company. She opened it and read the enclosed form letter.

Dear: Mrs. Breslin

Enclosed is the key #   A – 31
_____

for your deposit box that you hold in partnership

with   Charles McBride
_____

at the   Colorado Security Bank, Calpine, Colorado
_____

The enclosed key, in combination with the key held by your bank, will open the deposit box. If this key is lost or stolen, notify the bank immediately. Replacement of new keys or additional keys will be made at the expense of the boxholder.

Thank you,

Norma Helder
_____

Secretary of Security
Colorado Key and Lock Co.

"Damn!" she screamed as she threw the letter down. "Why did I ever let him in this house? Why did I fill out that stupid card?" She got up and walked around the house. "To hasten his exit," she answered herself.

She reached for the letter and ripped it up. "That's not going to end it," she yelled to herself. She sat down and lit a cigarette, then quickly reached for the phone.

"Barry Aston, please," she said as she drummed her fingers impatiently. "Barry, this is Lillian. I've done a stupid thing. Remember, I told you that an old school mate visited me a month or so ago, someone from Indiana? Well, to get this person out of the house, I agreed to sign on a deposit box with him. What? Well, this person didn't trust anyone else...No, I don't know what's in the box. I didn't want to do it. As I said, I did it just to get him out of the house ... Look, what are you doing for lunch? ... I'd love to ... No, don't pick me up ... I'll come downtown ... I'll see you then."

She put the phone down and opened the small package. She took the key and read the number, A-31, and the name Colorado Security Bank and Calpine, Colorado written on the side. Opening the china closet, she put the small key in an oriental-design cup and shut the door.

"Damn! He could have anything in that box," she said, gritting her teeth. "I could be an accessory to..."

The more she thought about it, the more upset she became. Consoling herself, she decided to wait and see what Barry would advise.

Chapter Fifteen

Cooper County, Arkansas

Sergeant Bud Freeman glanced at the wall clock as he entered the night report form in the office typewriter. He filled in the August 8, 1947 date, and the time, 8:15 a.m. A man in his thirties, wearing a sheriff's uniform with the nametag, Sergeant Gaylord, strolled into the office.

"Hey, Freeman. You're early. You're not off duty for fifteen minutes, Old Buddy."

"Then you won't mind covering for me, Gaylord. I need to get off now," Sergeant Freeman said without looking up from his typewriter.

"No ... no, Buddy, I got nothing better to do," the sergeant replied as he strolled up to a row of offices. He stopped at the door marked Sheriff John J. Bullard, then strolled back.

"Hey, Buddy? Is what I heard the God's truth?"

"Depends on what you heard, Gaylord."

Sergeant Gaylord bent down and whispered over the counter. "They're sayin' down at the courthouse that you done put your hat in the ring against the old man."

"Gaylord," the sergeant stopped typing. "you don't have to whisper. We're the only two in here."

Sergeant Freeman finished typing his report and zipped it out of the typewriter. "Yeah, it's true. I registered yesterday. I am officially a candidate for Sheriff of Cooper County."

"J—e—e—s--s—u—u—s Christ, Freeman! You got balls, I'll give you that, man! You got balls!" Sergeant Gaylord yelped as he walked back and forth smoking his cigarette. "Shit, man, I couldn't believe it! I mean, hey, that's really something! Does the old man know? Does Big J know?"

"Know what, Gaylord?" Sergeant Freeman answered as he pulled out the top filing drawer.

"Know what? Well, that you ... did this ... that you're trying to take his job ... that you're against him?"

"I'm not against him. I'm not against anyone," the sergeant yelled as he slammed the file cabinet drawer. "I just registered as a candidate for a public office. Anyone has the right to do it. Even you, Gaylord. It doesn't mean you're for or against anyone personally. It just means you're running for a public office."

"O.K., O.K., Buddy. Don't get so excited. No offense, Buddy. But, on the surface, it might be considered by some in the community like a personal affront to a ... well ... to the way things been run around here for the last twelve years."

"Well, maybe it's time for a change, Gaylord."

"Actually, Freeman, I'm surprised that you'd put yourself in such a position. Ain't you his ... what'd you call them ... a ... 'protégé' ... I mean, didn't he send you to school and then some, like gettin' you a scholarship to the academy?"

Sergeant Gaylord began to put his cigarette out on the counter ashtray, and Sergeant Freeman pulled it aside and looked straight in his eyes.

"Let's get this straight, Gaylord. I'm no one's fair-haired boy. Anything he might have done for me was done to smooth his conscience. Any favors he did for me have been paid long ago. Get that?"

"Sorry, I just thought you might be bitin' the hand that fed you ... I mean, if you ask me."

"Well, I didn't ask you, Gaylord."

"Sorry, no skin off my nose," said Sergeant Gaylord as he saw a large form open the back office door.

"The old man's here, Freeman. I'm anxious to see what he has to say on it."

A heavyset man walked into the room. He chewed on the stub of a cigar and wiped the sweat from his forehead with a red bandanna.

"Mornin', Sergeant Freeman. Sergeant Gaylord."

"Mornin', Sheriff," they both replied.

"It's early and as hot as the last of August," he said as he walked into his office.

"I'd be much obliged, Sergeant Freeman, if you would see me in my office before leaving this morning. I'm sure Sergeant Gaylord won't mind filling in the last of your duty while we talk."

"Oh, no ... no, Sir," Gaylord whispered. "Gimme' the keys to the patrol car and I'll make the last round. I don't want to be around here when he starts sounding off."

"Hey, you gonna vote for me, Gaylord?" he asked as he threw him the keys.

"Hell, Freeman, when he gets through with you, there won't be enough of you around to vote for," he snickered as he caught the keys and walked out the front door.

Sergeant Freeman looked at the wall clock. Fred Griggs was late. He had hoped to be picked up before Bullard arrived. Now he had to see him alone. He silently damned Fred for talking him into running for candidate. It was an exercise in futility. He was fully convinced of that before agreeing. Why did he accept it? He damned himself for being a part of something that would only end in personal embarrassment. Yet he had to be convincing to everyone else that he was sincere in what he was doing.

"C'mon, in, Bud," Bullard said as he stood looking out his window. He wiped the sweat from his forehead and throat while he chewed nervously on his unlit cigar.

"Y'know what?" the Sheriff said as Sergeant Freeman sat down.

"What's that, Sir?"

Sheriff Bullard bent his two-hundred-fifty pounds over his desk and looked straight into the sergeant's eyes. "I'm gonna make the damnedest fool out of someone in this here department, someone I most sincerely do like, around here. Did you know that, Bud?"

"No, I didn't, Sir."

"Why, yes, Sergeant. That's just what's gonna happen. And it ain't nobody's fault but the person that's gonna get hurt. That's what's so sad about it all."

"You wouldn't be talking about the up-and-coming election, now, would you, Sheriff?"

"Why, yes, I am, Bud. I was just informed that you are also running for Sheriff."

"That's correct, Sir."

"Well, now, tell me," the fat man said as he sat on the edge of his desk. "Are you serious about this election, or is it some kind of little joke?"

"No joke, Sheriff. I'm dead serious."

"Well, now, that's very interesting, Bud," he said as he lit the cigar stub. "I am curious as to why?"

"Why shouldn't I?"

"Well, Bud, it's premature to bring this up, but, well, boy, there is a time in the future, a time when, you might say, you'll take your place. Of course, that's well in the future, but a part of the plan."

"Well, Sir, I guess I can't wait."

The Sheriff threw away the burnt ash and paced the floor. "My, you young kids are impatient," he said, showing his irritation.

"Change is part of the political system, Sheriff."

"You think this county needs a change, eh?"

"After twelve years with the same Sheriff, yes, I do."

"Well, now, Bud, what makes you think you, or anyone else, can do a better job than what's been done around here?"

"Hell, anyone can."

The large man stopped short and looked at the sergeant. "Now just what the hell does that mean?"

"It means that there are a lot of people in town that are fed up with the way this office is handled, and after twelve years, want a change."

"Explain yourself!"

"You know damned well what I'm talkin' about. That cell back there is used as for your personal holding cell for ..."

"Now just a damned minute, there, Sergeant."

"...trumped up charges. Half the people that come out of this jail come out black and blue, which you attribute to resisting arrest or attempted escape, or 'accidents.'"

"Damn you! Can you prove anything you say?"

"Every time you shut your car radio off at night, everyone in the county knows some damned fool is going to suffer from your sickness to bully and violate people."

"You can't prove none of this!"

"...of course not. I can't prove it, Sheriff. You cover your ass very well."

"Why you ungrateful son of a bitch! After what I did for you after your dad's accident!"

"You didn't do a thing for me except quiet your own conscience."

"That there's your Ma talkin'! She never did trust me or my intentions!"

"It ain't all rumors, Sheriff. When I was sixteen, my old man caught you beating up the only jail tenant you had one night. You nearly killed him 'cause you were so drunk. Before you could kill him, my old man pulled you off him. My old man covered the whole thing up. I stood outside and heard my old man calm you down. Then he brought the man home, cleaned him up and put him on the next bus out of town."

"There was exceptional circumstances!"

"Your circumstances are always the exception! My old man covered up for you until it got to where he didn't know what was to be covered up and what was legal. That's when he ran one of your patrol cars off the reservoir cliff!" the sergeant yelled back.

"Your old man was a drunk, and I kept him on the books too long until he killed himself while on patrol. Now you and your ma are turning against me!"

"There are others out there that know the truth."

"You've just been hangin' around your nigger and newspaper friends too long, listening to the garbage they spew out about me and this department; just a bunch of kooks who don't like law and order."

"Well, neither do I. Not the way you run it, Sheriff."

The Sheriff's face turned red and he wiped his sweaty forehead. "You ungrateful S.O.B. I'm goin' to have to retire you early."

"You do whatever's necessary, Sheriff."

"No, wait a minute," the Sheriff yelled, "Oh, no...I ain't firin' you. That's just what you want, ain't it ... Oh, no, sir ... I got a better plan...I think I'll just do Mrs. Freeman's son a favor ... yes, sir ... a favor . . No, sir, you ain't gettin' fired. No, sir, you're gettin' a promotion ... to the day shift."

The sergeant turned red and looked at him. "You heard me right, boy. A promotion. If you're gonna resign, you're gonna have to give up more than you bargained for."

"I don't get it."

"You don't get it! Why, boy, you made some pretty disgustin' accusations. Accusations that you say you can't prove. Well, boy, I think people runnin' for office should air their views and accusations right out in front of people, people like the Masons, and Elks and Rotary. You and me is gonna go around to those people in those organizations and state our platforms, and I want you to tell those people in those organizations what you told me just now and see how much they believe you. And, you can do it as my first deputy ... on the day shift with me."

The Sheriff stuck his cigar in his mouth and came around the desk with his finger stabbing at the sergeant, exaggerating each spoken word.

"And, then, boy, you can explain to those club brothers of mine and to those clubs, of which I have been president, not once, but many times, just what kind of a change we need around here. You can tell 'em what you told me just now, and we'll see how much of a chance you have of gettin' elected anything in this town!"

"Is there anything else you would like to discuss with me?" the sergeant asked.

"Listen, you S.O.B., you just don't realize the power I got; but you're gonna learn the hard way. Now get the hell out of my office."

Sergeant Freeman left the office and walked down the street. "I knew it wouldn't work!" he swore to himself. A blue Ford pulled up next to him and he got in.

"Well, Bud, what happened?' asked Fred Griggs.

"Well, it's no good, Fred. It was a stupid idea to begin with, and it's not gonna get any better. He didn't fire me. I'm his first deputy. We work the day shift together ... right where he can watch me. It's either that, or resign."

"That's even better," Griggs said as he pulled into traffic.

"It's gonna be egg on my face."

"But we knew that, Buddy. We agreed that it was gonna be tough."

"I don't know, Fred. It all looked so possible at the organizational meeting."

Fred pulled the car to the curb and stopped. "Buddy, there are a lot of people counting on you. Since he didn't fire you, resign. We've set aside contributions for you and your family to live on. We counted on this..."

"That, and unemployment for being fired."

"Buddy, there's more riding on this than a job. We're counting on you to go through with this. People want a change. They want to break the hold that man has on this town. It's gonna be tough, but these people trust you. They feel you're the right man to break him."

Buddy looked out the window at the passing pedestrians.

"Yeah, and I'll bet there's a lot of people out there that won't vote for me because of the way they feel."

"Like who?"

"Like Gaylord."

"How does he feel?"

"Scared ...just plain scared."

Chapter Sixteen

St. Helena's

The nun walked into Sister Theophane's office and picked up the bundle of mail. She flipped through the envelopes, looking for anything other than the usual bills. One envelope with the return address of Breslin, Inc. caught her eye and she quickly opened it. From the envelope, she pulled out a note which said: "Please accept this contribution in our name. The individual donor does not wish to be named." The same note had accompanied each contribution. The nun quietly thanked Lillian as she grasped the check for five thousand dollars.

"Theo will be glad to know about this," she thought to herself. She carefully put the check and note in her purse and continued through the mail looking for anything unusual. She stopped at the envelope with the return address marked 8th St. Mission, Lovelace, Missouri. It was addressed to Frankie Phillips.

"Why should Frankie be getting a letter from a mission in Missouri?" she said to the empty room. Then she recognized the handwriting. Her first reaction was to open the letter and not show it to the girl. Frankie would be arriving soon, and it wasn't right. The nun put the letter aside and searched the mail again. "Surprises come in threes," she said.

"Oh, there you are, Sister. I went straight to the library where we worked yesterday." The pretty girl with brunette curls stood at the door. The nun thought she looked exceptionally pretty in her blouse and skirt. The thought to keep the letter from her passed through her mind.

"Oh, Frankie," the nun said, startled, "I didn't hear you come in." She picked up the envelope. "I have something for you. I believe it's from Johnny McBride," she said as she handed her the envelope.

"From Johnny?" she said excitedly as she tore open the letter.

The nun watched the girl's eyes glow with amazement and concentration.

"He's fine, Sister. Just fine," she giggled as she continued to read. Sister Maureen sat down as she waited for more of the letter to be revealed to her. "He says he had no trouble hitchhiking ... the rides come easy." There was a long silence while she continued to read, "... when he reaches a new town, he always goes to a mission ... they make him listen to a sermon before they give him something to eat or a place to sleep ... he says it's the first time he's had to read the Bible," she said and laughed. Her face frowned and she said, "Oh, my goodness."

91

"What is it, Frankie?"

"When he goes to bed, Sister, he always puts his wallet under his pillow, and in the other hand, he holds an open knife, so nobody tries to rob him. Oh, that's awful ... He hopes Sister Theophane is better, and he's sorry he left in such a hurry and hopes we understand ... Oh, I do, Sister. I do understand." She looked at the paper again and quietly folded it.

"He wants me to write him at his aunt's in Long Beach."

"Frankie," the nun said to get her attention, "he knows where his aunt lives because you gave him the envelope in the graduation file, didn't you?"

"Yes, Sister, I did. He was so desperate ... I didn't know what else to do. I'm sorry."

The nun looked concerned and said, "Well, it's all right; that doesn't matter now."

But there were other concerns that did matter. It kept running through the nun's mind: 'They're related. They're half brother and sister and they don't even know it. I have no proof, no right, and yet, she has become infatuated with him.' The thoughts frightened her; she felt a need to see Sister Theophane about it.

"Isn't he wonderful, Sister?"

"Why, yes, of course, Frankie."

"I'm going to write him, Sister."

It came to the nun that Lillian Breslin should be notified that the boy would be arriving. Suddenly she was becoming a part of something she wanted no part of.

"Frankie, I just remembered I have to go to the hospital to see Sister Theophane soon. We won't be working today ... we'll work tomorrow ... I'll have lots for you to do then."

"Fine, Sister. I'm going right now and write to Johnny. See you tomorrow."

The nun sat back and looked at the rest of the discarded mail. She felt guilty about giving the letter to her. Perhaps she should have just held it. But then there would have been more. Someone should tell them of their relationship. The nun felt powerless. It was only known to her and Sister Theophane. She got up and left her office. She would see her friend and they would come to some decision. As she left for the hospital, she felt assured that Theo would have a solution.

Sister Maureen approached the nurse's station. Visiting hours would not begin until twelve noon. She hoped they would let her see her friend immediately and not insist that she wait. On each visit, her friend's appearance worsened. Apprehension seized her as she thought of what she would gaze upon today.

"I'm sure it's all right, Sister, but please keep it brief," the nurse said as she looked at the wall clock.

Before entering the room, Sister Maureen prepared herself for whatever change she would see in Theo's appearance.

"How are you doing, dear Theo?" the nun said as she moved to her bedside.

"Mo!" the nun replied as she attempted to raise herself. "You're early today. Is everything all right?"

"Does something have to be wrong to condone an early visit? I just wanted to come over early." 'Must not overdo it,' she thought to herself as she pulled up a chair and reached out for her friend's hand. "Well, now, are you still giving Dr. Kilsner and the crew a rough time?" Sister Maureen said teasingly. The nun restrained from reacting to the gray pallor of her friend's face.

She would not mention the McBride boy or her concerns for Frankie. Today, the news would only be good news.

"One of the reasons I have come so early is to inform you that you were wrong ... a doubting Thomas ... Oh, ye of little faith," the nun went on in a dramatic flurry.

"What are you talking about, Mo?"

"Guess what arrived in the mail today."

"I give up. What?"

"A check."

"A check?"

"Yes, from your guardian angel."

"From Lillian?" the nun asked as she tried to sit up.

"None other, and don't tire yourself," Sister Maureen said as she fluffed her pillow.

"Oh, God bless that woman," she said as she lay back down. "How much was it, Mo?"

"Enough to take us smoothly into the school year, and maybe just enough left over to pay the monsignor's greens fees for a month or so."

"Oh, Mo, you're absolutely sacrilegious," Theo said laughing.

"I knew it would make you happy."

"It does ...It does ... Now, remember to pay the utilities first, then budget for food..."

"Hey, there, slow down. You're still on sick leave. I know what to do and how to do it. I've had a first-class instructor in financial budgeting for orphanages and other institutions."

They both laughed and Sister Maureen again arranged the pillows. Sister Theophane lay back and closed her eyes. They talked of unimportant things, and soon fell silent. Sister Maureen gazed out the window, and the realization of how sick her friend was came to her. She was much worse than she cared to admit, and it scared Sister Maureen to think of it. In the silence, Sister Theophane lay very still, and Sister Maureen thought she had fallen asleep until she called her name.

"Mo?"

"Yes, dear."

"Thank you."

"Thank you?"

"Yes."

"For what, dear?"

"For being such a wonderful friend."

Sister Maureen tensed at what she heard and went closer to the bedside.

"Hey," the nun replied lightly, "what's this 'thanks for being a friend' business?" Why, you'd think I was going somewhere."

No sooner had she said it, then she knew what Theo would reply.

"No, my friend, I am."

Sister Maureen pressed her friend's hand in hers and quipped, "Hey, you're not supposed to talk of such foolishness. First of all, no one around here is going anywhere, and, secondly, the crew around this hospital is not going to let anything happen to you." She cleared her throat to ease her tension. "Anyway, who's going to clean up the financial mess I'm making of the school in your absence? I'm afraid you're not going to get out of this that easily, Miss Know it all." There was no reply and she clenched her friend's hand as though to give her strength. Her only thought was to keep talking ... to talk of anything ... anything but her illness.

"Oh, by the way. You goofed," she began in a sarcastic tone, "I mean, you really goofed."

"You sound like one of the children talking, Mo," the nun replied without opening her eyes.

"Well, you did. You put me in charge of affairs while temporarily taking a respite, and well..." The nun bent down and, in a stage whisper, said, "I'm afraid Sister Wilma is a bit put out." The nun lay in bed very still, never opening her eyes, only smiling as she listened. "Oh, you laugh, my friend," Mo continued, "but Wilma, being the oldest, feels that she should have the responsibility." And, as though mimicking the villain in a melodrama, she squeaked, "Methinks she suspects favoritism."

Eyes closed, the nun acknowledged her friend's dramatics by slowly nodding.

"Theo," the nun continued, "you remember those new English books we ordered last May? Well, they arrived, and they are beautiful, absolutely beautiful. Not only that, the publisher gave us a much bigger discount than we expected. I do admit writing to him, explaining our circumstances. That is one of your tricks. Of course, at the time, I didn't expect Lillian's benevolence. Anyway, the books arrived, and, well, they are so well written, so well organized, the children will benefit so much from them!"

The woman in bed did not move. The smile on her face was replaced by a sober expression. Her color was gray, very gray. Sister Maureen walked to the window and said, "Theo, I nearly forgot. The date of the Order's Yearly Retreat has been changed. It seems many of the sisters are having difficulty getting to it in November. Mother General wrote and suggested that it be held between Christmas and New Year's. She also mentioned that she would be looking for a house to hold it in. It seems the Mother House is scheduled for an interior paint job over the Christmas holiday; and of course, it would be terribly inconvenient for everyone in the house. Well, I was thinking..."

The nun turned to look at her friend in bed.

"Theo, why don't we have the Order's Retreat at our place? It will be a lot of work, I know, but oh, it would be fun. We could re-do the third floor of the main dorm. The rest of the sisters could move in with us." Sister Maureen sat at her friend's side. "Oh, it would be so much fun. I would take full responsibility for it. You wouldn't have to worry about a thing.

There was no acknowledgement of what was said; only the faint smile on the nun's gray face showed any sign of life.

"1 haven't written Mother General about it, because I wanted to talk to you first, of course. But, oh, it would be such fun. What do you think of the idea, Theo?"

The smile was gone. Only the grayness lingered.

The nun lay very still ... too still.

"Theo ... Theo ... Did you hear me, dear? Are you asleep?" Mo leaned over her friend. She nervously bit at the side of her finger. She felt out of place. Maybe she should leave, but she didn't want to. She took her friend's hand. It seemed extremely cold. "Oh, God," she exclaimed, "Theo... Theo... Theo, dear," she called out, "Theo, are you all right?"

The nun lay in bed, never moving. Mo patted her cheeks as she felt terror rising inside her. "Theo...Theo ... Theo, dear," she repeated over and over. Then, getting no reaction, she felt for a pulse but could feel no life. The nun grabbed at the nurse's button and frantically pushed at it again and again. A nurse entered, and on seeing her concern, asked, "What is the matter, Sister?"

"I think she is unconscious, Nurse. I was just talking to her. She was just resting and then she didn't respond."

The nurse took the sick woman's pulse, and without answering, pressed the wall button. "I think it is best if you step outside and wait in the hall, Sister," the nurse requested.

Sister Maureen backed away from the bed as a tall man in a white jacket entered. The nurse again took Sister Theophane's pulse and said something to him that was inaudible to the nun. The man lifted her eyelid and whispered a response to the nurse.

"Sister, I think it would be best if you would come back at another time," the nurse said.

The man picked up the bedside phone, dialed, and said, "Stat." He put the phone down and listened for a heartbeat.

"I want to know what's goin' on."

"Sister, I am only an intern, but I'm sure Dr. Kilsner will be contacting your superior."

"You are holding my superior's hand in your hand," the nun shouted in desperation. "She has left me in charge."

"If you will wait in Dr. Kilsner's office," the intern insisted, "The doctor will explain everything."

The nun moved to the door, only to be stopped by two men bringing in a gurney.

"They're going to take her somewhere. Something has happened and they won't tell me," she said to herself.

"Please, Sister, if you will go to Dr. Kilsner's office, right down the hall. Office 81," the nurse insisted as she helped the men to transfer the nun.

Sister Maureen ran out in the hall, frantically looking for Office 81.

In her attempt to control her panic, she forgot the number, then realized she was going the wrong way. She asked a passing nurse for directions. Once inside the office, she sat down in a small waiting room opposite an old man who leaned against his cane. For fear of bursting into tears, she took a black rosary from her inside pocket and quietly prayed. Beside the old man, there were three others in the room. They all looked straight ahead. No one spoke. The old man with the cane saw the nun praying and was about to ask her to remember his daughter in her prayers when he saw she was crying. Realizing she had enough to pray on, he slowly lowered himself into a chair and picked up a magazine. As he paged through it, he glanced at the distraught nun. Then, turning to a specific article, he found himself distracted from his reading because he envied her for her faith and reliance on prayer for a solution.

Chapter Seventeen

Arkansas

Johnny stuck his thumb out as another car whizzed past. It had been a stupid thing to do, a real stupid thing. Now that the fields had been harvested, truckers, who were always good for a ride, were seldom seen. Cold weather had made other drivers indifferent to strangers on the road; so there he was, walking the side of the highway somewhere in Arkansas. Not a house in sight, not a porch light or a barn. The sun had set better than an hour ago, and it was getting difficult to see five feet in front of him. He thought of the down jacket he had thrown away somewhere in Illinois, a gift of a social worker in one of the missions. But, because it was hot, and cumbersome to carry, he had decided it was excess baggage. Walking at a fast clip, he cupped his hands and blew warm air into them.

As the last of the daylight vanished, Johnny knew he would not survive the night alongside the road wearing just a T-shirt and pants. Already the cold was becoming unbearable. Another car came in his direction, and he waved and jumped up and down, but his actions only caused the driver to speed up and pass him. He continued down the road, blowing warm air into his cupped hands and massaging his bare arms. For the first time in his journey, he had enough money to rent a room; but believing the weather would hold warm for weeks, he had hitch-hiked out of the last town wearing only his T-shirt and jeans. He felt for the packet of matches in his pocket and decided to go into the field and find a ravine, some corner to hide in from the wind and to build a fire. As he looked about, the lights of a car flashed in his eyes. If he was picked up, he would be returning to the town he had just left, but it didn't matter. He couldn't stay in the cold. He crossed the road, waved, and stuck out his thumb. The car approached slowly, then stopped. Without waiting for an invitation, Johnny jumped in and slammed the door.

"Thanks for stoppin'. I didn't think anyone was ever gonna stop," he said in one breath.

"That's all right, boy. Just doin' my job," the driver replied as he moved onto the road. It was the shotgun between them that Johnny noticed first. Then, as his eyes became accustomed to the dashboard lights, he could make out a silhouette of the driver and the insignia on his sleeve. He realized he was in a patrol car.

"What you doin' out here this time of night, boy?" the officer asked.

"Couldn't get a ride," he answered cautiously.

He watched as the officer lit a ragged edge of his cigar and took a puff. In the light of the match, the man looked very large.

"Where you comin' from, boy?"

"The last town."

"Your mommy and daddy know where you are this time of night?"

Johnny chose his words carefully. The tone of the man's voice scared him.

"Oh, sure. Y'see, I just came from my sister's place in the last town. She was havin' a baby, and no one was there to help her. Her husband's in the army, so Ma sent me to help out."

The radio blared out a series of numbers and called to be identified. The officer picked up the receiver and identified himself as Sheriff Bullard. He issued some instructions and shut the radio off.

"Now we won't be disturbed. Where'd you say you come from?"

"The last town."

"You mean Merlin?"

"Yeah, that's it, Merlin."

"And you went there to help your sister?"

"Yeah, she's havin' a baby."

"And now you're goin' to Paxton?"

"Yeah ..."

"Is that where you live?"

"Yeah, I live in Paxton."

"What's your sister's name, boy?"

"Hafley, Marylou Hafley."

The car suddenly stopped at the side of the road. The officer grabbed him by the throat. "Look, boy, I know every birth when and where in this county. We're headed toward Merlin. I just left Paxton, and there ain't never been anyone who lived in these parts name of Hafley that I know of. Now, I want some straight answers and I want 'em now," he yelled. Then he pulled him closer. "You're a runaway, ain't ya?"

"Yeah," Johnny choked.

"Where you from?"

"Illinois.

"You in some kind of trouble?"

Johnny shook his head no, and his eyes pleaded to be released.

"What's your name, kid?"

"John . .. . John McBride."

"You're not in trouble, McBride?"

"No, sir.

"That's easy to check. What you doin' in these parts this time of night?"

"Travelin'."

The officer shook him and yelled, "Travelin' where?"

"To California."

"What's in California?"

"My aunt," he said, afraid to give any more information.

"Where's your mommy and daddy?"

"Indiana."

"Where in Indiana?"

"Wilcox ... Wilcox, Indiana."

"And why ain't you with them, boy?"

He hesitated a minute, and then decided to tell the truth. "I ran away."

"That's what I figured."

For a moment, there was silence as the big man looked at the boy. Then he pushed him back and turned his attention to getting the car in gear and driving off. The man's perspiration was all over the boy's throat where he had held him. Johnny wiped it away; the distinct smell of stale beer permeated the car.

"Y'see, boy, we get all kinds like you, and every once in a while, we pick 'em up. The law says we got to turn 'em in. Lock 'em up until we can check out their stories. We got to see if there's any reason we should be holdin' 'em longer than for a vagrancy charge."

Johnny sat very still. He just listened. He did not move.

"As I say, we get these drifters. Usually not as young as you, but we get 'em. We don't mind if'n they come into our county, but we don't want 'em stickin' around. We're not partial to strangers hangin' around our towns and countryside. That is, unless they're relatives or friends of the county residents ... you understand our way of thinkin' on that, don't you, boy?"

He nodded yes, but didn't move. It wasn't what the Sheriff said but the way he said it. He was leading to something, but Johnny didn't know what, and it scared him. The Sheriff slowed the car down and turned off onto a dirt road. Pangs of fear gripped at the boy's insides.

"Y'see, boy, we believe in law and order, and punishin' the guilty and rewardin' the righteous. You did know that hitchhikin' is against the law in these parts, didn't you?"

Johnny shook his head quietly and said, "No, I didn't."

"Well, it is, boy, and ignorance of the law is no excuse."

The tone of the man's voice frightened him and sweat poured down his face. The smoke from the half-lit cigar was stifling. Johnny kept asking himself why they were going down a dirt road. He hoped against hope that it was some sort of a shortcut.

"Now, we don't need to get involved in all that paperwork just to satisfy the law. There are other ways of fulfillin' the requirements. All it needs is a little cooperation on your part, boy, and you can be on your way."

The car came to a stop. The road ended in an empty field. He shut the front lights off. "This here skirtin' the law can be mutually beneficial, son. All you got to do is just cooperate," he said as he slowly moved his hand onto the boy's leg and cautiously rubbed the boy's crotch.

Johnny pulled away and jerked at the door handle.

"You can't get out that door, boy. The only way out is across me."

"I ain't cooperatin'," he said over and over again as he pawed at the window, then at the door handle. "Oh, God," he yelled. He would rather have been left on the highway, he thought as he tried looking for a way out.

"I ain't gonna hurt you, boy. Just a little cooperation and you'll get no trouble from me," he said as he grabbed Johnny's arm and pulled him from the corner of the seat. Beads of sweat poured out of the sheriff as he pulled at the boy. The smell of stale beer and cigar smoke, along with the fear of what was going to happen, caused Johnny to gag. The only light was from the cigar stubs smoldering in the ashtray. Suddenly it came to him... so he grabbed for the light. While picking a cigar stub up, he burned his hand as he smashed it into the sheriff's face again and again. Sparks flew and the big man let him free. Johnny jerked at the door as the sheriff screamed and flung out at the burning ash against his face.

"You son of a bitch!" the man screamed. He yelled as he defended himself against the burning ash. Johnny turned to see the weapon between them being pulled from its place, and then felt the butt of the shotgun slam against his face. Over and over the butt slammed at his body and at his head.

"You bastard! You bastard!" the man screamed in time with the swats of the gun. Then he stopped attacking the boy and sat puffing to catch his breath.

"You bastard! You really hurt me! You burned me!" He grabbed the boy by the T-shirt and pulled him to him. "I ain't through with you yet, kid, and if anyone asks you how you got so beat up, it's 'cause you didn't cooperate like I told you to. Right? ... Right?" he screamed.

Johnny held his hands to his face to ward off another beating. The man shoved him against the car door. He took out a pair of handcuffs and handcuffed his wrists to the metal bar on the dashboard.

"I ain't through with you yet, boy. We'll just go on in to the jailhouse; then you'll cooperate ... yes, sir ... there's a lot more room for you to cooperate there, boy. But I'll tell you one thing, boy, your ass is gonna be mine! It's gonna be mine before this night is through!" the sheriff yelled as he pulled the car around and headed for the highway.

Johnny lay his head against the windowpane. It began to rain. He wished he had been left on the highway to take his chances, but he could not think of that now. He had to plan a way to free himself, some plan of escape.

Flashes of lightning lit up the rear of the Sheriff's office as the patrol car screeched to a halt. No sooner was the big man out of the car than he was opening the passenger's door and unlocking the boy's wrists from the dashboard.

"You son of a bitch, you gonna be mine in just a minute."

"God damn it! Leave me alone! You can't do this to me!" Johnny screamed as the man pulled him from the door.

"I can do anything I want to do to you or anyone else I see fit, you little bastard. Ain't no one gonna help you, neither," he said as he threw him to the wet pavement and kicked at him. Then, grabbing his handcuffed wrists, he pulled him up the back steps.

"You're gonna suffer for what you did to me," he repeated again and again as he threw the boy into the dark hallway. "You're gonna suffer for burnin' me, boy," the man said as he came into the hallway and shut the door. In the blackness, Johnny tried to get to his feet, but felt the man pull him down and fall on top of him. "You're gonna learn not to make fools out of your elders, boy."

Johnny was turned on his stomach. He felt the cold dull edge of steel against his buttocks as the man sawed at his belt and pants.

"Yes, sir. You are mine, boy. Your butt is mine."

Lightning flashed and lit up the darkened hallway as the Sheriff yanked the boy's belt and ripped his clothes, leaving his backside completely bare. Johnny screamed as the man bared himself and pulled the boy to him. Silhouettes of the two bodies danced against the wall, rocking back and forth as lightning flashed and flickered through the empty office.

"You're mine, boy ... you ... are ... mine, boy ... you ... are ... mine." Over and over the man repeated it as he pushed himself in and out of the boy.

Like some sustained victory, the man repeated it while Johnny writhed and screamed, and then vomited.

Lightning flashed, then flashed again, and then there was another flash, not unlike the lightning, but more engulfing. It wasn't unlike lightning, but it was not the lightning. It was something else. Again, in counterpoint with the lightning, it flashed again and again.

Then the sheriff knew it was not lightning. It was a bulb, and he knew that he was not alone with the boy. He dropped the boy and turned his face from the continuing flashes. He couldn't distinguish one flash from the lightning, or where the bulb was located, so he crawled into the first exit of the hall and slammed the door. Another man was heard running down the hall.

Then another bulb flash lit up the hallway, and the man was gone. A third man stood quietly in the hallway, his silhouette imprinted on the hall door marked Toilet each time the lightning lit the sky. He looked down at the boy who lay half-conscious in his own vomit.

"That's where you belong, Sheriff, in the can, 'cause you're nothin' but a god-damned turd!"

There was no reply.

"You know who's talkin' to you, Sheriff?" There was only silence.

"Hey, you know what I want to do to you, Sheriff? I want you to resign from the up and comin' Sheriff's race. I don't like competition, anyway."

Still there was no reply.

"Anyway, how could you explain them pictures that was just taken?" Especially to all your lodge brothers. Can you hear me, Sheriff?"

The only reply was the sound of thunder as it roared across the sky.

"I think I've made myself clear, Sheriff. Just think of it as sort of an early retirement. I'm gonna take your prisoner, now."

He waited for an answer.

"I think you've punished him enough for whatever it was he did, or was accused of."

In the silence, the man picked up the body of the half-conscious boy, who limply struggled to be free. The man carried him out of the door.

Lightning flashed in the empty hall and thunder roared as the screen door flapped in the rainy wind. From behind the door marked Toilet could be heard the faint sounds of someone standing, a zipper being fastened, and a buckle being snapped into place. Then there was a pop of a single snap, of metal brushing against leather, and of a trigger being cocked into place. Lightning flickered and lit up the empty hallway, and from behind the door marked Toilet resounded one ... loud ... Bang!

Chapter Eighteen

St. Helena's

Sister Maureen looked up from her typing as she saw the office door open. Frankie Phillips entered and shut the door behind her. She stood against the door. Her eyes were moist from crying. In her hand, she held a piece of paper. "Could I see you. Sister? It's very important."

The nun realized the seriousness of the moment and stood up. "Why, yes, Frankie, what is it? Come here and sit with me on the sofa."

The girl ran into the nun's arms.

"Oh, Sister. I just got a letter from Johnny. Oh, Sister, it's awful, just awful. He was beaten up by a policeman in a police car ... Oh, it was just awful," the girl cried out as she buried her head in the nun's shoulder.

"I'm so sorry, Frankie." It was all the nun could think to say. She felt so helpless.

"And ... and, he did awful things to Johnny ... Sister," she sobbed as she looked to be comforted by the nun. "I know ... I know ... he didn't explain ... he didn't say it .. but, I know, Sister ... I know," she said through her tears.

"Know what, Frankie?"

"It was worse ... he didn't say it, but from what he says ... the officer attacked him ... sexually ... I know...."

"Sexually?"

"Yes. He didn't want me to know, but I know in the letter. He says ... he was forced, forced to be a part of ... something ... something he couldn't talk about ... but I know...."

"How can you be so sure, Frankie?"

"Because ... because it ... happened to me," she cried. "It happened to me. I never told anyone, except a girlfriend, and then she wouldn't talk to me anymore when we started to school."

The nun looked into the tear-stained eyes.

"What do you mean, it happened to you, Frankie?"

"That's why my mom left South Bend and came here," she cried again.

"I don't understand, Frankie," the nun pleaded with her.

"We never told anyone, Sister. She just caught him one day."

"Who did, Frankie?"

"My mom. She just walked in one day when he was doin' it to me, and when I told her I'd written a friend about it, she got real mad, Sister, and made me promise to never tell anyone again. I didn't mean to do those things, Sister. He made me. Honest. He made me," she sobbed uncontrollably.

"Who made you, Frankie?"

"I don't believe my mom ever believed me, but he made me do those things, Sister, honest!"

"I believe you, Frankie ... but ... who made ... you ... do .. those ... things?"

The girl breathed heavily as she tried to control her hysteria. Then, as though unleashing years of kept-in trauma, she screamed, "My Dad, Sister. My Dad ... Oh, God! ... I promised I wouldn't tell ... I promised!"

The nun felt faint as she realized what the girl was saying and quickly said a prayer for strength. She pulled the girl to her and comforted her.

"Listen, Frankie ... listen to me. It's all right that you told me. I'm sure of that . . Please, just listen to me. It was good that you told me what happened."

The girl cried uncontrollably as the nun held her to her.

"I just couldn't keep it a secret any longer, Sister. Not after reading Johnny's letter."

"That's all right, Frankie. Tell me, did your mother talk about it after it happened?"

The girl wiped her nose and, like an obedient child, said, "No, Sister. When my mom saw us that day, she just called me to her; then she made me take a bath, and then she took me to a doctor. He examined me. When we got home, my dad was gone and my mom got real mad and said that I was never to tell anyone about it."

"Have you seen your father since?"

"No, Sister. Then, after that, we moved here to Grandma's."

"Your mother never talked to you about it from then on, Frankie?"

"No, Sister."

The nun held the child to her and winced while asking the next question.

"Frankie, did your dad do this to you more than once?"

The girl began to whimper and confessed, "Almost every time we were alone together." Then, breaking down, in uncontrollable sobs, she pleaded, "Please, Sister, don't tell my mom I told you ... please ... please don't tell her."

"It's all right, Frankie," the nun assured her, "You don't have to worry about that. Don't worry, I'll take care of everything. Just don't worry. You're not to blame," she said as she felt tears coming to her eyes. "Just stay right here and nothing will hurt you, child," the nun said as she waited for the girl to compose herself. They sat for several minutes in silence. The girl relaxed, sniffled, and wiped her eyes.

"Is there anything else you might want to tell me, Frankie? Anything that would make you feel better about all this ... anything ... anything at all?"

"Yes," the girl whispered.

"What is it, Frankie?" the nun answered as tears fell from her cheeks.

"I miss him, Sister. I miss him very much."

"I'm sure you do, Frankie," the nun replied. There was another long silence. Then it came to the nun that they might not be talking about the same person.

"Who do you miss, Frankie?"

"My Dad, Sister ... I miss him ... my Dad ...very much ... I miss my Dad very much," she said between sobs.

Chapter Nineteen

160 Willow Lane, Plainesville, Oklahoma.

Miriam DeWitt pulled on her leather glove and fit it firmly to her hand. She looked around her spacious living room. With each antique and furniture piece came a memory of the reason for its purchase.

Tears filled her eyes and she slipped on the other glove. She glanced at the full-length mirror on the wall and decided her matronly suit was the best choice to wear. A middle-aged man stood at the entrance dressed in old dirty pants and a shirt. He held a small garden hoe in his hand. He looked tired and older than his years, and his general appearance was in contrast to the luxurious surroundings.

"I've paid all of this month's bills and took out half of the savings account for myself," Miriam DeWitt said, and she checked her appearance once in the mirror.

"How long will you be gone, Miriam?" asked her husband.

"I don't know, Charles. All I do know is that I'm leaving."

"You don't have to," he pleaded.

"Oh, yes, I do, Charles," she said as she hurriedly pulled on the other glove.

"Please, Miriam. I want to talk to you about this."

"We've tried talking about it, Charles, but you don't listen ... nothing changes ... We talk and talk, and nothing changes. We just get upset and frustrated. Please, I just don't want to talk about it," she said as she put on her coat.

"After twenty-two years of marriage, you can't just walk out."

"Oh, but I can ... and will leave, Charles. I warned you it would come to this." Tears welled in her eyes and she wiped them away with an embroidered handkerchief.

"Let's not rush into this, Miriam."

"I'm not, Charles. I've thought about this for a long time."

"1 know things have been different between us since Billy's gone."

"Things changed before he died. It's not that he left, Charles. He died. You can't even say it or admit it..." She reached for her purse as she began to cry. "You've never completely admitted it ... You keep a memorial to him, as though it will keep a part of him alive."

"Miriam, what harm is that?"

"Charles, it is harmful ... unreal ... You can't give life to something that is dead. It's not wrong to remember, but it's wrong to memorialize it. You don't listen to me, and I won't witness your charade ... your mania," she cried as she moved her luggage to the front door.

"You're staying at Diane's?"

"Yes."

"She must really think me insane."

"My sister never was partial to you."

"You had to apologize to your whole family for marrying me."

"Now, Charles, please. Let's not bicker while I'm waiting." She went to the living room table and picked a rose from the bouquet and put it in her coat lapel.

"Your American roses are exquisite this year, Charles. How many varieties will you enter in the exposition this year?"

"Miriam, are we going to stand here talking about roses and entries right before your sister picks you up?"

"There's nothing else to talk about, Charles."

"It just doesn't seem right," he stammered.

"It's not right, Charles, but we have no one to blame but ourselves. I don't want to start on it. Nothing ever comes of it. We only disagree. I told you I can't stay under these conditions."

"You sound like I'm making you leave, Miriam."

"Well, aren't you, Charles? Aren't you?" she yelled. "I told you I would not stay as long as you insist on memorializing the past ... on keeping ... that ... thing!"

"I feel better for it ... better for having it here ... Better ... I feel better for it."

"It's sick, Charles ... sick ... Give it up ... Billy is dead. Nothing can bring him back," she cried as the phone in the hall rang.

"Yes, this is Mr. DeWitt. Yes, I could use some help around here next week. Look, I'm very busy at the moment. I'll call you later." He hung up the phone. Miriam looked away from him. She looked out the picture window at the freshly cut lawn that stretched before her.

"That was the damned mission calling, wasn't it?"

"Yes."

"And you're getting some volunteer from there to help you with the roses?"

"You know I get help from there."

"And some day one of those vagrants will take advantage of your trust and goodness and beat you up and rob you blind."

"Miriam, you know how I feel about the mission."

"Yes, I know. It's one of your favorite charities."

"It gives men that are down and out a sense of worth."

"I know ... I know," she yelled. "I don't want to hear it."

"We've been all through it."

"Yes, and like everything else, to no avail."

A car drove up and a horn beeped.

"I love you, Miriam," he said as she picked up her luggage. We could close up the house, go to Europe for the summer," he pleaded.

"We tried that months ago," she said as she headed for the door.

"Can I call you?"

"No," she said as she waited for him to open the door. "I don't want you to call me."

"You'll call me?"

"In time ... yes ... in time I'll want to make sure you've not been harmed by those mission vagrants working for you," she said as she headed down the stairs.

A middle-aged woman got out of the car and helped Miriam with her luggage. Charles waved to them, but both women quickly got into the car without showing any recognition of him. He shut the door and walked into the living room. The emptiness of the large room upset him. He would go to his club for dinner ... for the night. He would feel better if he stayed at the club for a couple of days. He would leave right away. As he went up the winding staircase, he admitted to himself that Miriam was right. It was not right to try to give life to the dead ... to consider the reliving of the past the better part of your day. But, he could not help himself. Before leaving, he would stay for just a moment ... maybe a few moments ... but he would sit with Billy until he felt better ... until he felt content ... until the feeling of emptiness left him.

Chapter Twenty

Sonora, California

Kelly wiped off the bar as he looked at the clock. He opened the small refrigerator below the bar to make sure there was plenty of bottled beer.

"I'll never understand why bottled beer is preferred during the day and draft at night," he said to himself.

The bright afternoon sun filtered through the cut glass windows that fronted the large room before him. He always enjoyed looking at the variety of colors that reflected throughout the room. Outside the front door, he could hear several trucks pulling up front. The boys from the mill were right on time. He reminded himself to ask Charley McBride for his rent money. There would be more drinking done today than the usual beers; today was payday.

"Hey, Kelly, my man! How about a bottle of your finest American made," yelled Cliff Hansen as he hit the bar with his fist. "Damn, it's hot today," he said as he reached for a bottle of Budweiser. Herb Belling and Mac Wells sat on either side of him. Kelly put two more bottles of beer on the bar.

"And how is the wood business today, gentlemen?" he asked.

"Hot and dusty, Mr. K," Mac answered as he grabbed a bottle of beer.

"Damn! That forest is ready for a big burn if the heat keeps up," quipped Herb.

"Where's my star boarder?" asked Kelly.

"Takin' a piss next to his truck," laughed Herb. "That guy is so soused! I mean, he drank more than his usual today. It's a wonder he didn't get himself killed."

"He just got out of the truck, and instead of comin' in here, he went across the street to piss in the park. Damn, he's drunk!" chided Mac.

"Did you see how much he put away today?" asked Herb.

"Damn near close to a quart of vodka," answered Cliff, "Hell, he puts it away and it makes him all the livelier."

"Listen. When we felled the big oak on Hill 24, that damned tree came within three feet of where he was guzzlin' it down."

"Hell! I don't think he even heard the thing hit the ground!"

Everyone laughed as Herb continued, "Cruthers was fit to be tied!"

"Cruthers?" asked Kelly.

"The woods boss. Hell, he nearly shit a brick watching that tree comin' within three feet of where McBride was standin'. I'm tellin' ya, Charley keeps drinkin' that way, he either ain't gonna have a job, or he's gonna get himself killed. This ain't the first time he had a close one."

> It's fornication I love above all,
> No matter if from Heaven my soul will fall.
> I'll gamble my life, my soul, seven come eleven,
> For who ever heard of a hard-on in Heaven?"

Charley McBride stood framed in the doorway raising his near-empty vodka bottle. "Hello, my friends, and hello, Kelly," he shouted as he entered.

"You got to admit, he's got a way with words," Herb chuckled to the group.

"Set up the drinks, Kelly," shouted Charley as he approached the bar and put his arm around his fellow workers. "What you guys want to drink? These guys are my friends, Kelly. Give 'em what they want and put it on my bill."

Kelly stood still. "Nothing, Charley ... you get nothing until I get my rent for the month and this week's bar bill paid."

"Rent ... bar tab?" Charley yelled, "Hell, is that all you're worried about? Shit! I got so much money ... your damned eye's would pop out if you saw how much money I really got!"

"How much you got?" asked Herb, to egg him on.

Charley smiled. "Never mind ... how much. I got it, and I'm gonna keep it in the bank until I need it ... Anyway, this old fart wants his money, so take it."

He reached in his pocket and threw a wad of bills on the bar. "Take it, old man. Give them guys what they want. I want ..." He swallowed to make his speech distinctly understood. "I want your finest Jack Daniels ... a quart, please."

"I thought you being an Irishman, you'd be drinkin' Scotch," said Mac.

Charley stumbled over to Mac, "Hey, listen, I like to drink vodka before Jack Daniels. That way it tastes better. I only sip Scotch on holidays."

The men laughed as Kelly took the bills and handed him his change and bottle. "Along with your bill, the damages come to exactly $32.50, and that's including your bottle, your Eminence," said Kelly.

Charley took the bottle from the bar and sat down at a table to open it. Suddenly, he grew very silent and put the bottle on the table. The men at the bar were taking bets on how quickly he would finish it. Sweat poured out over Charley. Suddenly, he had trouble breathing.

"Gotta go out for some air," he mumbled to himself, as a roar of laughter came from the crowd of men. Charley headed for the door and knocked into tables and chairs. "Gonna go and piss in the park again?" yelled Herb, and laughter came from the men.

Charley went into the park and sat on one of the benches. Slowly, the tightness in his chest passed. He noticed that the daylight seemed to fade and that he had trouble sitting up. Sourness formed in his stomach, "Got to stop mixin' the drinks," he said to himself. "Got to ... stop mixin' ... 'em."

Using the metal bench arm as a pillow, he laid his head down. The sourness came into his stomach again and he just wanted to sleep. If he could sleep, he would be all right. The daylight faded and all he could think of was to lie down, very still to ease the sickness he felt inside.

Bennie Campbell threw the football to his friend Bobby. Bobby missed it, and it flew past him and then rolled under a park bench on which lay a middle-aged man dressed in logger's clothes.

"Hey, Mister," asked Bobby, "can I crawl under the bench and get my ball?"

The man did not answer, but just stared, his eyelids half open. He did not blink or move.

"Can I get it, please?" the boy pleaded.

The man didn't answer, and the boy slowly crawled under the bench and retrieved the ball, then ran away.

As Sergeant Kilmer of the Sonora Sheriff's department slowed for a red light, he watched a small boy cautiously retrieve a football from under a bench on which a man slept. "Damned drunk," he said to himself. "If he's still there when I come back, I'll pick him up and run him in." And then, when the light changed, he made a right turn.

* * * * *

Lillian Breslin stood in her fur-lined housecoat, waiting for the postman to deliver the morning mail. It was at times like these, when nothing pleased her and everything bored her, that she tended to think of her past. It was times like these when she wished that she could do more with her life.

Everything had been a struggle until she had met Louie Breslin. Now she had more money than she had ever dreamed of, and she didn't know what to do with it. 'I need a purpose,' she thought to herself.

The mail car drove up the long curved driveway. She thought of her sister, and the farm in Indiana. She envied Vera for having someone else to care for. Damn her for not doing the same. With these thoughts came the memory of the orphanage girl, and, for a moment, she dared to wonder about the child she had given up. As the mail car stopped at the driveway, she quickly moved her attention to the packet of letters the young man handed her.

"Mornin', Mrs. Breslin."

"Hello, Joe. I appreciate your coming up the drive with my mail."

"No problem. You got some magazines here, too."

111

"Thanks," she said as he drove off. She entered the house and went into the living room. She flipped through the correspondence and stopped at a pink envelope addressed to John McBride. The handwriting and the postmark were the same as the last pink envelope. Undoubtedly, her oldest nephew was on his way. Or why would a Miss Frankie Phillips from Wilcox, Indiana, be writing him here? She wondered if she should call her sister. 'No, I'll wait,' she thought. 'I can probably expect a call from her.' She put the envelope on the top shelf with three other identical envelopes. The thought of her sister's son arriving upset and intrigued her. It was something to think on. It made her curious; and yet, it was something to fear. Her past was returning ... and she didn't like it.

Chapter Twenty-One

Plainesville, Oklahoma

The bus marked 'Kensington-Madison' stopped at the corner of Willow Lane and Hyde Avenue. "It's right up that street there," the bus driver said as he pointed out the door. Johnny McBride nodded a 'thanks' and got off. As the bus moved on to Hyde Avenue, he stood looking up Willow Lane. The street was narrow, just big enough for one car to pass another. It wound up a hill and homes on both sides were fronted with large, manicured lawns. The houses were Victorian estates nestled among landscaped shrubbery.

Johnny began walking up the hill. He walked past several homes. One that especially impressed him was brick, and the front lawn was many times larger than his Indiana farmhouse and barnyard. At the top of the hill was a park. Several boys his age were playing ball and when they noticed him watching them, they stopped and stood still, looking at him. Two of the boys wore jackets bearing athletic letters from Jefferson High. He looked at the boys as they gawked at him. His uncut hair and dirty clothes made him stick out among the well-kept surroundings. One of the boys said something and they all laughed.

"Up your ass!" Johnny yelled. They continued to laugh as he crossed the street and proceeded on Willow Lane. He took a piece of paper from his pocket. The minister of the mission had written '160 Willow Lane.' The street numbers of the houses were difficult to see. After walking another two blocks, he stood in front of a three-story brick house that was covered with ivy. He went up the driveway and onto the large front porch. He was about to knock on the front door, when a man dressed in dirty overalls and carrying a plant stepped from the side of the house.

"Did you want something, young man?" he asked.

"Yeah," replied Johnny, "You called the Plainesville Day Mission?"

"The mission? ... Why, yes."

"Well, they sent me," Johnny replied.

"You? ... But I asked for a man to help with the gardening."

"Yeah? Well, they sent me."

The man looked puzzled for a moment and then replied, "I'm sorry, they usually send someone older."

"You don't think I can do it?" Johnny said defensively.

"Oh, no," the man replied as he came closer, "It's just that they usually send someone older..." He stopped and looked intensely at him. "Yes ... yes, I'm sure you'll do just fine."

Johnny became uncomfortable as the man gazed at him.

'I could take him in a minute,' he thought to himself. 'I could wipe him out in a minute if he tried anything.'

"I'm sorry for staring at you, but you resemble someone I know. My name is DeWitt ... Charles DeWitt," the man said as he ungloved his hand and held it out.

"Johnny. Johnny McBride," he replied as he shook the man's hand.

"Please, come in, John. I'm here alone and am in the midst of transplanting my roses."

Johnny followed him into a large living room. The room was enormous, and a wide winding stairway led to the upstairs. He followed him through the dining room in which was centered a long table surrounded by high-back wooden chairs.

"New plants must be transplanted and fertilized at a specific time of the year for their greatest potential growth." DeWitt continued to talk as they entered the kitchen. It was almost as large as the orphanage kitchen. Johnny followed him as he went into a hallway which connected to a long hothouse.

"It's always best to transplant and fertilize by hand as quickly as possible, so as not to upset the flower plants."

Johnny looked at the rows of flower plants. The length of the greenhouse reminded him of the orphanage dormitory.

"I'm sure with your help, young man, we can complete this work this afternoon," DeWitt said as he looked at Johnny with that strange gaze.

Johnny walked among the trays of plants.

"Each plant must be put in a pot and fertilized," DeWitt said. He watched Johnny walk down the aisle. There was a long silence, and Johnny realized the man was staring at him. He turned and looked at him.

"Well, what do you want me to do?"

"Do ... oh, yes, of course," DeWitt said as he broke off his daydreaming. "Yes, just come along over to this box of plants and I will explain what has to be done."

The man showed him how to separate the plants and place them into individual pots. "The fertilizer goes in the bottom of the pot... Once the plant is in, this other brand of fertilizer goes in around it. Then, very carefully, put black dirt into the pot until it is full." The man worked very carefully, with understanding and sensitivity. "Always make sure the plant is upright and that it's roots are pointed straight down." DeWitt potted several plants and then watched Johnny follow his example. When he was convinced that the boy understood what to do, he busied himself with a group of larger rose plants at the other end of the greenhouse. From the amount of plants to be transplanted, it was obvious to Johnny that it would take the better part of the afternoon.

Several times DeWitt checked on him to make sure his directions were being correctly followed. "Not too much fertilizer, John. Just around the sides. You're doing fine, John, just fine."

After the third inquiry, the man said something about bringing yard plants into the greenhouse and was gone. Johnny looked at the long row of plants to be repotted and began daydreaming to avoid the boredom of what he was doing. He thought of how nifty it would be to live in a house like this. He didn't think he would like the local kids, but it would be fun to live in such a rich neighborhood. He wondered if DeWitt was married, if he had any kids, if one of the kids in the park today was his. He looked at the long row of plants again. He didn't think he would finish them all today. If old DeWitt liked what he did, maybe he'd have him back tomorrow. The work wasn't that hard; he liked the surroundings. "Hell," he said to himself, "maybe I'll just take my money and hop a train tonight."

It was while he was reminding himself to check the trains and the departure times that he felt an uneasiness. He sat at the table of flowers. To all appearances, he was alone, but he didn't feel alone. He had acquired a sixth sense while sleeping in mission dormitories, a sense of being observed by someone unnoticed. A sense of being watched by someone in hiding flooded him. He continually dreamed of someone watching him sleep ... someone standing at the end of his bunk watching him sleep; and, on two occasions, he had wrenched himself from sleep to find a vagrant standing over him, just watching. And now he had that feeling again. He was sure of it. He stood up to make sure there was no one in the aisles and then turned quickly to the steam-filled glass panels at his back. Through the moisture and dirt on the window, he could make out the shape of a man just standing in the outside yard, looking at him. Johnny stood gazing back at him. The face was not recognizable, but the man's shape was close to that of DeWitt. Then, the figure turned and walked away.

Johnny sat down and, at different intervals between potting several more plants, would turn quickly to see if the figure had returned. When he had finished potting fifteen, he turned and stopped to rest as Mr. DeWitt came in from the house entrance.

"Could you eat a sandwich?" he said as he put two plants down.

"Yeah, I could," Johnny replied.

"Then follow me, my boy," he said with a smile.

Johnny followed him into the kitchen, and DeWitt had him wash his hands in the sink while he prepared a sandwich.

"Like a Coke?"

"Yes, sir," he said as he shut off the faucet and wiped his hands.

DeWitt got himself a glass of buttermilk and sat opposite Johnny. They sat in silence for a minute. Johnny decided not to ask if he had been watching him. He looked up from his plate to see Mr. DeWitt staring at him. He stopped chewing and said, "Why do you look at me like that?"

"Look at you? I'm sorry, John. I was not aware of it. Please excuse me today. I'm not quite myself."

There was a long silence, and then Mr. DeWitt asked, "Tell me, Johnny, why are you working out of the Plainesville Mission?"

"'Cause I just got here last night."

"You got here last night?"

"Yes."

"You live there?"

"Yeah."

"But why?"

"I can't afford nothin' else right now."

"You can't afford ... but where is your family, John?"

"Ain't got none."

"But surely you have some family ... are you from Plainesville?"

"No, from Indiana. I left home a couple of months ago."

"You left home? Why?"

"My stepfather and me didn't get along ... I left, that's all."

The man could tell his questions were antagonizing the boy, so he put into words the answers he wanted to hear.

"So you just travel around living in Mission Houses?"

"Yeah, sort of."

"Haven't you got anywhere to go, John?"

"Yeah, I got an aunt in Long Beach, California. I'm headed out that way."

"California's a long way, John?"

"I know." He took a bite from the sandwich. "But I'll make it."

"Does she know you're coming?"

"No ... I guess, I'm gonna surprise her. Hey, you got any kids?"

"Kids?" he said, as though surprised to be asked.

"Yeah, kids."

"Yes ... one, John. Are you going back to that mission tonight? After you're done working?"

"Yeah, I might ... I guess I will ... I don't know ... I might ... I might take the money you give me and head out of town." he said independently.

The man looked at him and then he quickly walked over and poured himself another glass of buttermilk.

"How old's your kid?"

"Kid?" he asked, "Oh, yes. I have one child. A boy. You're going back to the Mission?"

"Yeah, I guess."

"Well, if you're staying at the Mission ... I mean ... there's really no need to return there ... that is ... if you wished to work tomorrow ... what I'm trying to say is ... why don't you stay here this evening ... that is ... for the night?"

A cautious look crossed the boy's face.

"Oh, look." the man pleaded, "I'm not some sort of pervert. I mean no harm to you, John. It's just that, well ... I'm lonely ... so lonely. It would be so enjoyable to have someone else ... some company ... believe me, I'm just looking for an evening's conversation with what looks to me like a very independent, industrious young man."

Johnny half smiled at the compliment. "Yeah, well, maybe for dinner."

"Oh, we can have so much fun! We'll go out. Then we could come back here and pop popcorn." he exclaimed as though finding a new toy. "Actually, I would have gone to my club tonight. You can come with me," he said excitedly. "And, if you wish, you can stay the night; you have six bedrooms to choose from."

"There's no one livin' here but you?" asked Johnny.

"Not exactly ... not exactly," the man turned toward the kitchen window, more to avoid looking at the boy than to look out. "My son..." He stopped in mid sentence as he thought of what he would say. "My son ... has a room upstairs," he continued quietly.

"I saw some kids playing in the park when I was coming here. Was one of them your son?"

The man turned and looked at Johnny. "No ... no ... none of them was my Billy, I'm afraid. No." It was as though he had difficulty talking about his son. There was an apparent change in his tone. It made Johnny uncomfortable.

"He looks so much like you, John."

"Yeah, I think you told me that already."

"I couldn't believe it when I first saw you at the front door. It was as though Billy had come home."

"Come home?"

"Yes," DeWitt said. There was an uncomfortable silence between them which made Johnny more uneasy.

"Look, I think I ought to go," he said, getting up.

"No! Please, John. I'm sorry I make you uncomfortable talking about him. Let me explain."

"Yeah, well, I..."

"You see," he interrupted, "he was born with a brain tumor. That's what the doctors told us. It didn't affect him until he was thirteen." The man talked softly as though in his own world.

Johnny sat down and listened.

"It was futile to operate. He lost muscular control first, and was in terrible pain. Right before our eyes, his condition worsened with each passing day; then

117

he went into a coma ... he was supported by a life-support system while in the coma. DeWitt stared into space as he continued. "My wife begged that we take him off of it. But he lived, Johnny ... he lived," he said excitedly. "They took all the tubes out of him and he lived!"

"He has his room upstairs, John. In fact, I have to check on him. Oh, you do look so much like him. Why don't you come with me? You can clean up upstairs and then we can go to dinner at my club."

"Hey, Mr. DeWitt, I'll just wait here."

"Please, John," begged the old man, "just indulge me. I'm just an eccentric old man who's lost a great deal. Please pamper an old man's request."

"There are some clothes in his closet you are surely welcome to. You're his size," DeWitt said as he led him up the circular staircase. They walked down a hallway and stopped at a door mid-way.

"This is Billy's room," DeWitt said as he took a key out and unlocked the door. He let the door swing open and stood at the doorway for a moment. "You'll like Billy. Everyone likes my Billy," he chanted in a low tone.

Johnny was sorry he had agreed to see his son. He followed the man into the large sitting room. The walls were full of pictures of a boy his age. Some of the portraits so resembled Johnny that there was little difference except the length of hair and the angle of the chin.

"I told you there was an uncanny resemblance, John," DeWitt said in a low tone.

Banners and different placards describing events at 'Wilson Elementary' and 'Jefferson High' decorated the walls. DeWitt handed him a picture of a graduating class.

"This was taken when he graduated from Wilson Elementary. He was in high school just three months when he became ill." DeWitt moved around the room, lightly, reverently touching different objects. It reminded Johnny of Monsignor Sabin blessing medals on holidays. The whole room was like a sanctuary. A single sanctuary candle flickered under one large picture of the boy.

"I've kept in contact with his school mates ... his teachers ... since he fell ill ... I know he'll wake one day. I will be his continuity with the present while he sleeps ... and when he does wake, I'll have all the resources and knowledge he'll need to pick up where he left off. He'll catch up with the rest. I have faith in that." A typewriter and pad and pencil were carefully stacked on a new desk. Textbooks from Wilson High were neatly piled next to them.

"My wife has given up hope, John. She calls this my living memorial, but I can't help it. I believe he will return to me someday, and I have to have everything in preparation for when he does."

DeWitt opened a sliding door to a large closet in which hung new shirts and pants of various sizes. Pairs of boy's shoes and boots covered the closet floor.

"This is Billy's wardrobe, John. I'm sure Billy won't mind your taking what you need. They're all brand new. As he grows, I buy him the newest styles of boy's wear so that, when he is ready, he looks just like all the other boys his age. Here, take this." He handed Johnny a pair of corduroy pants and two shirts. The man stood aside. "See what else you'd like, John. You're welcome to any of it. Billy will be more than happy for you to have something of his."

Amazed at what he saw, Johnny perused the contents of the closet. In back of the closet were drawers filled with many brands of sweaters, socks and underwear. He became so engrossed in deciding what he would take that he was not aware that DeWitt had left the room until he heard him whispering and quietly talking from within the adjoining room. He went to the doorway and saw the old man sitting by the shape of someone lying in a large bed. The old man was seated at the head of the bed and blocked the view of whom he was talking to. The mound in the bedspread outlined the waist and legs of a still figure. DeWitt bent down and kissed the hidden fingers and mumbled something. Johnny knocked lightly on the door.

"Oh, come in, John ... come in," he said in a whisper, "I was just talking to Billy. He would be more than happy to have you use some of his clothes."

Johnny stepped into the room clutching a pair of pants and two shirts he would ask permission to take.

"Billy is still asleep, but I know from his reactions when I talk to him that he would be more than happy to have you take any of his clothing."

Johnny stepped forward and looked down at the figure in the bed.

"... and I'm sure that he would be so very happy if you were to stay with us tonight, John. Billy and I are very lonely in this big house with just the two of us to keep company." The man was grasping the figure's hand and gently brushing the hair from the forehead. Johnny looked at the figure in the bed. The light was dim, but there was little resemblance to the figure in the pictures on the wall. The face, its eyes closed, did not resemble him. It was the probably the sickness that gave the figure in the bed that unreal look. Johnny stepped closer.

"See, I told you there was an uncanny resemblance." DeWitt said.

Johnny stared down at the still figure. It's skin was pale and unreal looking. And then it came to him. It looked unreal because it was unreal! That wasn't skin, not human skin! Not real hair ... the thing was made of rubber ... or plastic ... or whatever they made store mannequins out of ... and that old man was holding its hand and talking to it!

"Please stay the night, John. Wouldn't you like John to stay the night, Billy?" DeWitt asked the still form.

Johnny felt sick to his stomach and put the shirt to his mouth for fear of vomiting on the floor.

"I might even bring you downstairs tonight if Johnny stays," the old man said as he grasped the lifeless hand. "We could pop some popcorn. It could be just like it was for us, Billy." He turned to Johnny and said, "Please reconsider, John. We could have so much fun!" But the old man found himself alone in the room. He heard the boy running down the long stairway and the front door open. DeWitt went to the window and saw Johnny running across the front lawn, still clutching the pants and shirts. One of the shirts fell from his grasp and became entangled in a rose bush. DeWitt returned to the side of the bed. He took the figure's hand in his, and bent down and kissed the forehead.

"John won't be staying with us tonight, Billy. I'm sorry about that. I guess he had to leave ... maybe another time." Then he brushed the hair from the forehead. "It's all right. We have each other ... he doesn't understand ... your mother doesn't understand ... nobody understands."

Chapter Twenty-Two

Long Beach, California – August 1949

Lillian Breslin sipped her martini and looked over the sprawling front lawn of her estate. It was the first week of August. She couldn't bring the exact date to mind, but she was sure of the month. Like a never-ending cycle, it was the same recurrence in the beginning of August, the continual relapse in the past, the remembering of insignificant trivia, triggered by a conversational response or the viewing of a landscape, or just by day dreaming as she was now. It was as though the mistakes of her past were amplified when the heat of the end of summer was at its peak.

Lillian detested the month of August and the mental anguish the end of summer brought her. For it was this time of year that most reminded her of the farm, Indiana, and the child born in the first week of August. It was not that she felt guilty for giving the child up, or that she wanted to know more about it. On the contrary; under the circumstances, it was the wisest decision she could have made. As she thought of it, she reasoned that it was not what she remembered that so upset her, but the premonition that, somehow, past events would all return to haunt her. This she greatly feared. It was nothing you could put your finger on, but somehow, it was already beginning to happen. According to Sister Maureen's letter, she could expect a visit from her nephew. Somehow, it had begun and Lillian could not turn her back on it. So, to pass the time during these threatening days, shopping for outfits of uplifting colors and designs filled her waking hours as did a frenzy of social commitments which filled her days with people and events so that the nights alone were more bearable.

She drank the rest of her martini and, handing the glass to Barry, she smiled and said, "I'll have another."

"Another? I've never known you to have two martinis before dinner."

"I'm a changed woman," she snapped.

"That's all well and fine, Lillian, but we do have the board meeting within the hour."

"Don't worry, I'll not embarrass you," she smirked, taking her drink.

"I'm sorry, darling. I didn't mean it that way. I just thought we ought to get going. Actually, you can get as sopped as you want. I just feel it's important that you make an appearance."

"How do I look?" she asked, modeling a brown and yellow outfit.

"Very convincing. They won't be able to decline any of our recommendations."

"They'd better not. I own sixty percent of the stock."

"Sixty-four, to be exact. Counting my votes. Isn't that a new outfit you're wearing?"

"I decided to give myself a present," she said, drinking half the martini in one gulp.

Barry went to her and held her in his arms. "Anything the matter, Lillian? You seem preoccupied, a thousand miles away."

"Nothing I can't handle, Barry."

"You want to talk about it?"

"No, it's just that some people have a difficult time getting through the Christmas holidays; my miseries begin in August ... about August the fifth." It was said before she realized it ... the birth date of her child. At this moment, it stuck out in her mind like a beacon, and yet, she had not intentionally thought of it for years ... until now, when she repeated it in idle conversation. She held onto Barry and he had the feeling that she was deeply hurt and scared.

"Is there anything I might do, Lillian?" Barry asked as he held her.

"Just be here when I need you, that's all."

They kissed and Lillian smiled at him. Then she handed him her empty glass and walked to the end of the patio. "Just cover the bottom, not too much, please."

As he poured the martinis from a large glass pitcher, Barry had the distinct impression that Lillian held a mental weight she could not confide to anyone. He handed her the drink and put his arms around her waist. For a long time they stood looking at the manicured lawn that stretched before them.

"You know, Lillian, you really ought to marry me. I could take you away from all this. The serenity, the huge estate, not to mention the gorgeous view, the country air. Think of it, you could give all this up for a luxurious apartment in a high-rise smack in the middle of Long Beach with as much smog and congestion as you could bear." Lillian lay her head on his shoulder.

"Oh, it's not the place ... or moving ... or you. I'm just not ready yet, Barry ... you know what I mean?"

"Time is running out. I might stop asking you one day." he answered, half smiling.

She pulled away from him. "I guess that's a chance I'll have to take."

Barry took a sip of his drink. "You don't think I'd fit in your world?"

"To the contrary, Barry. I don't think I'd fit in yours."

"Then I'll give you all the room you want, no questions asked."

"I know you would. That's what makes it all so difficult."

"Look. We'll live here, in Long Beach, go out with my friends, your friends, I don't care." He kissed her gently. "Just marry me, please."

"I do love you," she said quietly, "when I love you."

"Now what does that mean?"

Laughing, she lay her head on his chest.

"I'm just stupidly independent ... stubborn ...I don't know ... marriage seems so confining right now."

"You married Louis Breslin."

"I didn't marry Louie. I married a corporation. Breslin, Inc."

"What about your independence?"

"I was a lot hungrier then, Barry. Money meant something to me, or the absence of it meant more. Louie wanted a woman to fill out the picture of a corporate executive. Do you know how I met him?"

"Didn't you work as a typist in the pool? That's where I remember meeting you."

"It started earlier than that. Louie put me in the typing pool after we had initially met. Before that, I was a clerk at the L.A. Times. I took ads for the paper and quoted prices for printing them. One day the mail brought this ad to be put in the personal column. It ran something like, 'unusual man of the executive type seeks special young female companion. Must be trim, bright, sensitive, interesting.' He didn't care if you were pretty, but went on to say that 'clothes, travel and car are yours if the chemistry is right.' Then he described himself as a highly educated white male, a leader in the business world. He described how he was bored with women he was associated with and wanted 'something new.' He asked that whomever he picked would correspond with him before an initial introduction was arranged.

"Well, the ad really interested me. I could see myself fulfilling the requirements, along with a good percentage of the other young ladies that would apply. I had to figure an angle, something that would set me apart. And then it came to me. I would put an ad in the same paper with the same requirements for a man. To make a long story short, after Louie and I were married, I told him what I'm telling you now. He laughed. He loved it, and confessed that after seeing my ad, he immediately wrote me and disregarded the rest of the applicants. And so, for all those years I was his legal wife, the inheritor of all he possessed, which was part of my agreement. God knows, no one expected him to die so suddenly. The real point of the partnership was that this, the facade of the wealthy executive and financier, happily married, was to be upheld at all costs. It was Louie's theory that the family-man impression was a help in solidifying bigger and bigger financial ventures. In short, potential backers trusted him and, thus, his ideas for making money."

"Did you love him?"

"Did I love him? ... Let's say I was not meant to love him. I had little choice in the matter. I remember once after he had been through a rough evening of corporate bigwigs, counseling them to come around to his way of thinking, we sat down to dinner with all of them and their wives. It was just after we had been married. One of the fat cats that was going to back Louie in a new venture sat next to me. He was very drunk and obnoxious. Turning to me, he put his arm around me and hushed the general conversation at the table by announcing at the top of his voice, 'Well, Lil, can that big hulk of a business man keep a smile on your face every morning?'

"The dinner guests were embarrassed by his loud outburst and each in his own way dismissed it. I turned to him, and in the same volume and obnoxious attitude, announced, 'Not only do I smile, sometimes I think I've died laughing and gone to Heaven.' Well, Louie roared and they all started laughing. That night, on the way home, Louie put his arm around me and said, 'Lil, you know just what to say to those money-hungry fools. Thanks.'

"He got his backing; I had been instrumental in helping him. There were a few other times I was of such help, but after he made it to the top, my presence wasn't needed. But he never reneged on his promise. Even after he had exceeded his wildest dreams, he gave me anything I wanted ... anything but his love ... my own charge accounts, travel expenses, lovers, and being the sole beneficiary of his will, which included this place and the majority of Breslin, Inc. stock."

"Why not his love?"

"He couldn't. You see, he took lovers, too, and sometimes it got very confusing in the late evening around here. When a man rang the doorbell, you weren't sure just who he was calling on."

"Louie Breslin was a queer?"

"About as heterosexual as a three-dollar bill is negotiable."

"I was his lawyer for eight years and never knew it."

"Of course not. That was my job, to make sure that neither you nor anyone else ever even had a hint of it."

Barry swallowed his drink and made another. "That's quite a revelation. That's a side of Louie I never realized, and I thought I knew him."

"Then you must have some doubts about me, since I've bared my soul, too."

"No," he said, "I know you, and I don't give a damn about what I don't know. I do know that I love you very much. What I want to know is, do you love me?"

"In a way. And, because I do, I don't want to hurt you."

"Lillian, that's a chance people take in love."

Lillian sipped her drink. "I guess that's a chance I'm not willing to take. It's a chance I didn't have to take with Louie."

"Well, I want to chance it," Barry said, turning her toward him.

"Barry, there are a lot of things in my life undone."

He held her in his arms. "I'm willing to take you, independent, undone life and all." He cupped her chin in his hands. "I tell you what. You can be as free as you want. Take lovers ... We'll have the first marriage built on infidelity ... I don't care, but make me happy ... seriously consider it ... marry me."

She threw her head back, laughing. "All right, I'll think on it, I promise."

They kissed and then stood very still in each other's arms, then in silence walked to the edge of the patio.

"What's so important about today's meeting?"

"Transistors."

"Transistors?"

"It's part of the new experiments of Cal-Ex Corp. These transistors will revolutionize communication – radios, television, you name it. We want in on the ground floor. I mean the experimental stage, patents, the final product."

"Isn't it chancy?"

"It's what Louie would have done."

"Then let's do it," she replied. As she watched, Barry became concerned with a figure on the bridge of the highway. "What are you looking at?" she asked.

"Tell me, Lillian. Has anyone been following you?"

"Following me?"

"Yes," he asked as he concentrated on the figure on the bridge.

"Why would anyone follow me?"

"See that boy on the road, throwing rocks at the road sign?"

Lillian looked in the direction he was pointing.

"Yesterday, when you were getting your hair done, I parked outside Henri's salon. You know how I hate to go in those places. I was sitting in my car going over some briefs when this kid comes up and looks in the window. I didn't recognize him, and I didn't think it unusual; then he did it several times, as though he recognized someone he knew. When you came out, I noticed that he looked straight at you. You didn't notice him, and I was going to say something to you, but you kissed me and suggested we go to my place and bed down. That threw him right out of mind until now. But there he is again, the same kid. I'm sure of it."

Lillian looked at the small figure that occupied himself by throwing rocks into the river. Her heart thundered, and she rubbed at the goose pimples that rose on her arms. She knew her premonitions were correct. It had begun and she could not turn her back on it.

Feelings of joy and fear rose in her at the same time. Inside, a voice kept saying, 'Run from it!' But she knew it would only extend what inevitably had to be faced.

Lillian turned to Barry. "Do me a favor, Barry. Go down to the road and ask him if his name is John McBride. If he says yes, bring him up the hill. Tell him who I am and that his Aunt Lillian would like to talk to him."

"John McBride?"

"Yes. Charley and Vera's boy."

"Isn't he supposed to be in that orphanage you send a check to every month?"

"Yes, but I've been told by the authorities there that I could expect him here."

"You're kidding!"

"No, please go down and ask him. I'll explain later."

She watched as Barry climbed down the front steps toward the road. As he grew closer, the boy stopped throwing stones. They talked for a minute and Barry pointed toward the patio. The boy hesitated and then slowly ascended the hill. His right foot pigeon-toed inward, and there was that light bounce of his step that reminded her of another afternoon years ago when she first saw such a young man climbing the hill toward her farmhouse. He stopped at the edge of the patio, as though afraid to enter. His clothes were dirty. He was in need of a bath. He carried an old, dirty army jacket over his shoulder.

Behind the dirt and uncut hair that hung down over part of his face, Lillian could recognize Charley's son. He stood at the end of the patio, unsure of his presence there, fearful of not being welcomed. Barry walked past him, saying, "Lillian, this is your nephew, John. I'm sorry, kid. All we have to drink is beer and martinis." Lillian and the boy stood looking at each other. She didn't know what to say. The more she gazed at him, the more she recognized Charley in him.

The boy half smiled and said, "You're my Aunt Lillian?"

"Yes, John, I am ... Oh, please ... come in ...sit down," she replied, unsure of what to say.

He hesitantly moved toward her and sat down at the patio table.

"Can I get you something to..."

"A beer is O.K.," he replied.

Barry opened a bottle of beer and gave it to him. "Oh, this is Barry Aston, my ... lawyer," Lillian awkwardly introduced him.

"I would rather be introduced as her fiancé, but that hasn't been decided yet," Barry interjected to break the tension.

"Well," said Lillian, smiling, "Barry said he saw you yesterday in town."

"As a matter of fact," interrupted Barry, "now that I've gotten a look at him, I've seen you several times in town. How long have you been around here?"

"Two weeks," he replied.

"Two weeks!" asked Barry, "Why didn't you just announce yourself?"

"Because he wasn't sure," Lillian answered for him.

"Yeah, I just wanted to look around first."

Again Lillian could not help but stare at the boy, and then she turned to Barry. "If you don't mind, Barry, I'd like you to leave us. Go to the meeting without me."

"What?" he gasped.

"You have my proxies. You said there was no problem, that I'm not needed ... Please, Barry go without me."

He hesitated and then said, "You'll be all right here?"

"I'll be fine," she said while looking at her nephew.

"I'll call later." Barry took a swallow from his drink and said, "I can you see you two have a lot to talk over." He pecked Lillian on the cheek and left. It was the drone of his car that awakened her as she looked at the boy.

"So, you're Charley and Vera's oldest."

"Yeah," he said as though unsure of what to say.

"Well, I'm your Aunt Lillian. Please just call me Lillian."

"O.K."

"Tell me," she began in an attempt to make conversation, "How did you come to California?"

"Hitchhiked."

"All this way! ... by hitchhiking?"

"Yeah, most of the time. Sometimes I took a bus, if I had money."

"But why ... to California?"

"I got your letter to me about my graduation, and the money too. Your address was on the back of the envelope. And you said if I should ever come to California to look you up."

"You weren't supposed to see that envelope or letter."

"I know, but he ... Hank was hittin' on me and Tommy, and then somethin' happened, and I didn't have anywhere to go. And then I got your letter and decided to come here."

"What happened?"

"Somethin' I'd rather not say, but I wanted to get away from him ... and she wasn't much better."

"She ... you mean your mother ... my sister?"

"Yeah, and that guy she's living with."

"Oh," said Lillian, surprised. "How long has he lived with Vera?"

"I don't know. He come up to get Tommy and me with Ma. He's damned mean, so I came out here to find Pa. I didn't want to stay around the farm with him there."

"The man is mean, you say?"

"Yeah. He liked to beat up Tommy and me. She never did nothin' about it, so I left to find Pa. Do you know my Pa?"

"I know him. We grew up together ... Charley, your Ma, and me."

The resemblance to Charley was uncanny, and Lillian could not keep her eyes off him. It was not just physical appearance, but his stance, the gestures of the arms as he took another drink of beer, the tuft of hair that hung over the eyes. He got up and walked around the room.

"This place is big. It reminds me of a place I worked. Some crazy guy owned it. I'll bet this place is even bigger."

He walked up behind the patio chair that faced Lillian and looked right at her.

"Aunt Lillian," he said, as though trying out the name, "You seen my old man when he come out here? Did he stop here?"

Even the way he spoke, the timbre of his voice, took her back to a Sunday afternoon in Indiana when she walked down a railroad track arm in arm with Charley.

"I figured I'd come here first."

"Yes, as a matter of fact, he did stop in on a Sunday afternoon. Oh, it must've been about three years ago. I haven't seen him since."

The boy became excited at the news. "Did he say where he was going?"

"Yes. A place called Sonora. I looked it up on the map once. It's up North in the woods."

The boy smiled and an expression of hope filled his eyes.

"I don't know if he's still there, John. Three years is a long time."

"I know ... I know, but it's somewhere to look," he replied.

Lillian made herself another drink and offered him another beer.

"I knew you were coming, John. A Sister Maureen wrote after you left the orphanage and said that I could expect you."

"Maureen. She's O.K. Did she say anything else?"

"Yes. It seems that your mother returned Tommy to the orphanage after you left."

"Hey, that's great! Then Hank can't get his hands on him and he's all right."

"Yes. Sister indicated that he was very happy to return."

The boy walked around the room as though caged, cursing at Hank Kidder. She watched as he moved and listened to him talk. Glimpses from the past kept clouding out what the boy was saying. A wall of cement and an iron staircase. Charley was in back of her, leading her down below a bridge that trestled the river. It was their meeting place, their secret place, and no one else knew about it.

"What was my Pa like?"

His question interrupted her train of thought.

"Didn't your mother ever talk about him?"

The boy stuck a wad of gum in his mouth and said, "Naw, she was drunk most of the time. She didn't talk about much of anything."

She could not remember the last time she had thought of those days, of that room of metal and cement. She could picture herself kneeling before him on a hot Sunday afternoon, each disrobing the other until they were both nude, kneeling there, touching one another, surrounded by cement and metal girders, neither of them talking, just touching slowly, experimenting with one another. And then, when the touching could no longer satisfy them, they placed their clothing on the cement floor and lay together. Only the sounds of the rippling water below them could be heard as they pressed their sweating bodies together.

"What was he like, Aunt Lillian?"

128

"Your father?" she began, to put from her mind what she really wanted to think about. "We dated a few times, before he began going out with your mother."

"Maybe he should've married you."

She was a bit taken back by his response. "Well, that's not the way it worked out," she said.

"Say, I'll bet you're hungry," she said, to change the conversation.

"Well, I haven't eaten since this morning."

"Bring your beer and follow me into the kitchen. I'll fix us a French cook's delight. One thing I'm good at is cooking."

They went in the kitchen and they talked of his experiences at the orphanage and at home. He helped her with the meal preparations by slicing French bread and preparing vegetables and fruit for a salad. Over steaks and salad and potatoes, they became well acquainted. During a dessert of cherry pie, they discussed their reasons for coming to California.

"I was also looking for someone or something when I came here, John," said Lillian as she sipped her coffee. "Why did I leave Indiana? Well, let's just say the Midwest didn't agree with me, and leave it at that. Fortunately, there were friends here that helped me get started. I worked in a secretarial position until I became competent at shorthand and typing. Later, I applied for a full-time position at Breslin, Inc. It was just a small company. Louie Breslin, a very imaginative young man, took a liking to me. We married and the rest is history."

Lillian began clearing dishes when John said, "You sent money for Tommy and me to go to the orphanage, didn't you?"

"Yes," she replied.

"I guess you knew Sister Theophane, then?"

The name brought back images of nuns in black and white scurrying about in their convent.

"Yes," she replied, "I knew her before she entered the order. Her name was Jeannie Miller. Her family lived in back of our farm."

Johnny continued to tell her of how Sister Theophane had worked with him so that he might skip a grade, and Lillian could well imagine the charitable attributes of her novitiate friend as he described how she went out of her way to help him. As he talked, her mind wandered to another small room and two young girls chatting into the early morning, of Jeannie comforting her when she first came for help and gaining permission for her to stay at the convent until the baby was born.

"After she went into the convent, I left the Midwest."

"I guess I owe you something for sending money for us to stay at the orphanage."

Lillian was surprised at what he said. "You owe me nothing, young man. I sent contributions to that orphanage long before you got there. You see, after I married Louie Breslin, I could well afford it, and the orphanage was just a tax break the corporation needed. Believe me, you owe me nothing."

They walked into the living room and went out onto the patio. The sun had gone, and an orange glow penetrated the countryside. "This is the time of the evening I like most," Lillian said, "the time just before dark."

Johnny sat opposite her, sipping coffee and smoking a cigarette. "It's a lot prettier here than most places I've been lately."

There was a long silence between them as though there was little more to say. Then Lillian said, "You haven't talked about your mother."

"Nothin' to talk about."

"How is she?"

"Probably drunk ... like most of the time."

"I thought you might like to call her and let her know you're here ... that you're all right."

Johnny got up and walked about agitated. "Hell, no! She never cared for me or my brother when we were home ... I got nothin' to say to her now."

Because of his obvious agitation over his mother, Lillian changed the subject. "How about a brandy? I always have one about this time of the evening."

"Sure," he said in a more restrained manner. Lillian poured two glasses of brandy and handed one to him.

"There is someone I would like to call, though."

"Oh, and who is that?"

"Her name is Frankie ... Frankie Phillips."

Lillian sat and lit a cigarette. The name sounded very familiar, but she could not understand why. "Is this a school friend of yours?"

"Yes. She said that she would write to me when I left."

"Write you! Oh, of course!" yelled Lillian. "The pink envelopes!" and she leaped up and went to the china closet. "There are eight of them, John. They have been arriving here regularly for months. I've not opened them. They are just as I received them," and she handed the letters to him.

He hurriedly opened the first and quietly read it. Lillian sat back and watched him. His resemblance to Charley filled her with memories she had long forgotten and could not help recalling.

"She misses me and ... is worried about me," he said, smiling.

"What?" asked Lillian, as she was brought out of her daydreaming.

"She misses me and she wants me to contact her when I can. If it's all right, I'd like to call her."

Lillian looked at her watch, "I don't mind, Johnny, really, but there is three hours difference between here and Indiana. I think it would be better to call tomorrow."

130

"Oh, sure," he said as he ripped open the second letter. Lillian watched him excitedly read it. She recognized the same excitement and zest that she remembered when Charley was a young man.

"She wrote me ... I didn't think she would."

"You like this young lady?"

The question embarrassed him and he hesitantly answered, "Oh, we're just good friends."

As he continued to read, the expression on his face changed, then he slowly put the letter down. "Aunt Lillian, I got bad news for you."

She sat up. "Yes?"

"Sister Theophane is dead."

"Dead!" The news so surprised and shocked her that she spilled her drink. "Jeannie is dead?"

"Yeah. Frankie says that Sister Maureen told her she had a tumor in her head, that she went into a coma." He looked at the letter to get the exact words. "They took her to St. Vincent's, but she never regained consciousness. Do you want to read it? Here."

"No ... no, that's all right," Lillian said as she thought of her friend. "Jeannie always blamed those headaches on the intense heat of the summers ... she'd never report the headaches when they came ... I told her so many times ... there's more to it ... there was always more than just headaches from heat."

Lillian smashed her cigarette out as she visualized her friend lying on her cot, her head covered with a cool damp cloth. "Every time I wash my face with a hand cloth, I think of Jeannie and those damned headaches."

"Frankie says here that Sister Maureen will be writing to you about her death in more detail at a later date."

Lillian got up and sipped her drink. She lit another cigarette. Waves of desperation engulfed her as glimpses of a small cubicle came to her. Two teenaged girls whispering in the darkness...

"Lillian, you shouldn't be here. It's after hours. If one of the sisters hears us..."

"Shh, then don't be so loud," the girl reached into her pocket and pulled out a cigarette. "Want to share, Jeannie? That's all that's left."

"No, Lillian. Oh, dear God, open the window," the girl pleaded as she laughed at her friend.

"Relax, there's no one around. They're all in the chapel for vespers."

"I'm glad Mother Superior let you stay, Lillian. I mean, until the baby is born."

"She only did it because she likes you, Jeannie."

"What do you want, a girl or a boy?"

"I just want to have it and leave," the girl said as she puffed on the butt.

"I'll be sure to call her tomorrow before I leave."

Lillian snapped out of her daydreaming, "Leave? What do you mean, leave? You just got here."

Johnny put down the letter in the envelope. "I'm sorry, Aunt Lillian. I'd like to stay, but I want to find my old man. I'll come and visit you sometime," he said as he opened the last letter.

She could tell from his tone that he was adamant. "Well, you must at least let me buy you some clothes."

"I never object to a handout," he said without looking up from his reading. "Hey, guess what! It's her birthday!" he yelled. "That's something."

Lillian froze at the mention of the word birthday. When she allowed herself to think of it, the memory was always the same. It began with a hazy fog that seemed to surround her. She recalled the distinct sensation of someone talking to her, and then something being pulled from her loins. Then she was conscious again, and then unconscious. She remembered hearing a baby's cry and trying to locate its origin. Then the haze engulfed her and only passed through a doorway; the last image she saw was a small wall clock above which were the numbers and date, August 5, 1933. The images stuck out more than the clock hands...

"Can I see the pool?" His question awakened her from the daydream.

"Pool?" Lillian looked up to see him standing over her.

"Could I see the pool in back, Aunt Lillian?"

"Oh, of course. In fact, I'll give you a short Cook's tour of the place."

They walked out in the back, past the tennis courts and stopped by the pool. Johnny knelt down and splashed water with his hand.

"Do you want go for a swim?" she asked.

"Tomorrow ... first thing tomorrow ... I'm sort of tired."

Lillian showed him the rest of the house and, lastly, his bedroom and bath.

"It's my husband's room. I'm down the hall. If you need anything, just help yourself."

Before closing the door, she stopped and turned to him. "I'm glad you came to see me, John. I'm sincerely glad you came. It's made me very happy. I know you want to get on your way, but I do want you to know that you're always welcome here."

Her eyes began to tear and she quickly shut the door before he had a chance to thank her. Johnny undressed and got into bed. He would take a swim first thing in the morning. His last thoughts were of what he would say to Frankie when he called Wilcox, Indiana.

The soft knocking at her bedroom door awakened Lillian and she turned over and said, "Come in."

The door opened and a petite Spanish woman entered holding a tray.

"Time to get up, Miss Lillian."

"All right, Mariana. I'm up."

"You told me to get you up at seven this morning."

"I did?" She couldn't remember why, but, with her nephew's arrival, she had changed any and all plans of her own. As she sat up, she took the small rose from its vase and smelled it as the maid poured her black coffee. "The advantages of having money," she said, smiling to herself. At the sounds of someone splashing in the pool, she was reminded that her nephew was in the house.

"There is a young boy swimming in the pool this morning. He says he is a relative of yours, Miss Lillian."

"My nephew, Mariana ... he arrived yesterday."

"O.K. That's good, 'cause he made a long-distance call, too ... somewhere in Indiana. I told him he should wait, but he..."

"It's all right, Mariana," Lillian said, smiling to herself, "I told him to call first thing this morning." She smelled the rose again and sipped her coffee, and Mariana laid out an outfit for the day. "No, dear. I'm going into town with my nephew ... Something colorful ... flashy." Mariana displayed another outfit, and Lillian nodded her head in approval.

"That's it," she said as she drank her coffee. Then, putting on her robe, she walked to the French doors and let herself out on the patio which overlooked the pool. Johnny was just diving off the board. When he surfaced, she yelled, "How about some breakfast?"

"Sure," he yelled and jumped back in the water.

As Lillian returned to the bedroom, Mariana was running her bath.

"We'll have breakfast after my bath, Mariana." She drank the rest of the coffee and again put the rose to her nose. "There are advantages to having money, and this is definitely one of them," she said to herself. And outfitting her nephew in the best she could afford was another.

"I'll buy him anything he wants," she said to herself as she stepped into the warm bath water.

"There's a men's clothier in the shopping center just a few miles from here, John. I would suggest that we just burn your old clothes and we go there with you in those swimming trunks." They laughed as they ate. Johnny sat across from her, dripping wet and still in his bathing suit.

"While I was getting dressed, I made plane reservations for you to Sonora."

At the sound of the word 'plane,' his eyes lit up.

"I'm sorry, John; the plane service will get you to San Francisco, but from there, I'm afraid it's going to be a bus into the hills. But it's not much more than a hundred and twenty miles. It was the best I could do."

"I've never been on a plane before, and it's neat to see the countryside from a bus."

They ate and left. After being fitted for several pairs of pants, shirts, socks and shoes, they packed what he would not be wearing into a new suitcase and headed into downtown Long Beach. While lunching at Frederick's, Lillian showed off her nephew to the headwaiter and some acquaintances at the next table. After sightseeing and more shopping, Lillian realized it was time to head for the airport.

Lillian drove the car past the parking lots and to the airport entrance.

"If you don't mind, John, I'm going to say goodbye out here. These damn places depress me." She began to tear, something she hadn't expected to do. "I'm sorry, John."

He smiled and thanked her again for all she had done.

"You'll call me when you get there?"

He nodded yes.

"It's just that I want to know that you're safe."

"Aunt Lillian, a lot of unsafe things happened to me that you don't even know about since I left home."

"Well, now that I know you, I don't want anything unpleasant to happen to you." She smiled and wiped away the tears. "I'm really sorry, John. Your aunt is just a self-centered, wealthy widow who's found someone she likes making a fuss over ... If it doesn't work out, I mean between you and your father ... well, you're always welcome at my place."

He grabbed his suitcase and said, "I'll come visit you, Aunt Lillian, after I get settled." Lillian kissed him on the cheek, and without saying a word, he got out and shut the door.

While driving back toward her estate, she berated herself for getting emotionally involved. "Damn! I should've just packed him a lunch yesterday and sent him on his way. He'll bring Charley around. I know it! Damn it, I just know it! God damn! You can't get away from your past ... Damn! I hope I never see him again. Charley will just take advantage of the situation ... He'll talk the boy

134

into moving in ... so he can move in ... I just am not going to be a part of it ... any of it. God damn Vera and her kids!"

As she drove into the driveway, she decided to fix a pitcher of martinis and call Barry. She walked into the living room and fell into a chair. The silence of the large house depressed her, and she began to cry. "Damn it, I miss him ... already ... I miss him," she sobbed.

"I waited until you came back, Miss Lillian, before I go." Mariana entered from the dining room.

"Oh, thank you, Mariana," Lillian said as she wiped her eyes.

"There are lamb chops in the oven. All you need to do is warm them up. There is a salad in the refrigerator. You O.K., Miss Lillian?" she asked.

"I'm fine, Mariana, and thank you."

"Oh, I almost forgot. Here are some letters and envelopes I find in your nephew's room in the night stand." She handed the letters to Lillian. He had forgotten two of the letters.

"I'll make sure he gets these. Thank you, Mariana."

"O.K. I go and I see you tomorrow."

Lillian began to put the letters in the envelopes, but stopped as she noticed the words, 'St. Vincent's Hospital' on one of the pages. His friend must be describing Sister Theophane's last moments in the hospital. She did not like to pry, but was curious to see what was written about her old friend. She began at the top of the page.

> It's not only my birthday, August 5, Johnny, but, since I am sixteen, my mother thought it was the time to tell me that I am adopted. I've always wondered if I was. I guess everyone does. Anyway, she told me that I was adopted right here in Wilcox, from St. Helena's orphanage. She told me I was born at St. Vincent's hospital. Isn't that something! She doesn't know who my real parents were, but that doesn't matter. The Phillips' raised me up, and I love them very much. When she told me, I felt funny, not like a different person, but funny. I'm still not used to it. Please don't tell anyone. I'm still getting used to it myself.

The image of the clock with the date 'August 5, 1933' rocketed through her mind.

"Oh, my God!" she gasped. Lillian felt cold, alone and scared. "No, it couldn't be," she told herself, "It couldn't be." In a fit of panic, she ripped up the letters and envelopes as though the act would diminish the possibility. "No, I didn't ask for any of this. I don't want to know!" she shrieked, "I don't want to know. I don't want to know!"

The phone rang, and it so startled her that she screamed. She grabbed for it. She wanted there to be another person's voice ... anyone ... just so she would not have to think of what she had just learned.

"Hello, there, you budding aunt. How's the new relative working out?"

At the sound of Barry's voice, Lillian began to cry. "Barry, I need you ... please come over ... please ... I need you ... now!"

Without questioning her, he said, "I'll be right there," and hung up.

Lillian fell against the sofa pillow of the large chair and cried hysterically.

Chapter Twenty-Three

Wilcox, Indiana — September, 1949

Dancers wiggled and gyrated to the music of the three-piece band that played at the end of the Cedar Inn bar. Hank Kidder made his way through the crowd that stood at the edge of the dance floor, clapping to the beat of the music. Men greeted him and several women asked him to dance. Joe Betton chided him by asking if he was going to drink the two whiskies and bottles of beer on the tray. He returned their greetings and smiled to others as he found his way to the booth where Vera sat smoking. As he approached, she shoved a plate of food aside in disgust.

"I thought you was hungry. Ain't you gonna eat nothin'?"

"It's late. I wanna go home, Hank."

"Damn it! You said you was hungry. I bought you a steak. Hell, you didn't touch it! And now you wanna go home!" he yelled as he put the tray of drinks down.

"Hank, I put the baby down three hours ago. He's gonna be wakin' up and wantin' me."

"Damn it! You said you wanted to get somethin' to eat!"

"We ain't been eatin', we been drinkin' and I've had too much. Now I ain't hungry and I want to go home!"

"God damn it! We get a little money ahead and try have a good time, and you got to ruin it 'cause that little bastard is uncomfortable."

"I ain't stayin' around here and listen' to this," she said as she got up to leave.

"Damn! I told you I didn't want no kids! You should've listened! You should've given it to that orphanage like you did the others." He grabbed her arm. "We ain't goin' nowhere!"

"Hank, shut up and leave me go ... people are looking." Vera pulled away from him and headed for the door.

"You just damned well find a ride home. I ain't comin'!" he yelled after her. Several people looked in Vera's direction as she headed out the door. Bill Hendricks danced his wife over to where Hank was standing.

"What's the matter, old man?" Can't keep the little woman happy these days?" he laughed.

"You just keep your goddamned mouth shut, Hendricks!" he shouted back as the man danced his wife back to the middle of the floor. Hank sat down in the booth and guzzled both whiskies. His face reddened and then, with a bang, hit the table with his fist. A waitress walked by with a tray full of empty glasses.

"Helen, leave those beers on that table and add two more whiskies. I'll be right back."

He caught up with Vera in the parking lot, and they walked toward the truck.

"All right, God damn it! I'll take you home. If you think that baby's more important than one night out. I'll take you home ... you bet! I'll take you home!"

"You said you'd get me something to eat and that we'd go right home, not goin' out drinkin'. That baby's gonna wake up with me not there!" she yelled at him as she got in the car.

"You and those fuckin' kids! I got you something to eat!"

"But you been doin' nothin' but drinkin'. So have I, and I don't want to get stinkin'. I got to feed the baby."

"You been shit to live with ever since that little crapper came along," he screamed. "I was glad when you lost the last one ... I should've made you get rid of this little brat, too."

As he pulled out on the highway, he yelled, "You're nothing but a damn weight on a good time. Well, I don't care! ... I'm takin' you home, but I'm comin' right back! You can be sure of that!"

As they approached the highway, a semi-truck roared in front of them. Hank slammed on the brakes and they both lurched forward.

"Watch it, Hank! You'll get us both killed!"

"What's the matter? I thought you was in such a goddamned hurry to get home!" He slammed his foot down on the accelerator, and the truck screeched onto the highway.

"Not so fast, Hank. You're drunk."

"You're goddamned right, and I'm gonna get drunker."

Hank accelerated the truck and it vibrated as he raced down the highway. "Hell, I thought you wanted to get home! Well, that's where you're going ... just as fast as I can get you there."

"Damn it! Hank!" Vera demanded. "If you're gonna act like a kid, just let me out!" Vera pulled at his arm to get his attention. "Damn it, just let me out, Hank ... let me out!"

Hank pushed her off him and slammed the accelerator to the floor. "I ain't goin' fast enough for you!" he yelled sarcastically. "Well, I'll just show you how quick we can get there, Vera." The cab of the truck shook with the mounting speed. Coming toward them were the yellow and white lights of a semi-truck. "I'm gonna get you home in record time!" Hank yelled as he laughed at her.

"Hank, stop this truck ... I want out now!"

"Hell, I wouldn't think of it, Vera. That baby's probably cryin' for you right now ... Hell, I can hear it ... sure enough. That baby's cryin' its eyes out for ya!"

"Stop it ... stop it, Hank!" Vera grabbed for his arm, "I want out! Just stop it now!"

The semi's lights came on them. Hank pulled away from Vera, lurching the truck into the opposite lane. He pulled at the steering wheel as the semi bleeped his horn. The truck loomed upon them and Vera bowed her head. On impact, she felt her body crash through the front windshield. The sound of metal and glass scraping and slamming was heard by the patrons of Cedar Inn as the two vehicles collided.

Someone walking on pieces of glass and warm metal against her cheek were the first impressions of consciousness. As Vera awoke, she realized that she was lying on the hood of the truck. Hank was nowhere in sight. Water hissed below her, and the smell of gas and antifreeze permeated the air. She could not move. She felt nothing. People silently walked past her line of vision.

Someone touched her, others talked to her, but she could not understand what they said. She was unable to answer them. She wanted to tell them that her baby was home alone, and waiting to be fed, but she could not speak. Revolving lights threw patches of red around the area in a steady tempo. In the pulsating light she could see the outline of a face staring up at her. The flesh was punctured and cut. Pieces of glass protruded from the face everywhere. She was reminded of a dirty piece of clay that children might discard.

People and voices and a high eerie siren pitch came and went. She blinked her eyes and looked at the face. The lips of the face trembled and teeth and blood poured from the mouth. A man in white stood next to the disfigured face and pushed a cab mirror aside which had been twisted to a reverse position upon impact. He talked to her, but Vera could not understand what he was saying. As she watched the mirror swing back and forth on a loose screw, it came to her that the face she saw was her own reflection. Black patches of unconsciousness began to form on both sides of her and she took a breath so as to scream her baby's name before becoming completely engulfed.

Chapter Twenty-Four

Sonora, California

The bus jumped forward as it crossed the bridge into town. The jolt woke Johnny, and he sat up and looked out the window. It was pitch black outside. He could make out the metal frames that sided the bridge; beyond them was blackness. He rubbed his eyes and realized the seat next to him was vacant. The fat man that had gotten on in Sacramento was gone. He wondered what time it was.

"Sonora. We're in Sonora," the bus driver said into the microphone. "There'll be a ten-minute stop." The bus turned left and came to a stop in front of a drugstore that had a Greyhound bus sign extending from its front.

"Ten minutes, and then we'll be on our way," the driver repeated as he opened the door and got out. Johnny picked up his new suitcase from the rack and followed the driver. He stood out in the street and looked both ways. The driver began pulling baggage from the compartment of the bus as the passengers emerged.

"They got an all-night mission in town?" he asked.

The driver looked up. "Isn't someone coming to pick you up. Sonny?"

"I'm supposed to meet my old man, but he doesn't know I'm coming."

"You'd better get off the streets, kid. There's a curfew in this town for kids of your age."

"Curfew?"

"Yeah. They're not allowed out after ten p.m. You'd better get ahold of your dad," he said as he slammed the compartment door and locked it.

The driver got on the bus, and Johnny watched as it took off down the street and disappeared around the corner. He stood for a moment and then decided to walk to the center of the town. He walked to the end of the block. As he walked down the street, a patrol car pulled up beside him.

"Hey, kid!" an officer yelled, "You know what time it is?"

Johnny walked to the side of the car. "I just got off the bus from San Francisco."

"You supposed to meet someone?"

"Not exactly. My old man doesn't know I'm coming."

"What's your dad's name?"

"McBride ... Charley McBride."

The officer turned to his partner and repeated the name, then they mumbled something to each other.

"Did you say, 'McBride'?"

"Yeah. Charley McBride," Johnny answered.

Again they mumbled something back and forth, and then the officer reached back and opened the back door. "You wanna come with us, kid?"

"Why?" Johnny asked suspiciously.

"It's O.K., kid. We aren't takin' you in. I think we can locate your old man. That's all."

"You just got in to town?" the officer who was driving asked.

"Yeah," Johnny replied.

"We're gonna take you to Kelly's. It's just at the end of the block here."

"Why there?" Johnny asked.

"Kelly rents rooms. He rented one to your old man a couple of months ago. He's a friend of your dad's."

"He can tell you about him," the other officer agreed.

The boy picked up the air of uncertainty in what they said. "What do you mean, 'He can tell me all about him'?"

"Here we are," interrupted the driver. The car stopped in front of the blinking 'Bar' sign. The officers got out and escorted him into the bar. A few people were dancing to the music of a jukebox that was playing in the corner. The man at the bar stopped his conversation and headed their way.

"And what glorious occasion brings two of California's finest into my place tonight?"

"Hello, Kelly. How's it goin'?" the driver asked.

"Fine, Joe. And how're you and Jerry? You men got time for a brew? ... On the house?"

"Thanks, Kelly. We're workin'. Some other time. We brought this young man here. He just got off the bus from the Bay Area. Seems his father is Charley McBride."

Kelly looked at Johnny and then at the men. "What's your name, son?" he asked.

"Johnny McBride," he replied.

"Johnny McBride, you say." Then he looked suspiciously at the officers.

"My dad came out here to cut wood in the forest."

"That he did, young man. Look, why don't we sit down over here in the corner, away from the noise?"

"Kelly, we're gonna leave him here with you. He just got into town. Give him one of your rooms. We'll pay for it. We got to go. You got any money, kid?"

"Yeah, about two hundred and fifty dollars."

"You're doin' better than I am," the other officer replied.

"Where did you come from?" inquired Kelly.

"Long Beach. My aunt lives there. She told me my old man came here."

"Oh," said Kelly, nodding his head.

"As I said, Kelly, we're going to leave him with you to fill in the rest about his dad. Welcome to Sonora, kid."

Johnny watched as they nodded to the other customers and walked out.

"Hey, I'll bet you're starved. Let me get you something to eat." Johnny watched as the man went behind the bar and fixed a sandwich and slowly withdrew a dill pickle from the large jar. "Here's a Coke, too, young man."

Kelly watched him as he ate.

"My old man lives here?" Johnny asked.

"He did, Johnny, he did ... the truth of the matter is ... my two officer friends recognized the situation when you identified yourself as Charley's son. That's why they brought you here ... You see, your dad did rent a room from me ... up until about two weeks ago."

"He moved? Where is he?" Johnny asked with a mouthful of food.

"No, boy ... he ... I'm sorry ... he died."

Johnny stopped chewing.

"I'm sorry to have to be the one to tell you, Johnny. He came back from work. He'd been drinking. Of course, that was nothing new. Anyway, he excused himself from the bar and walked across the street to the little park there. They found him an hour or so later. It seems he had a stroke. He was stone dead, lying on the park bench with a drink still in his hand. Joe, the man that brought you here, tried to wake him, but it was apparent he was dead."

Johnny continued to eat. "So. He's dead?"

"I'm afraid so, Johnny. Oh, he was some character. Always kept us entertained with his songs and tricks. I'm sorry, Johnny. The officers left you here for me to tell you ... your dad talked about Indiana and some family. We all just figured it was a long time ago, that they were all grown up or dead. He never talked of anyone in particular. There was no address left or anyone to claim him, I'm afraid. Your comin' here is quite a surprise."

Johnny finished the sandwich and took a sip of Coke.

"Where is he?" Johnny asked.

"In a pauper's grave outside town. I'm sure the officers will be glad to take you there. Father Benedict, our priest, said some words over him, and myself and two of the officers that knew him and some of his friends were at the graveside. It was a lovely funeral."

Johnny took another sip of Coke.

"When was the last time you saw him?" Kelly asked.

"A long time ago. I was about ten when he left.

There was a long silence between them and then Kelly said, "He always talked about a family in Indiana, but, as I said, he never mentioned anyone in particular. There was no one to contact. He worked in the mill, as I told you. When he came to town over a year or so ago, he was such a spirit, always jokin'. He never bothered anyone, only liked to play tricks and such ... of course, him bein' Irish didn't hurt his chances of gettin' along with me, so he had a room upstairs for the better part of his stay with us."

Johnny sat very still and finished the Coke.

"Hey, I got some things of his. They told me to hang on to them in case someone like you was to show up. They're in a closet upstairs. I found them in his room."

"I'd like to see them," Johnny replied.

He followed the man upstairs and into a darkly lit hall. Kelly stopped at a door mid-way down the hall and pulled out a leather suitcase.

"This is it. I put it right in here after your dad died. I never touched it or even looked inside. It was the only thing in the room, besides some dirty clothes I threw away."

Johnny looked at the suitcase. It was very old and on the top were three letters on a metal plate.

"Let's get you into a room, young man. You must be exhausted."

Kelly opened the door at the end of the hall. "It was your dad's room before he died. It's not much, but I try to keep a clean place. You can be sure of that, young man."

Johnny put the suitcase down by the bed and looked around.

"It's better than a mission barracks."

"What?"

"Nothin'"

"Now, I'll be right downstairs, Johnny, for about an hour. If you want anything, just call. My room is behind the bar. I'm here after I close up. The toilet is just two doors down the hall. I've got to get back to my customers."

Johnny nodded and half smiled. He could sense the man was in a hurry to leave him. It had been difficult to tell him of his father's death. He wanted no more of a depressing situation.

"You just yell if you're wantin' anything else, young man. I'm right downstairs."

Johnny thanked him and closed the door. He sat on the edge of the bed and thought of what Kelly had told him. The anticipation of meeting his father had turned to depression. He was tired and the room was dark and depressing. He lay back on the bed. He felt let down. He had come a long way and had always anticipated that he would see his father. Tomorrow he would take the first bus out of town. He was thankful that he had his aunt to return to. He sat up. "I'll call her," he said to himself. He wanted to hear her voice. The thought of contacting her relieved his depression. He looked down at the suitcase, and then slowly unbuckled the leather strap at the top.

He opened the case and the smell of moldy wood and leather filled his nostrils. On the top was a clean white shirt and a pair of men's underwear. Under the clothing were two pieces of metal and one of wood. He picked them up and slotted them together. The pieces fit together to form a sawed-off shotgun, which he laid on the bed.

Rolling around at the bottom of the case was a marble. Johnny picked it up and then realized that he held a glass eye in his hand. He looked at the objects and became depressed again. He had truly hoped to meet his father, and this was all he had of him. Before closing the lid, he reached in a cloth pocket on the lid of the suitcase. He pulled out a napkin which held a brass key. The number on the key was A-31. As he returned the objects to the case, he wondered at the unusual shape of the key. He put the case under the bed and opened the door. He could see a telephone at the end of the hall. He was in need of hearing his aunt's voice.

When the operator answered, he told the number, reversed the charges, and identified himself.

"Hello?"

"Aunt Lillian, it's me, Johnny."

"Will you accept the charges, ma'am. The call is from ...." continued the operator.

"Yes! Yes!" she screamed. "Johnny, is that you?"

"Thank you," interrupted the operator. "Go ahead."

"Aunt Lillian, it's me."

"Oh, Johnny, are you all right?"

"Yeah."

"I'm so glad you called. Where are you?"

"Sonora. I just got here."

"Oh, Johnny ... Johnny. I have some bad news for you. You'll have to tell your father. I just heard from St. Helena's in Wilcox. I'm so very sorry to have to tell you over the phone." There was a long silence. The news of his mother's death had no more effect than when Kelly had told him of his father's dying.

"Johnny ... Johnny," his aunt called out, "are you all right?"

"Yes."

"Johnny. Remember what I told you. Anytime you want to return ... well, you know you are more than welcome. Johnny, I'm so very sorry to have to tell you about your mother. You'll have to tell your father."

"I can't. I can't tell him."

"Why not? Isn't he there?"

"He was, but..."

"Oh, Johnny, if he's not there, just come back. Just come home. I miss you so much."

"Aunt Lillian," he began.

"Yes?"

"He's dead ... my old man is dead."

"Dead?"

"He died two weeks ago. A man named Kelly told me, and gave me a suitcase full of his things."

Lillian began to cry. "Oh, Johnny, I'm so sorry. Oh, my God! ... you poor dear. They're both dead ... and you just found out. Oh, I'm so sorry, Johnny. I'm truly sorry ... Johnny, I love you. Just come back ... please, come right back," she pleaded. "Just come back and live here with me. You're more than welcome. Oh, you poor dear," she cried between sobs.

"Aunt Lillian, listen to me," he said.

"Yes?"

"Aunt Lillian, did my old man have only one eye?"

"One eye? ... I ... don't know," she said, "why do you ask?"

"I found a glass eye in the suitcase with some other things."

"I don't know," she said as she gained control of herself.

"There is a gun, too . . a sawed-off shotgun, some underwear, and a key."

"Key?"

"Yeah, a brass key. It was in the lid of the suitcase."

"Johnny, this is important," she said, controlling her emotions, "What kind of key is it?"

"I don't know. It looks different from most keys. It has a number on it."

"Wait a minute," she shouted and then put the phone down. He wondered what made it so important to her. She returned and picked up the phone.

"Is the number A-31?"

"Yeah. How did you know?"

"Never mind. Just come back. I'll explain everything ... No, better yet, I'll meet you I'll meet you in San Francisco."

"You'll meet me?"

"Yes, Johnny. It is imperative that we go to Wilcox ... to the farm. I'll explain why when I see you. We'll make a vacation out of it," she said excitedly.

"Yeah, sure, O.K., Aunt Lillian."

"Oh, I am sorry about your parents' deaths, Johnny, but I'll be so glad to see you. I'll explain everything then. All right?"

"Yeah. I'll get the first bus out of here tomorrow."

"Yes, the first bus. I'll check the arrival time, when I reach San Francisco, and meet you at the bus stop. Oh, it will be good to see you."

"Yeah."

"Oh, Johnny, I almost forgot. You have a baby brother. Your mother had a child by the man she was living with. It's at the orphanage at Wilcox with Tommy."

"Did they say how Tommy was?"

"They said he was fine. I'll call them tomorrow to tell them to expect us."

"Yeah, O.K."

"I'll see you tomorrow, Johnny. I'll explain everything then. Goodbye."

"Goodbye, Aunt Lillian."

He hung up the phone ... so much had happened, and so quickly. He entered the room and shut the door. He lay on the bed and realized that the news of his mother's death had little effect on him. It was all so confusing. He had a half-brother, who was at the orphanage with Tommy. He took the key out of his pocket and looked at it.

"How in hell did she know the number on it?" he said to himself as he turned off the light.

He thought back on all that had happened and welcomed the return to Indiana and the chance to see Tommy and Frankie again.

"Jesus Christ! The first thing I tell him is about Vera's death, and he's just found out Charley is dead! ... Damn! ... That is rough! ... and him sitting up there in some damned hotel room alone."

Barry took the phone from her and hung it up. "You're going to Indiana?"

"Yes. I'll pack tonight. I will meet John at San Francisco, and from there we'll go to Indiana."

"You want me to go along?"

"No," she said with a start. "Thanks, but no, Barry. I want to go alone ... there's something I've got to do on my own ... but there is something you can do."

"You got it."

"Barry, I need to find out something about Vera's boyfriend. When the orphanage called, they said he was in the Wilcox hospital, that he had just regained consciousness."

"Since Charley and Vera are dead, you're concerned about what happens to the farm," he replied.

"That farm belongs to John and his brother," she yelled.

"...and Vera's common-law husband and their heir," continued Barry.

"Maybe," Lillian said as she got up and quickly lit a cigarette. "I want the place for Johnny and his brother ... not for some bum that bought Vera a couple of beers and fixed a few fences. And, now that he sees a possibility of inheriting a few-hundred-acre farm ... No, Sir!"

"Hey, wait a minute, Honey. It might not be that simple. Are they married? Is there a will?"

"That's why I want you to find out about this guy."

"What's his name?"

Lillian went to the phone and picked up a piece of paper. "Kidder. He's registered at the hospital under the name of Hank Kidder."

"What else do you know about him?"

"Nothing, damn it, nothing," she said as she paced the floor. "All I know is what was included in letters pertaining to the children's care at the orphanage.

After Charley left, she took up with this guy. I was always under the impression they weren't married. Once Vera showed up to see the boys about two in the morning. She introduced him as just "Hank" to a Sister Maureen. This nun talked them out of trying to see the boys. Hell, I really don't know anything. When John first arrived, he talked about this Kidder guy. I got the distinct impression they weren't married then."

"O.K., let's not jump to conclusions," replied Barry. "I have an old classmate who has a law office in Louisville, Kentucky. I'll ask him to send an investigator over to Indiana to check this guy out, and to check all the legal ramifications."

"Just pay him off, Barry. Whatever it takes, just pay him off," she cried as she paced.

"Hey, Honey, it may not be that easy."

"Everyone's got a price."

"Since when did you become so concerned with your family and all the trappings?"

Lillian stopped short and glared at him. "Listen, that's my homestead. I was born there, and got thrown off the place. I got another nephew who left there in fear for his life. I can't let some bum take it over. I'll fight this or any son of a bitch in any court to get control of what rightfully belongs to my nephews."

"O.K., O.K., Lady," Barry laughed, "It's great to see you so excited about something ... I was just playing the devil's advocate."

"Well, the more I think if it, the madder I get. I want him out of the picture ... completely. Offer him enough to just disappear, and disappear before I get there."

"Look, I can't perform miracles. I'm going to need time. Take your time getting back to Indiana. You're going to have to stop in Colorado and check out that safety deposit box."

"That's right, and John has the other key. Thank God I won't be legally connected to Charley anymore."

"When you get there, empty the box and mail the contents to me, no matter what it is. Then show him the Grand Canyon or something until I know what kind of animal we're dealing with in Indiana. We'll keep in contact."

Lillian smashed her cigarette out in the ashtray and sat down.

"Barry, there's something else," she said quietly.

"Isn't there always?"

"No, I'm serious. I never told you ... not everything anyway."

"You have another reason for going?"

"Yes. As you know, I've donated to that orphanage because of what they did for me after having the baby."

"Yes," he replied quietly.

"Well, that child grew up."

"... as children are wont to do," he replied.

Lillian went to the china closet and pulled a letter from it.

"Look at this." She handed it to him. "John's girlfriend, Frankie, has been writing to him since he left Indiana. They were in school there together. The girl's mother originally lived in Wilcox. Her mother adopted her from the orphanage and moved away. Later, she returned to Wilcox. In that letter, the girl tells John about her birth ... and her adoption."

Barry looked at Lillian.

"Barry, unless there was another child born in that hospital at the same time and on the same day, and adopted out of the same orphanage, I have every reason to believe that she is the child I gave birth to."

"You're telling me that your nephew and this girl have been writing each other and they don't even know they're cousins?"

"That's another thing," Lillian puffed nervously on a new cigarette. "They aren't just cousins."

"Aren't cousins ... Hell! If they're not cousins ... they could only be ..." Barry looked hard at her.

"Yes. Charley is her father, too."

"Does anyone know this?"

"Sister Theophane ... my friend Jeannie knew it."

"Anyone alive?"

"Not to my knowledge."

"And you want to see this girl?"

"Very much ... I want to see the child just once ... just once..." she fell into his arms. "Oh, Barry. I'm so scared, but I've got to do this ... it's my only chance."

"What are you going to do once you see her?"

"Oh, I don't know. All I know is that I want to see her."

"O.K.," he said as he held her. "Let's agree on a few things. First of all, as I said, I don't want you showing up there until I know what this Kidder's legal rights are. Maybe he can be bought off, and maybe he wants all of the rights of a 'grieving husband.' Secondly, I wouldn't say anything to anyone about this brother-sister relationship. And, thirdly, I think you and I ought to have a drink."

Lillian held him tightly and laughed; she kissed him passionately. "I do love you, and when I come back, when I resolve all this, I promise to seriously think about us."

"O.K., you got a deal."

They kissed again, and she reached inside his shirt and massaged his chest, whispering, "Take me upstairs ... make love to me." Barry picked her up and walked to the staircase.

"You complicated women. You certainly take advantage of us simple men."

Chapter Twenty-Five

Paxton, Arkansas

It was that pit-of-the-stomach feeling that came first; the cramps at his mid half even before the figures emerged from the fog. The figures, each recognizable, appeared as the fog swirled around, standing like statues, still and unmoving, standing on the gray highway that stretched to the horizon. Motionless ... dead ... each was dead and Johnny knew it, but he couldn't help running to them, asking their help ... begging them to help him. Little Tommy lay in the ditch, his face bloodied and grotesque. Sister Theophane sat still at her desk. Behind her he could see his mother, motionless. As he went to each, he could feel the terror behind him.

He had dreamed the dream before. It was always the same. The car was coming out of the fog, time and space seemed to stand still. Only the car had motion, and it would soon be upon him. As he struggled to move from it, Sheriff Bullard appeared, the cigar dangling from his mouth, the smile and smell about him that gripped the boy and sickened him. The faster he moved, the closer the Sheriff came until he felt the hand on his shoulder. Straining with every inch of strength, he could hear the man as he panted, "I got your ass, boy ... boy, you hear me ... I got your ass."

The screeching of the air brakes muffled out his cries for help as the hand tightened on his shoulder ... "I got your ass, boy ... your ass ...your ass ... your ann ... your aunt ... your aunt ... to ... wake ... you ... to wake ... you ... your aunt to wake you ..."

Johnny sat up with a start. The train conductor was shaking him.

"Sorry I had to wake you, son. Your aunt asked me to wake you before we leave the station." Sweat poured down the boy's face. His surroundings slowly became familiar to him.

"Where's my aunt?" he gasped.

"She's out in the station making a phone call. She asked that I wake you before we leave in case you want to get off the train for a minute."

Johnny looked around, still confused. "Where are we?"

"Paxton. Paxton, Arkansas," the conductor said. "We got a twenty-minute layover, but you only got a few minutes before we take off."

The word Paxton rang in his head like a distorted bell. He looked out the window at the station platform. Passengers moved quickly about. Memories of another day came to him as he watched the people scurry about. Memories of himself and Sergeant Freeman standing on that platform waiting for a six a.m. train sprang up in his mind.

"Sorry to have to wake you, son," the conductor continued, "I'm sorry to have to wake you, but you'll have to get off now. You only got a few minutes before we leave again."

'Sorry, son ... sorry...' It was a familiar phrase, one that had been said over and over that early morning as he stood with the sergeant.

"I'm sorry, son ... sorry this happened to you." He repeated it over and over as though it was supposed to make the boy feel better. "I'm sorry, son, really sorry." Over and over the man said it. He remembered gritting his teeth and wishing the man would shut up. Then the man handed him a twenty-dollar bill. "Oh, it ain't mine, boy. The department pays for this. You got enough to pay for the ticket and then some. As the train approached, he remembered the sergeant stopping him and saying, "Don't go away from here thinking we are all perverts like Bullard ... we ain't ... if it is any consolation, he's dead." Johnny looked at the man in surprise. "Yeah, boy, he's dead ... shot himself right afterwards ... after he got caught with you ... couldn't face bein' found out ... don't feel that you're to blame, boy ... I just thought I'd tell you ... you ain't the first, you know..."

Johnny stopped before getting on the train.

"I ain't the first?" he asked.

"Nope. There's been others I've put on the train out of town the morning after..." The man stopped in mid sentence as though embarrassed to admit it.

"The morning after what?" Johnny screamed.

"You know ... the morning ... after ... what happened to you."

He remembered anger growing in him in those early morning hours as he heard the sergeant explain away his own guilt.

"There were others ... others that went through what I did!" he screamed at the sergeant. "This happened before, and you let it happen ... and then just put them on a train!" He remembered the sergeant not understanding why he couldn't accept his benevolence. The man looked at him as though insulted.

"Hey, kid. I do what I can ... I did what I could under the circumstances," he shouted back in frustration.

Johnny remembered getting on the train and then turning to the sergeant and yelling, "Well, it ain't enough! You should've shot the son of a bitch the first time!" Then he headed down the aisle and sat on the opposite side of the train until it left the platform.

The conductor walked toward him from the end of the coach yelling, "Transfer. Transfer. Tickets, please ... final destination, Chicago ... all transfer tickets, please."

Johnny reached in his pocket and pulled out a handful of tickets. "This is for me and my aunt."

"You're both going to Chicago?"

"Yes," he replied as the conductor wrote something in his book.

Johnny looked out the window at the platform. Anger and frustration swelled as memories of that morning came to him again. He watched as his aunt scurried to the newspaper stand and then got on the train. Seated in front of that station brought back too many memories he did not want to recall ... other familiar faces ... people and places he did not want to think about began to flicker across his consciousness."

"John, I have wonderful news," Lillian said as she hurried down the aisle and took a seat opposite him. "It's the most wonderful news! I've just called Barry. He received the package of money we found in the safety deposit box ... he said there was over twenty-two thousand dollars in that box."

Now he could not help look at that platform and the grotesque figures it brought to mind. He could picture Hank thrashing at little Tommy ... beating away at him in the same tempo as the sergeant repeated, 'I'm sorry ... I'm sorry ...'

"Barry suggested we put it in a trust fund for you and your brother. He asked if I knew where your father had gotten the money. I told him it was a surprise to both of us when we opened the box. I didn't quite understand, but he said it was yours."

Johnny hardly heard her as other images performed their rituals like actors on a stage. He could see his mother standing there crying as he heard his brother's cries for help. He could see DeWitt sitting next to a bed of roses ... roses that covered a grave, a boy's grave.

"This Hank, your mother's boyfriend, is gone, John ... he left ... he took the money we offered him and left ... he admitted he had no right to the farm since he and your mother weren't married ... he wants nothing to do with his child."

She went on in a droll tone that only seemed to give more life to the imaginary figures that moved on the platform. One image, a man that resembled Sheriff Bullard, appeared to walk by the window, stop and look at Johnny. He just stood there looking at him, and events and emotions he had long hidden began to emerge.

"Barry said the farm is legally yours and your brothers'. I will be your legal guardian, yours and Tommy's and your half brother's."

He felt tired and resisted emotions that he had for so long been afraid to express. And now, try as he may, he could not hold them back. The harder he tried, the more he felt them swell within him.

"A Mr. Morris will meet us there, John. He has a paper that Hank Kidder has signed giving up all rights."

Johnny could feel himself breaking up inside. It seemed to just hit him that his mother was dead; she wouldn't be there when he arrived. His father had died. Sister Theophane was dead. He felt alone and cheated.

"... someone is being sent to the farm to clean it up before we get there."

His chin quivered and tears began to form in his eyes as frustration and loneliness overran him.

"They buried your mother last week. Your half brother is at the orphanage ... I told them we'd arrive in about..."

"It ain't fair! ... It ain't fair!" he screamed as he began to cry, "It ain't fair!"

"What?" yelled Lillian.

"It ain't fair! I didn't ask for none of this. It ain't fair!" he cried.

Lillian stared at him. It was obvious he had heard nothing of what she had said. He put his hands to his face and blotted out the imaginary forms on the platform.

"Why don't people just leave me alone, goddamn it! he cried, "I didn't ask for it!"

Fear clutched at Lillian as she became aware of his emotional state.

"Oh, my dear, what's the matter?" she exclaimed.

"Goddamn it! I didn't ask for none of this!" he yelled again as he hid his face.

"Oh, John, it's all right," she said as she sat next to him and put her arms around him.

"Nobody asked what the fuck I wanted!" he cried, "Why didn't they just leave me alone?"

His aunt held him and began to cry. "Did I say something, John? I'm sorry ... I'm sorry ... did I say something I shouldn't have?"

"No . . No ... Me and Tommy didn't want to go that orphanage ... I didn't want to go home when our old lady came for us ..." He looked at his aunt. "My old lady should've stuck up for me and Tommy ... She shouldn't've let Hank do that to us ... goddamn it, it ain't right! ... it ain't right ... she never did right by me and Tommy," he cried.

"Oh, yes. I understand, John," his aunt said while blotting her tears and holding him. But she didn't understand. She didn't know what had brought it all on. She was at a loss for words, at a loss for what to do but hold him until it passed.

"... then, goddamn it, she gets herself killed before I get home ... it ain't fair! ... it just ain't fair!"

Lillian held him to her and said, "I'll take care of you ... you and your brothers, John. I'll take care of you ... you don't have to worry. I'll take care of all of you."

Johnny wiped his eyes and calmed himself, then he quietly leaned against the windowpane as the train slowly left the station. Lillian sat across from him. "Is there anything I can get for you, John?" He didn't answer, but kept looking out the window. "I'm sorry if I upset you, John."

"No," he said quietly, looking out the window, "I was just thinkin' about some of the things ... things that had happened to me..." He took a long sigh. "Aunt Lil, I've learned one thing from all of this ... one thing."

"Yes?"

"One thing. You gotta watch out for yourself ... no one else ... but yourself."

"Oh, John, I know you're upset ... a lot has happened to you, but don't be too quick to judge ... to judge your ma ... I wasn't your ma's favorite person, nor was she mine, but she did what she had to do ... we do that ... we all do..." Memories of standing in front of a Justice of the Peace with Louie Breslin came to her ... of leaving her baby at St. Helena's ... "We all do ... what we have to ... to survive ... we all do what we think's right ... or best ... in times of crisis ... even if it's not best for everyone involved ... we do it."

Johnny wiped his eyes again and sat up. "Well, I learned one thing. I'm doin' my own biddin' from now on. I'm doin' what's best for me, for Tommy ... I learned that much."

Lillian could see the bitterness he felt, the betrayal, and felt helpless. The determination in his voice sent a chill through her. She wanted to convince him he was wrong, but there was no convincing him of anything at the moment. She was not sure she was convinced herself.

"I bought a local paper. Maybe you want to read something," she said, handing it to him.

On the back page was a picture of Sergeant Freeman being congratulated by the Mayor of Paxton. Under the picture, the caption said, 'Sergeant Freeman is the new Sheriff due to the untimely death of incumbent Sheriff Bullard.' Johnny stared at it and began to giggle, then laugh.

"What's so funny?" Lillian asked.

"Untimely ... the word is 'untimely'," he said as he roared with laughter that untied the knot in the pit of his stomach.

"I don't understand," she said.

"Untimely! There's only one thing untimely about his death."

Lillian looked at the picture. "Yes?"

Johnny stopped laughing. He stared out the window ...he gritted his teeth in anger and spit out, "Hell! He should've been shot a long time ago!"

Lillian bit her lip. 'Something must've happened to him,' she thought. 'Something must've happened here in Paxton ... it must've been terrible.' It was all she could figure out, and it was all she wanted to know.

Chapter Twenty-Six

Wilcox, Indiana

The Yellow Cab turned down Michigan Avenue, the main street of Wilcox. Except in her memory, Lillian had not viewed the town in over twenty years. Aside from a new facade here and there, the Hooks Drug, the Sillman Brothers Department Store, and the courthouse all stood as she remembered them. Johnny sat next to her, excitedly showing her the different stores and shops.

"That's the Five and Dime where we bought model airplanes!" he shouted.

Seeing it reminded Lillian of the time her mother had given her money to buy candy at that store. "Just don't tell your Dad; he'd think it a waste of good money," she would always caution her, "... and eat all the candy before coming home." It was one of the many ways her mother "made up to her" for "surviving" the Ben Roberts house rules.

Perspiration poured from her as she viewed the familiar storefronts, each reminding her of a day or time in her childhood that she had long ago avoided remembering. Although most storefronts were the same, a whole new generation of people busied themselves along the sidewalks. Hesitantly, Lillian looked for a familiar face among the shoppers. If she should recognize someone, it was a relief to know that her long absence would hide her identity.

The cab stopped for a red light.

"Look, Aunt Lil!" Johnny exclaimed. "There's the Grand Theatre. The sisters took us there for Saturday morning kids movies."

Lillian's eyes met two middle-aged women who stared at her as they talked. Although she did not recognize them for a moment, she believed they recognized her, and that they were talking about her. ("Oh, yes ... yes, that's the Roberts girl, yes, Lillian Roberts ... Oh, that one was no good, I can tell you that.")

The acceleration of the cab broke her concentration as it skirted around the corner and stopped at a very familiar building. 'Stop the paranoia,' she thought to herself as the cabbie opened the door.

"We stayin' here, Aunt Lil?" asked Johnny.

"Yes, John, is that all right?"

"Yeah, I guess. It's just that I want to see Tommy right away and stay with him."

"Of course, John, but let's just get settled, change clothes and freshen up a bit before going to the orphanage." Lillian couldn't decide whether she needed a respite from the early morning bus ride from Chicago, or if she was trying to avoid her visit to the orphanage, but she knew she needed time—time to realize that what she was about to venture into could change her future.

Lillian and Johnny entered the LaSalle Hotel lobby. It was as she remembered it. With the exception of new furniture and fixtures, it was the same. Time stood still, and for a moment she was taken back to a Saturday afternoon outing with her mother, an unusual occurrence, a luncheon date for just the two of them at the LaSalle Hotel restaurant. They had been in town to do some necessary shopping and, on the spur of the moment, her mother had exclaimed, "You and me are goin' to lunch right here. I don't care what your father thinks, but don't be talking about it to no one, Lillian. What he don't know won't hurt him. It's just that he wouldn't understand about us sittin' and talkin' away an afternoon, over a meal bought with his money, when there's plenty of food at home."

Even as a small child, Lillian always understood her mother's "cautions" against her father and his rules. And now that she had returned, she had begun remembering incidents ... episodes in her childhood which brought with each memorable recall a heavy sense of guilt.

'Why should I feel guilty?' she thought to herself. 'Was it for breaking my father's house rules, or for running away ... for not putting up with the male-dominated social mores women were expected to adhere to in those days. Why do I feel so guilty?'

And, deep within her, a tiny voice answered, 'Because you left your mother to take the blame and punishment for all your independence, Miss Smarty.'

At her own revelation, Lillian thought of the saying, "You can never really go home."

'The hell you can't go home,' she thought as she approached the reservation desk. 'You can't go home because it never really leaves you.'

"May I help you?" asked a man in his early thirties. He was dressed in a brown, double-breasted suit, and he sported a congenial smile. Lillian recognized Arnold Wells, a classmate and childhood playmate. As a boy, he had worked her father's fields during peach picking. Now he stood before her, still redheaded and freckle-faced.

"Your name, please?" he inquired.

Lillian tensed, almost afraid to answer.

"Breslin, Lillian Breslin. I have a reservation." As she signed the registration, he looked at her intently, as though he was about to ask her something; then, changing his mind, he reached for the room key and said, "Oh, yes, here it is, Room 210 for two. Have a nice day. If there's anything we might be able to do you for you, please call on us."

'Just don't recognize me,' she said to herself. Relieved that she was unidentified, she took her key, thanked him, and headed for the elevator.

155

As she and Johnny entered the elevator, he reminded her that the orphanage was just a few blocks away. His pronouncement caused her to break out in perspiration. As they left the elevator and walked toward their room, Lillian came to the realization that being recognized by Arnold Wells was irrelevant compared to what lay ahead. Certainly there would be nuns at the orphanage, novices in Sister Theophane's class, possibly "help" who still worked for the organization and would know her, and who would know why she had first come to the convent and why she had left. And then there was the child, Frankie ... her child.

While laying out new slacks and a shirt for Johnny to change into, she became aware, for the first time since the boy had entered her life, that she was about to meet the child she had possibly given birth to and later abandoned. A child who would not know her, and who quite possibly might be surrounded by individuals who knew more of her beginnings than the young girl knew of herself. 'And my returning will conjure it all up,' she said to herself. For a moment, the possibilities of what she might encounter overwhelmed her, and she stopped unpacking and sat on the side of the bed to steady herself.

"You okay, Aunt Lil?" Johnny asked as he came from the bathroom. "You look sort of sick."

"Yes," she said haltingly. "Yes." To change the subject she handed him his new clothes. "You'll look fine in these, John."

The boy took the clothes, thanked her, and headed for the bathroom. Lillian sat on the edge of the bed. The revelations of what she was about to encounter sapped her of her strength. For the first time, she was not sure she could go through with whatever new events lay ahead. Some primal instinct told her to just get up and run, walk out of the room, leave money and a note for Johnny at the main desk, and get out of town.

"How do I look, Aunt Lil?"

Johnny stood before her in his new clothes. To her he resembled her Charley. His face was younger and his body smaller, but there he was, as Charley was when she was a teenager. He stood in front of her with the same stance and body stature, right down to rolling the ends of his shirtsleeves to accentuate his budding arm muscles.

"Who showed you this?" she asked lightly, touching his folded sleeves.

"I don't know. I just thought it would look neat," he replied.

"It must be in the genes," she said as she pulled him to her.

"What?" he asked.

"Nothing, you look just great, young man," she continued as tears flowed down her cheek.

Johnny pulled back. "What's wrong, Aunt Lil?"

"Nothing ... nothing." She held him for a quiet moment and then said, "You won't understand what I say, John, but ... thank you ... thank you for coming into my life and for bringing me home."

"Gee, I'm sorry, Aunt Lil, did I do something wrong?"

Lillian hugged her nephew and said, "No, no ... never mind, let me get dressed while you call a cab." Then she kissed him on the forehead and headed for the bathroom.

As the cab entered the iron gate of St. Helena's Orphanage, Lillian felt knots tighten in her stomach. Johnny was so excited that he didn't wait for the cab to come to a complete halt. He opened the door and ran along as the cab slowed to a stop. A nun was seated at the top of a pair of stairs which led into the institution. Johnny ran to her; she shook his hand and spoke to him, then pointed down the entrance hall. Johnny scurried into the building.

Waves of loneliness, indecision, and insecurity rolled over Lillian as she paid the cab fare and prepared to meet the approaching nun.

"How do you do, Mrs. Breslin. I'm Sister Maureen." Lillian extended her hand and greeted the nun.

"Johnny looks so well ... so happy. We were all so concerned about him," said the nun. "How was your trip?"

"Fine ... just fine." Lillian was nervous and knew it showed.

"Monsignor Sabin was to be here to greet you, Mrs. Breslin, but something came up. Where is your luggage?"

"We're staying at the LaSalle Hotel in town."

"We would be happy to have you stay here. There is more than enough room."

"Thank you, but staying in town is fine."

The nun ushered her into a small room off the main hall. Lillian remembered it as a music room. Now it was used as a reception room.

"Would you like a cup of coffee, Mrs. Breslin?"

"No. No thank you, Sister." Lillian could feel the strain of the moment and knew the nun was uncomfortable, too.

As the two women exchanged small talk, voices and laughter could be heard outside the room. Then Johnny ran in with another boy. Lillian immediately recognized the McBride resemblance. He had brown eyes and a somewhat darker complexion than his brother, but Lillian knew he was a McBride. His facial features resembled Vera more than Charley, but his inward step, a McBride trait, gave him away as Charley McBride's son.

"Aunt Lil, this is Tommy."

"Hello, Tommy. I'm your Aunt Lillian."

As they shook hands, Tommy said, "Thanks for helping Johnny, and for all the money you sent here."

"What?" she said, surprised.

"Mac told me to say it."

"Mac told you?" For a moment the name did not register ... then laughing, she said, "Of course, Mac ... Well, I enjoyed doing it."

The boy was so open ... so outgoing ... much more of an extrovert than his older brother ...another characteristic she attributed to Charley McBride.

The door at the other end of the room opened, and a pretty brunette of about fifteen or sixteen came into the room. She wore a blue skirt and patent leather shoes and was surprised to see all the people, for she obviously expected the room to be empty.

"Frankie!" yelled Johnny. "Frankie!" he yelled again as he ran to her.

Lillian froze at the recognition of the name. It was so unexpected. She was not prepared to meet this child unannounced ... and yet, there she was.

Lillian watched as the two children clasped hands. Johnny thanked her for writing, as he told her about reading all of her letters at once. Lillian studied the girl, her every motion, the sound of her voice...

"Aunt Lil, this is Frankie," Johnny said. "She wrote all those letters you got."

The girl's sudden appearance had taken Lillian's breath away, and she replied in a small whisper, "Hello, Frankie."

"Johnny has told me so much about you I feel I already know you," the girl replied.

"And I have heard so much of you and read your letters that I feel I know you."

But it wasn't the letters or anything that Johnny had said. It was the girl herself, standing there in front of her. Something from the past, some maternal instinct, some interrupted time warp, some Voice saying yes ... yes, you know this child, you have a connection, a common bond...

"My mother is very interested in meeting you, Mrs..." The girl hesitated and looked at Johnny.

"Just call her Aunt Lil like I do."

"Aunt Lil ... my mother said she would like to talk to you as soon as she gets off work. She works at the courthouse."

"I would be more than happy to meet your mother, Frankie," Lillian said.

Lillian was so intent on observing every detail of the young girl that she hardly realized what she had said, and just for a moment Frankie gazed at Lillian as though there were more to their knowing each other than this first introduction.

"Hey, Mac, did you really hitchhike all the way to California?" asked Tommy.

"Yeah. All the way and then some."

"Next time, I get to go with you."

"Okay, but I ain't goin' back. I just want to stay with you here."

As he said it, the boy realized he was answering the question Lillian had so many times asked.

"Now that I'm here, Aunt Lillian, I think I want to stay here ... for a while."

"Of course, John. I believe I will be staying longer than expected myself," said Lillian. "I want to get acquainted with my new nephews, and their friends."

"Speaking of new nephews," exclaimed Sister Maureen, "I forgot about Joey. Frankie, would you bring the Kidder child downstairs so that Mrs. Breslin and John can meet him?"

"Sure, c'mon, Mac, I'll show you the new building they just finished. It's got the little kids' and babies' rooms."

"I'm coming, too," said Tommy as the children ran out of the room.

"Frankie works for us here, besides attending school," the nun said. "She is a big help. I'm of the understanding that Frankie's letters were the first announcement of Sister Theophane's death, Mrs. Breslin."

"Yes."

"Frankie told me she had written you. It was then I realized I had not informed you myself. I am so sorry I didn't write or even call. Her death was such a shock to all of us here that ... I'm afraid I was remiss with regards to informing you..."

"Please, Sister," Lillian interrupted, "Please, no apologies."

"As it turned out, when I did write, I had to also include the sad news of the death of Mrs. McBride. There was only a short service for Mrs. McBride. Later I will show you and the children the gravesite."

"Sister, I too have been just as insensitive. When Johnny went in search of his father, he went to a town in California called Sonora. I told him to call me when he arrived. I was so concerned about his safety. He, of course, is so assured of everything he does. Well, he called, only to tell me of his arrival, I thought. I wanted him to know immediately of the death of his mother. No sooner had I told him than he answered by saying that he would be returning to Long Beach, and then told me his father had died two weeks earlier."

The nun grimaced at the news. "He has suffered so much, Mrs. Breslin ... so much."

"Yes. I've only myself begun to realize the injustices done to both children all these years. I have always been embarrassed by my sister's propensity to get herself involved in matters over her head and then look to relatives or this institution, or even total strangers for a solution. Fortunately, I have been wealthy enough to be of some assistance."

"Let me say that, in the name of Sister Theophane and this order, we are most appreciative of all the years of your contributions to St. Helena's."

"Please," Lillian insisted, "I'm not looking for thanks ... just a ... resolution to all this. That's why I've come to Indiana with my nephew ... not for thanks for what I may have done."

159

"With regards to your coming, Mrs. Breslin, a Mr. Morris will be meeting with you here. He did call and notify us as to your being the legal guardian of the children. It seems Mr. Kidder has left the area."

"Yes. I was told he gave up all rights to the farm and to his child."

"Oh, Mrs. Breslin, their child is beautiful, a boy. His name is Joey. He is such a beautiful child. Almost a year old." Then, much to Lillian's surprise, the nun deliberately went to the entrance door and closed it. At her action, Lillian froze in a state of fearful anticipation. "I am so glad you're here, Mrs. Breslin, and that you are now the children's legal guardian. And, because you are here, I need to discuss in private something Sister Theophane confided to me."

Lillian tensed at the idea of Sister Maureen being a confidante to her dear friend.

"Mrs. Breslin, what I am about to say is really none of my business ... it's just that I feel a moral obligation to inform you ... to tell you something ... something that I can't prove as a fact ... something that Sister Theophane told me in strictest confidence."

Lillian's first impulse was to stop her and tell her to just forget it, but it was obvious that would not satisfy the situation. Reaching for a cigarette, she remained silent as the nun continued.

"Sister Theophane and I were close friends, closer than our order allowed within the community, or that our superiors would have preferred. Let me begin by saying that if she were alive, standing here today, she would inform you of what she had unintentionally learned, and what I am about to say."

'She knows,' Lillian said over and over again in her mind. 'She knows. Sister Theophane told her, and now she feels obligated to tell me.' Lillian cupped the cigarette in her hand and sat very still, listening and waiting to see how the nun would phrase it, and wondering what her reply would be.

"When Frankie came to us, it was Sister's definite impression that she was ... she was the same child adopted from here sixteen years ago."

"You mean my child," interrupted Lillian.

"Yes, Mrs. Breslin. Sister had no proof, no solid proof, just facts. She accidentally found out that a couple named Phillips was inquiring about adopting a baby from here at about the same time your child was made available for adoption. Then there is the place and date of birth."

"They coincide with the place and date I gave birth."

"Yes ... the results being, Mrs. Breslin, that Sister Theophane was of the belief that John McBride and Frankie Phillips are related."

Lillian sat in silence for a moment. The ticking of an antique regulator clock resounded like an amplified metronome.

"Do you have an ashtray?" Lillian asked as she lit the cigarette.

The nun opened a small drawer and placed a glass ashtray on the table.

Lillian inhaled the smoke once and then again before deciding on her response.

"Did ... did Sister discuss this ... this possibility with anyone else besides you, Sister?"

"No, Mrs. Breslin ... no one."

"And you are saying that Sister told only you of her belief in this matter?"

"Yes, only me, but it was more than just her belief. Sister Theophane told me she was convinced that Frankie was your child."

"And you are telling me this because..."

"Because you are the legal guardian of John, and John is striking up a relationship with a young lady who could possibly be his half-sister."

"Then Theo told you who fathered my child?"

"Mrs. Breslin, I am not here to make judgments on what I was told, but because these children have 'found' each other, and because they have an interest in each other, I, as would Sister Theophane, feel a moral obligation to inform you."

"What do you mean, 'found each other,' Sister?"

"Before John left for California, they became fast friends. I do not believe that Frankie has anything but feelings of friendship for John. I am concerned about his feelings toward her. After he left, they wrote to each other ... in one letter he told her of being sexually assaulted by some police officer in Arkansas."

Lillian gasped.

"You didn't know?"

Recalling the strange behavior on the train layover at Paxton, she said, "No, but it explains something I now understand."

"Frankie confided in me that she and her mother left her father and their home in northern Indiana because her father had been sexually abusing her. These identical misfortunes will give them reason for their relationship to be even closer. This is why I feel it is imperative that you know about their possible relationship."

Lillian inhaled on the cigarette and then stomped it out in the ashtray. She got up and went to the window. A small breeze blew across the front lawn. "Thank you for telling me this, Sister. I mistakenly read one of Frankie's letters to Johnny and in it she told of how her mother had told her she was adopted, and that she was born here. She also included the date of birth. I was aware of the possibility. It was one of the reasons I came to Indiana ... I've thought a great deal about this. I am going to take Joey back with me. I can give him a life in California. I can make up for a mistake I made a long time ago. What I don't know is ... if ... if it would serve any purpose to ... to..."

"To tell Frankie?" the nun asked.

"What would you do, Sister?"

"Mrs. Breslin, as I said, I in no way mean to judge you or infer by telling you these things that you should do something. You will have to determine what should be done. It is just that I feel a moral obligation to inform you since the children have formed a close bond."

"I understand, Sister. I realize it is my decision. If I might use you as a devil's advocate a bit more? Do you think Frankie would benefit from knowing who her real mother is?"

"I can't answer that, Mrs. Breslin. Since she has a good relationship with her mother now, I don't know that she is curious to know. She never told me she was curious to know."

Lillian walked over and took the nun's hand. "Thank you, Sister, for telling me ... and for your discretion in this matter; be assured that it is now my obligation to make the right decision."

For the first time since they had met, the two women smiled at each other with a real sense of sincerity.

"Well, here he is," yelled Tommy as the children entered the room. Frankie wheeled in a little crib. "His name is Joey," the boy continued. "I don't like the name. We ought to call him something else."

"I think Joey is just fine," Lillian laughed. Sister Maureen picked the child up and handed him to Lillian. Feeling out of place and totally inadequate, Lillian accepted the smiling infant.

"Mrs. Breslin, your new ward."

"They're so very tiny ... so very helpless," Lillian said. She couldn't remember the last time she had held a child so small. How old did you say he is, Sister?"

"Just about a year old."

Tears began to form in Lillian's eyes. "Is he all right? I mean physically."

"Our doctor gave him a complete examination the day he arrived. He is just fine, Mrs. Breslin."

"Why are you crying?" Tommy asked.

Lillian smiled as she held the child. "Well, Tommy, I've never been a mother before. I've always wanted the chance to be one."

"My Ma is dead. She died in a car accident," Tommy said.

"I know, Tommy." Then, looking at Frankie, and then to the nun, she pressed the child to her and said, "You know, Tommy, just because a woman has a child, it doesn't mean she is going to be fortunate enough to be able to bring it up."

"Motherhood is in the love and caring of a child," the nun said to the children. Then she returned Lillian's gaze. "Not just in giving a child life."

"Yes, Sister, you are so right." The women smiled at each other as the baby began to whimper and then to cry.

Lillian felt helpless and it was obvious to the nun.

"Here, Mrs. Breslin, let me take him."

"I have a lot to learn."

"You ain't used to kids?" asked Tommy.

"I ain't used to kids. I have a lot to learn if I'm to be the legal guardian of all of you."

"Tommy has the propensity to say exactly what comes to his mind," the Sister laughingly noted.

"I'm not used to being with children, Sister."

"You'll do just fine, Mrs. Breslin," the nun said as she put the baby back in his crib.

"Sister, I would like to accept your invitation to stay here a bit longer. I do want to get to know the children and their friends."

"Oh, we would enjoy having you stay. The other sisters are anxious to meet you. Lunch will be served soon."

"Yes. Yes, that would be fine." Lillian said with real determination.

"The place is okay, but I don't like the food," interrupted Tommy.

"Well, good or bad, I'll stay. And now, I need to make a phone call."

"Right there," Sister Maureen pointed to a phone on the desk at the end of the room.

"You children come with me and we'll make sure that Joey gets some lunch, too."

Before shutting the door, Johnny turned to Lillian, saying, "Aunt Lil, I guess I wasn't sure until I got here. I meant to tell you later, but I'm sure now. I'm not going to want to go back to California."

"Whatever you want, John. We'll talk about future plans later."

"You're going to take Joey with you when you go?" asked Johnny.

"As soon as I feel comfortable in taking care of him." Then she kissed him on the forehead. "Thank you. Thank you for coming into my life, John McBride ... for disrupting my self-centeredness, for ... for making a real person out of me."

"I don't understand, Aunt Lil."

"You don't have to. Someday I'll explain. Tell Sister I'll be there in just a moment."

After he closed the door, Lillian looked at herself in the wall mirror. She straightened her shoulders and flared her hair with a few whacks of the comb. "I should have worn that red suit. Brown never did show my best," she said to herself. She realized she felt better in that moment than she had in years; then she picked up the phone and dialed the operator. "A Barry Aston, Long Beach, California. The number is 1-42360.' As she waited for the connection, Lillian realized that she felt as if a great weight had been lifted from her.

"Barry Aston."

At the sound of his voice, Lillian began to cry. "Oh, Barry, it's so good to hear your voice."

"You all right, Lillian? You sound like you're crying."

"Yes ... yes, I am, but it's all right. So much has happened; I have so much to tell you."

"Has a man named Dan Morris contacted you with regard to an individual named Kidder?"

"Yes ... yes, I have been informed. Barry, something else has happened."

"What, honey?"

There was a long pause so that Lillian could pick her words carefully.

"I've met her."

"Who?"

"Her ... Frankie. Johnny's young girl friend, I've met her."

" ... And?"

"She's mine, Barry. I just know it ... she's my child," Lillian said as she wept quietly.

"Lil, I think I'd better come up there. You sound pretty broken up."

"NO ... no, believe me, I'm all right. I'm just getting used to facing up to some pretty important events in my past that I've avoided... Barry, do you love me?"

"What kind of question is that? Of course I do."

"Yes, I do know that," she said as she laughed through her tears. "But things here are changing so rapidly for me. I've seen Vera's child, the one she had by this man named Kidder. The child is a beautiful boy named Joey."

"Congratulations. You're an aunt again."

"I've found I'm more than that ... Barry, I'm going to need more time here. I'm staying longer; how long I don't know."

"Take all the time you want, honey. Just promise to marry me when you return."

"Oh, yes ... yes," she cried. "I promise you that now ... but ... when I return, I won't be alone. I've decided to bring Joey with me."

"Just as long as you return with him. I love you, Lil. You do what you need to do, but just be my wife."

"Oh, I love you, Barry, so very much."

"What can I do to make things easier for you out here?"

"There's nothing you can do now. I have to make some hard decisions, with regards to myself, and my new-found relatives ... But just be there when I return, that's all I ask."

"You know that I will."

Lillian jumped as she heard someone knock on the door.

"Please wait, I will be right there!" she called out.

"What is it, honey?" Barry asked in response.

"Someone is knocking. I've got to go. I'll call again tomorrow. I love you, Barry."

"I love you too, babe."

Lillian put down the phone, wiped her face with her hanky, glided a comb through her hair quickly, and said, "Come in."

Sister Maureen entered, accompanied by a tall, thin, middle-aged woman. Her hairstyle and suit gave her a professional appearance. "Mrs. Breslin, this is Mrs. Phillips, Frankie's mother."

Something told Lillian the women had come to meet her for other reasons than simply social.

"Hello, Mrs. Breslin. I'm Ann Phillips. I'm sorry, am I interrupting you?"

"No ... no, please sit down," Lillian begged. "I was just making some phone calls. I'm so glad to meet you."

"Frankie called me at work and said you were here, so I came over on my lunch hour."

Lillian became immediately curious as to why the woman was so much in a hurry to meet her. As she listened to her, Lillian felt that this woman would be a major influence in future decisions that she would make.

"I'll get lunch ready," said Sister Maureen. "You'll stay for lunch, Mrs. Phillips?"

"Oh, please do, Mrs. Phillips," urged Lillian.

"Please, call me Ann, and yes, Sister, I would like to stay."

"Then I'll leave you two alone," the nun said as she shut the door behind her.

"Did you have a nice trip here?" inquired Mrs. Phillips.

"Yes ... yes, and I just met your daughter Frankie. She is a beautiful child."

"It is because of her that I so wanted to meet you, Mrs. Breslin."

"Please call me Lillian. I know we're going to be good friends."

"I so hope so, Lillian. Since hearing of your coming, there is so much that I needed to talk to you about; and of course, not knowing you, I wasn't sure you even wanted to talk to me."

Lillian took Ann's hand in hers and said, "Oh, Ann, I think we both have a lot to talk about to each other."

The women sat down, and Lillian told her of Johnny coming to her home and involving her in his life. Ann Phillips listened intently. When Lillian finished, Ann stood and walked around the back of her chair and looked directly at Lillian. "I know we have just met, Lillian, but under the circumstances, time is limited. I work at the courthouse. I am a legal secretary. My brother Jake is a defense lawyer for the county here. He got me the position when I decided to move from upstate. Lillian, I'm going to confide in you as you have in me, for I believe we both realize it is in the best interests of the children ... Johnny and Frankie, and of course, Tommy."

"I must first tell you that I moved two years ago to Wilcox within a twenty-four hour period, because I had found out that my husband was molesting Frankie. I was so distraught, I just picked up and left him. I moved in with my mother. One of the sisters here, Sister Maureen, was good enough to counsel

Frankie. My husband has agreed never to enter our lives again. In turn, I have agreed not to prosecute him. The horrendous situation gave rise to problems with Frankie, but many conflicts are being resolved, many questions answered. But one question she asks I am able to answer but cannot because..."

Lillian could see that the woman was obviously troubled and had difficulty continuing with her story. Mrs. Phillips got up and walked back and forth as she continued.

"I must digress and also confess an impropriety. When my brother got me the legal secretary position at the courthouse, I took it upon myself to find out who Frankie's real parents were. Being in a confidential secretary's classification, I found it easy to probe sealed files and, without anyone else's help, to find the information I wanted to know. I apologize to you, Mrs. Breslin."

"Lillian. Call me Lillian, please."

"Lillian, I apologize to you for what I did. It was really none of my business but, because of what my child had just experienced, her coming of an age where she wanted to know more of her past, so as to know more of herself ... I don't know, I really have no business telling you this, asking you..."

Realizing the woman's dilemma, Lillian rose and went to her and took hold of her hand. "Ann, you have nothing to apologize for; you are a Godsend, the person to give me courage to do the right thing, to say the right words to these children. You wish me to tell Frankie who her real parents are, don't you?"

"Oh, yes, Lillian, yes. When I saw your name on the birth certificate, I concluded you to be Vera's sister. I had known Vera slightly. We were in the seventh grade together, until my family moved. I had known her as Vera Roberts, but knew she had married a McBride in her sophomore year of high school. I then concluded that you were Frankie's mother and, since Vera was Johnny's mother, the children were first cousins. When Frankie told me you were coming to Wilcox, I knew I wanted to talk to you about this and prayed you would be susceptible to talking to me."

Lillian guided her to the couch. The women sat down. Lillian found the words she had for so long wanted to forget. "Ann, the children are more than first cousins. Charley McBride, before becoming Vera's husband, was my lover and the father of the child I left at St. Vincent's to be adopted. The same child you adopted and mothered all these years. Frankie and Johnny are half brother and sister."

The two women fell into each other's arms. Ann repeated again and again, "I knew there was more. I knew it ... I knew it."

When they had wiped their tears, Ann rose and paced the floor, then said, "What are we to do, Lillian?"

"I know this, Ann. We can no longer let the improprieties and secrets of the past generation affect our children. I'll need your help but, thanks to you, I've found the courage to face the truth and tell the children."

As tears fell from their eyes, the women held each other for a moment, and released the fears and doubts they both had felt for years. Clasping each other's hands, Lillian said, "Thank you again, Ann. You have made me face the past and accept the present. Would you ever have believed that we would meet under these circumstances?"

"No ... no," laughed Ann. "Oh, Lillian, I am so grateful for your coming to Wilcox."

"Let's talk to the children over lunch," Lillian said. "I need to set things straight as soon as possible. Will you help me?"

"Of course, Lillian," Ann said as she wiped tears from her eyes.

A quiet knock was heard. Sister Maureen entered the room. "The children are here, and lunch will be served momentarily."

"Sister," Lillian asked, "do you think it would be possible for Ann, the children, and I to eat lunch in private?"

"Sister Maureen smiled and understood the reason for the request. "Not only do I suppose, but I insist."

The nun led the children, Lillian, and Ann into a small private dining area. Steam tables heated vegetables and hot dogs. "This is the executive dining hall where our Mother Superior always says, 'Big decisions are made by little people.'" Sister Maureen chuckled. "There are plates and ice tea. I'll be right down the hall if you need anything."

As the nun closed the French doors to the dining area, she could barely hear Lillian saying, "Kids, I have a story to tell you while we eat."

"Is it true?" asked Frankie.

"Very true, Frankie, replied Lillian. "In fact, you are involved in this story, and so are you, Johnny."

"What about me?" asked Tommy.

"Oh, yes, your re in the story too, Tommy."

The nun placed the "LUNCHEON CONFERENCE — DO NOT DISTURB" sign in front of the door and proceeded down the hall to the main dining room. She smiled as she thought of the day's events and what was being said behind those closed doors. She wished her friend, Sister Theophane, could be present, but realized that the spirit of her dear friend must have had a great deal to do with the lives of all the people in the Executive Dining Hall.

Having other important matters to attend to, Sister Maureen walked down the hall. "My, what a lovely day it is, and I am so very hungry for my lunch," she said to herself as she turned toward the main dining area.

Epilogue

Despite his volatile and turbulent youth, Johnny Mac not only survived but prospered. He served with honor in the military, attended college and enjoyed a career that was both professionally and financially rewarding.

Johnny has retired and lives with his wife of many years in a large urban community.

ABOUT THE AUTHOR

Although this is John Probst's first novel, he has been a prolific writer and composer throughout his life. John has composed numerous choral compositions and has recently authored a mass based on famous Gregorian chants with varying rhythms.

John's professional life has always been as a teacher. After graduating from the University of Notre Dame with a Bachelor and Masters Degrees, John began his teaching career in various parochial high schools throughout the Bay Area. His expertise was in the fields of music, drama and English.

In 1980, John became an instructor of fine arts at Feather River College in Quincy, California, where he continues today teaching a wide spectrum of classes in music, drama, English, film and philosophy. As part of his drama instruction, John has directed numerous stage productions ranging from Shakespeare plays, dramatic presentations, to musicals like *The Sound of Music.*

John has also authored and directed two of his own full-length plays, *Environmental Alternatives* and *Abuse.*

John, who is widowed, has four children, four grandchildren, and resides in Quincy.

CPSIA information can be obtained
at www.ICGtesting.com
Printed in the USA
BVHW081034171021
619134BV00006B/294